DEVIL'S BREATH

THE VOODOO BAYOU SERIES

ANNA PAXTON

About the Author

Anna Paxton can usually be found on her porch with a cup of coffee and her laptop as she creates her world of evil villains and strong heroines trying to kill each other. She sometimes takes inspiration from her villainous cat and three heroic dogs as they act out the "murder" scenes for her.

When not on her porch, she might be anywhere, as she loves to head down the highway in her motorhome with those furry heroes and villain to the peaceful world of nature. She finds witnessing a sunrise breaking the horizon or a pristine lake inspirational.

The odd thing is all that natural beauty and tranquility inspires her to write about murder and mayhem.

DEVIL'S BREATH

THE VOODOO BAYOU SERIES

ANNA PAXTON

BELLA
BOOKS
2024

First Edition - 2024

Editor: Cath Walker
Cover Designer: Hampton Lamoureux of TS95 Studios

ISBN: 978-1-64247-621-7

Acknowledgments

A big thanks to the Golden Crown Literary Society that helped me grow as a writer and showed me how to finish the darned book rather than tossing it to the side. Tammy Bird and my classmates have helped me grow in so many ways, including technique, resources, and just as importantly, self-confidence.

Tons of gratitude to my editor at Bella Books, Cath Walker. She helped me take my manuscript and transform it into something I'm proud of. Her sense of humor never faded as I floundered with the computer software, putting us behind schedule. Best of all, she didn't run away screaming when we discussed working together again.

Bella Books. Publishing my work is a dream come true for me. Thank you for giving me this opportunity. I sent my manuscript to Bella Books because of the great authors I saw on the website. Since then I have found support and community with Bella and am so happy to be a part of the Bella Books team. Jessica Hill and her staff are wonderful to work with. I consider myself very lucky to be working with them.

Dedications

This book is dedicated to my niece, Grace. I'm so proud of you and how you have grown into a courageous, compassionate woman. You're able to retain kindness and generosity without letting negative people change you. You're who I want to be when I grow up.

To my sister, Kim. You've gone through so much, yet here you still stand. Each day you urge us forward in faith and endurance by living your life. Wow...just wow.

PROLOGUE

October 2011

The bayou was still. No clouds drifted between the moon and the earth. No breeze rustled the leaves on the trees draped with Spanish moss. A mirror of the sky, the black water's surface was broken only by the eyes of an alligator guarding its territory. The full moon cast enough light to make its reptilian eyes glow red as it scanned the night.

Above it, along the limb of a live oak, a snake lay coiled among the leaves, keeping warm on this October evening. It watched a bullfrog waiting for an insect, but none stirred on this night. Perhaps it was the chill in the air or something instinctual. No matter the cause, it was deathly still during this witching hour.

A slight hum began, softly at first, then slowly grew louder. The gator dropped beneath the surface as the vibrations in the water signaled someone was near. The water moccasin remained coiled, even its tongue still as the small craft trolled by, black water rippling in the wake of the motor's thrum.

The dark figure in the boat used only the moonlight to guide him. Many years had passed since his summers fishing and hunting in the bayou, but his memory served him well. As a boy, he had traversed the blackwater in darkness many times. Tonight, he chose this forgotten piece of the swamp because few knew of it and fewer still bothered to come here.

He slowed near the bend where the water had gouged out the sand so deeply. The boat bumped against the bank where exposed tree roots tangled themselves as they fought their way to the water. The man rose from his seat, ignoring the gentle rocking of the flatboat. The lifetime away from the bayou melted away as he immersed himself into the night, the odor of decay and black mud as welcome to him as others might enjoy the scent of fresh-cut grass. He was finally back where he belonged, back where his purpose would be fulfilled. With little effort, he picked up a large burlap sack, the cloth saturated and dripping blood. He tossed it into the water. Soon the gators would investigate and make a meal for themselves, most likely destroying any proof of its existence.

His job now complete, he took a moment to plunge his hands into the briny water to rinse away the blood. Under the moon's light, the water bloomed red, a small copy of the large one that marked the sack's resting place below. He took another deep breath, savoring the earthy scents of his youth. It was good to be back. So many years had passed, learning, growing, and preparing for his triumphant return. His day was nearly at hand.

Reluctantly, he pushed away from the bank. The sun would breach the horizon in a few short hours, and he needed some sleep before starting his day. He began the long return trek, not looking back even when the water came alive as the alligators competed for their unexpected meal. He smiled at the wild splashes and relaxed, taking in the beauty of the surroundings.

His destiny drew near.

CHAPTER ONE

May 2018

Seven Years Later

Deputy Sherriff Claire Duvall jogged along the familiar path that ran on the outskirts of the small parish in Louisiana. The crunch of her shoes on the asphalt was rhythmic, showing no hint of stress from the mile she had just run. She was in the runner's zone, her long strides effortless as she crossed yet another bridge that straddled the slow-moving water of Kalfou Bayou.

She stopped when she reached the weathered sign that should read Welcome to Kalfou Parish. Instead, thanks to a vandal, it read Welcome to Voodoo Parish. Beneath it all was a drawing of a Voodoo doll, complete with pins sticking out of its body. She pulled errant strands of her black hair back into a neat ponytail before a glance at her watch sent her on her way once again. A frown marred her features as she thought about the vandal.

When will people realize that Voodoo is a religion meant to help people? Only a Voodoo witch would use black magic to harm others.

Living in rural Kalfou Parish, Claire had been exposed to Voodoo from an early age. Like many residents in Louisiana, she understood most of the Voodoo gods, called loa, were similar to the Catholic saints while other more prominent loa represented the Virgin Mother, and even Jesus. Claire was a believer in both Catholicism and Voodoo. She reckoned it might seem odd to an outsider, but it was routine for many throughout rural Louisiana.

In the Voodoo religion, Kalfou meant a crossroad between good and evil, a sacred place where believers lifted sacrifices to their gods. The Haitian slaves that worked the plantations named it. The owners defined the word literally and embraced it as simply a crossroads, appropriate for the prosperous trade associated with the bayou's booming transport hub. Kalfou became synonymous with both the bayou and the parish, and it stuck.

She supposed the parish was now at a crossroads of sorts. The once-thriving population was now less than a thousand. It had dwindled as transportation changed from water to road, and later, modernized farming reduced it further. But it was Hurricane Lionel that may have dealt the final blow. The 2007 storm tore through everything in its path and raised nearby waters to levels never seen before. The devastation was enormous, and many chose to build a life elsewhere.

Claire was also at a crossroads. Since her mother's death a couple of years ago, little held her here. She wanted a change. She needed a change, but something held her back. As much as she itched for something better, her prayers for guidance went unanswered. Both Voodoo's Legba, and the Catholic Jesus remained silent on the matter.

Oaks and pines changed to a large field of sugar cane, the healthy green stalks growing nicely in the warm May weather. At the edge of the field sat the weathered and battered home of Mr. Henri Trahan. It was no surprise to see the elderly gentleman placing crawdad baskets into the bed of his ancient pickup. "Mornin' Claire." His gravelly voice, thick with its Cajun cadence and dropped endings was reminiscent of her mother's. Perhaps more pronounced in the older generation, the lyrical sound was as flavorful as the cuisine that made the Cajuns famous.

"Hey, Mr. Henri." She always used the respectful term with Henri Trahan. His weathered skin and white hair attested to his life of hard work while his integrity attested to his faith. Anyone that held no bias for his poverty, or the color of his skin knew Mr. Henri was worthy of respect. "Looks like you're going to catch some crawdads today."

"I thought I'd set out some traps while I gather some goat seed and manglier. I can get my crawdads for my supper while I'm getting herbs for my medicines."

A couple of elderly women in the parish sold herbals to the sick but no one came close to Mr. Henri's knowledge. His mother had been an influential Voodoo priestess and Mr. Henri had learned at her knee everything from how to cast a spell to which plant helped with an upset stomach. Claire had seen the results of his work many times and trusted his expertise and his desire to help. "Claire, you coming to the Healing Service this week?" he asked as he lowered the tailgate of his old Chevy pickup. "There is so much cancer popping up in the parish, Father Higgins felt we should pray over the sick."

Claire refrained from rolling her eyes out of respect for Mr. Henri. "Mr. Henri, you know some people wouldn't be happy to see me cross the threshold of their church."

"Now Claire, it ain't up to you and them people. It's up to you and God. Anybody that wants to be thataway ain't there for the right reason, now are they?" He stopped loading his truck and walked over to her. "I promised yer mama I'd keep after you but you sure are a stubborn young thang." He smiled to take away any sting from his words. "I guess you take after her, huh?"

"Mama had me beat by a mile, Mr. Henri."

He laughed out loud. "I'm guessing yer right about that. She always had a mind of her own."

A sudden caw drew their attention. Up in Mr. Henri's huge oak tree sat a huge crow. It perched on the highest branch looking down on them and cawed several times before flying away, its black feathers shining in the morning sun.

Mr. Henri's expression darkened as he stuffed his hands in his pockets. "A bad sign, Claire," he said softly. "A big crow means big trouble is coming." He looked at her, his dark eyes seeing far too much. "Yesterday, as I prayed, Legba came to me and told me to make these gris-gris, one for you and one for the sheriff." He pulled two small muslin bags from his pocket, each attached to thin leather strips.

She immediately put hers around her neck, accepting it without question, but she gingerly accepted the Sheriff's pouch. A gris-gris carried power, and she wasn't sure how it might react to someone other than the sheriff or Mr. Henri.

"Is the crow forewarning trouble?"

Mr. Henri gazed in the direction of the big crow's flight, cypress trees standing tall at the edge of the bayou. "Not for me to say," he replied. "But something dark is about to touch you both, sooner rather than later." He turned back to Claire and patted her arm." 1 ain't sayin' anything you don't already know, but it never hurts to remind you. Make sure you tell the sheriff to keep the gris-gris in his pocket or around his neck. The bag must remain in contact with him for it to do its work."

She stared at the pouch, its plain fabric giving no hint of what was inside. With a little trepidation, she placed it in the pocket of her jogging shorts. She nodded. "I'll tell him, Mr. Henri. But I'm not sure if he will—"

"It's his choice, of course. But Papa Legba told me he's in danger. He said nothing about what was coming, only that it was very serious."

A sudden chill ran down Claire's spine. Anyone that needed to contact any of the Voodoo gods went to Mr. Henri to invoke their help. It was rare indeed for his requests to go unanswered. It would be prudent to listen to him. She grew more aware of the touch of the muslin around her neck.

He looked beyond the sugar cane to the forest where he spoke to the loa, the gods of Voodoo, and performed his rituals. Turning toward it now, he said, "I saw a dark cloud hanging over our bayou. While I watched, the cloud grew darker and bigger." He turned back to Claire. "Papa Legba's brother, Kalfou, must be growing strong. Papa Legba is having trouble keeping things balanced. I'm thinking the crow is a sign about trouble brewing in the swamp since he flew thataway."

Claire listened intently to the wise old man. Unbelievers might scorn his words, but she had seen him call the loa too many times to disbelieve anything he said. She began to ask what his vision meant but the sound of a car on the quiet country road caught their attention.

A patrol car came into sight and Mr. Henri's frown deepened. "Here comes Lester. Looks like he got hold of a sour persimmon."

She turned and saw her nemesis, Deputy Lester Henderson, in one of the Kalfou Parish Sheriff's Department squad cars. As usual, he sported a frown, indicating an insult would probably be coming her way in the next few minutes. As he drew close, he ran his fingers through his greasy strawberry-blond hair making it stand on end, a sure sign he was aggravated. He pulled the car up so close she was forced to back away. Claire refrained from rolling her eyes at his peevish display. She didn't want to start an argument.

When she leaned down, he lowered the window and glared at her.

"What's up Lester?" No smile for him.

"I thought I'd find you here," he stated as if it were a bad thing. "Come on and get in. The sheriff has been looking for you and sent me to find you." He pushed his sleeves up out of habit as his slight frame didn't fill out the uniform properly.

Claire wasted no time arguing and got in. "See you later, Mr. Henri," she said as she was closing the door. He answered with a wave as Lester turned the car around, throwing gravel as he spun from the driveway.

"Hopper Beaumont was caught poaching about an hour ago. They found some things we need to check." For once his chronically sulky expression lifted, curiosity piqued by the mysterious items that were important enough to warrant both deputies' attention.

"Where was he? Where are the suspicious items?" she asked.

"Down at the boat ramp off of Breaux Road."

"All the way down there?"

He shrugged. "I guess Hopper was trying to be off the grid since he was poaching."

Claire sighed heavily. "Okay. Drop me by home. I need to change into my uniform. Besides, I want my truck in case we need to split up."

"Dammit, Duvall! I ain't never getting home if you slow me down. I've been on patrol all night. I'm ready to go home and sleep." His ruddy complexion reddened further.

She didn't bother to remind him it was still over an hour before her shift began. She had every right to take her morning jog and talk to Mr. Henri. "All the more reason for me to drive my truck. You won't have to bring me back home later." She remained calm which agitated him even further.

"Fine. But you'd better hurry your ass. I ain't waiting all day until you get there!"

Claire swallowed the words that sprang to mind. The two of them had never gotten along. In Lester's world, being female made her unfit to be a cop, but being a lesbian made her unfit for polite company.

Thankfully, it took just a few minutes to cover the distance home and soon he was pulling into the driveway of the updated farmhouse-style cottage where she had lived all her life.

"I'm telling you," he warned. "Get your ass down there quick."

She ignored him and jogged onto the porch to unlock the front door. Lester showed his irritation by backing into the road and gunning the motor with tires squealing in protest.

Asshole.

Claire showered quickly even though she would still arrive at the landing before shift change. A tiny sheriff's department meant being flexible. They were divided into active deputies and those working with the courts. A total of three active deputies meant everyone jumped in to help, with the sheriff usually running the investigation.

As always when in uniform, she pulled her wavy dark hair into a tight knot at the back of her head. The academy instructors emphasized that rule to avoid it being used against the officer during an altercation. She often took guff from Lester for being a stickler for the rules, but it made sense to do things the right way. Maybe Lester might get more responsibility if he proved he was deserving of Sheriff Willis's confidence.

At five feet five inches and a woman just a couple of years out of the academy, parish citizens often considered her to be the weak link among the deputies. Thankfully, her fellow officers knew better. Slowly but surely, the citizens were also becoming aware of her abilities.

She glanced in the mirror to ensure she hadn't missed anything. She touched the silver cross hanging from her neck, the last birthday gift from her mother. Her dark hair, brown eyes, and tanned skin contrasted nicely, making the cross gleam more brightly.

As she looked in the mirror, she caught sight of her mom's picture where it sat on her nightstand. She shared so many features with her mother. Except for her eyes. Her mother's eyes had been a pale blue while Claire's were deep brown. Claire had always assumed her father's eyes were brown.

Frankly, she wished she had inherited nothing from the man she believed to be a coward. He had enjoyed her mom as a very young woman but hadn't the courage or morals to help raise their child. Consequently, her mother had led a difficult life, working multiple jobs ensuring Claire was well provided for. Her mother had never said an unkind word against her father, but Claire imagined he was a jerk who used women and then tossed them aside when they became inconvenient. That's what Claire was to the man, an inconvenience. She hated him and didn't even know his name. Her mother had taken that knowledge to her grave.

The watch her mom had given her upon graduating beeped as a reminder of the time. She grabbed her keys and both gris-gris, eager to start her day.

CHAPTER TWO

As always, Claire felt a weight lift as she entered the bayou. Cypress trees joined the live oaks, and hints of water began to appear whenever there was a break in the forest's undergrowth. The Breaux Road boat launch was one of the grassy areas that opened to a path leading to the water. It widened just enough to park a couple of trucks and still have room to back a boat onto the ramp. She parked beside Lester's squad car facing a small dock.

An airboat, sporting the Wildlife and Fish Service logo, sat aground at the water's edge. She headed toward her friend, Ranger Hollis St. Martin, easily recognized by her long blond braid extending below her cap. Hollis and Lester leaned against the truck while Hopper sat in the truck's bed, shoulders hunched forward, his head hanging.

"About damn time you showed up," Lester snapped as she got out of her truck.

As usual Claire ignored his ill temper. "Hey Hollis. Long time no see."

"It has been a long time," she acknowledged with a welcoming smile. "I just wish it was for a friendly conversation."

"What's up?" Claire walked up and leaned against the truck's bed, copying the others.

"I caught Hopper putting out bait for gators this morning. But he'd come across something that you'll find interesting." She moved to the side door of her truck and pulled out a large trash bag.

"Sorry I don't have something more appropriate. It's the best I could do." She set the bag gently on the ground and peeled it back while Claire and Lester looked on. The grayish curve of a small skull came into view.

"What the hell? Where did he find it?" Lester knelt down to get a closer view.

Hollis remained on her haunches. "He was deep in the swamp. He had gone all the way to 'Gator Alley', then made a few twists and turns farther southeast. He was setting up gator bait when he found the skull poking out of the mud. I picked him up just as he found it."

Claire nodded, her mind racing with questions. "Did Hopper act suspiciously in any way? Is it possible he was aware that you were watching him?"

Hollis shook her head. "Not a chance. Hopper nearly wet his pants when he heard me shout. As far as acting suspiciously—not at all. He gave no indication that he was searching for anything and seemed surprised to find the skull."

"Did you flag the spot?"

"Yeah. I tagged the tree but also put a flag right where he had dug it out of the mud. I didn't want you on my ass so I followed all protocol." She winked to show she was teasing. "It looks like it's been there a while."

Claire turned to the large man, sitting patiently in the truck's bed, his wrists in handcuffs. "Hopper. You got anything to say? You seem to be knee-deep in trouble."

He looked to the side not making eye contact with anyone. "Aww...I reckon I don't got nothin' to say, Ms. Claire. I better get the lawyer to do my talking. Last time he said I shoulda got him right off."

"The last time should have been the last time," Hollis snapped. "Hopper, you can hunt and fish. You just have to do it when it's legal. You know better than that."

Hopper's face flushed. "See what I mean? I just need to keep my mouth shut."

Claire stifled a laugh at his words while Lester stood and opened the tailgate of the truck. "All right. I'm taking you and that garbage bag in with me. I've already worked my shift and am ready for a bed." He glared at Claire as if his lack of sleep were her fault. "You need me for anything?"

Glad to be rid of him, Claire shook her head. "Nah. I can handle things here. I'll go set up the area and see if I can find anything else out there."

Lester put a hand on the back of Hopper's shirt to guide him toward the car. "Don't take all day. You'll probably need to be around to take Hopper's statement."

"Sleep well, Lester."

She watched them get in the squad car before allowing her exasperation to show. "Why can't Lester retire instead of Sid? Sid is a sweetheart." She was referring to the gentle soul that had served as deputy even longer than the sheriff had been on the force. Claire was twenty-four years old, and Sid Rochon had begun wearing the badge decades before she was born.

Hollis flipped her braid over her shoulder. "When is Sid's last day?"

"It's supposed to be at the end of the month, but the paperwork is being a little slow right now. He's on pins and needles about it."

"I can't blame him. I bet he's just itching to spend more time with Blanche and not have to do night shifts." She waved an arm toward the airboat. "Come on and I'll take you to where Hopper found the skull."

"Thanks for the assist, Hollis. Let me get my kit."

When she returned, Hollis was sitting in the boat's tall driver seat waiting patiently. Claire strapped down her gear, and took the headset Hollis offered before taking her place on the bench seat in front. As soon as the giant fan began turning, they were on their way.

Hollis seemed content to be quiet, allowing Claire to enjoy the beauty of the bayou as they sped along the narrowing channels of water. Live oaks covered with the gray beards of Spanish moss maintained a boundary between the muddy water and cloudless sky. At the roar of the airboat engine, alligators ducked beneath water lilies while birds bolted into the air.

As she so often did, Claire closed her eyes for a moment and said a prayer of thanks to Jesus, and then to Damballah, the Voodoo god who'd created the bayou. Damballah was aptly represented by a snake, beautiful but dangerous if disrespected… just like the bayou.

Hollis spoke through her headset, her voice clear in spite of the roar of the boat's motor. "What do you think about the skull?"

Claire blinked as she tried to bring her focus back to what lay at the end of her ride. "It's in pretty bad shape and there's not much of it. Hopefully, we'll find some more of it. It's easy to tell that it's a human skull and based on size it's probably a child."

"I don't remember having a child go missing since the tourists quit coming. Wasn't that little girl about seven or eight years ago?"

"Yep. The summer before I graduated high school."

Hollis took a right at a split in the water channel. "How soon will you get the autopsy report?"

"I don't know, but I'm sure Dr. Avi will be as quick as possible." Claire looked at the narrowed channel of water. "The drought is sure taking a toll on the bayou, isn't it?"

"Yeah." Claire could hear Hollis' regret. "I hope we get more rain than they project for this summer. Another hot summer like last year and we'll begin seeing the mud stretching across some of the channels."

"Wow. That would be a first, as far as I know."

Hollis took a second to answer as she maneuvered yet another sharp turn. "At least since they've been keeping records."

As they came out of the hairpin curve, Claire saw the chicken hanging from the tree limb and the small fluorescent-yellow flag stabbed into the mud. "Let me out over here if you can."

Claire pointed to a bank that was easy to access from the boat's platform.

"Sure. What do you need from me? Should I get out here too?"

"Why don't you bring the boat over and be ready to help if I need it."

"You got it Officer Duvall." She grinned when Claire raised a middle finger in her direction before heading toward the flagged spot.

Claire concentrated on the task at hand. She needed to set up a police investigation perimeter. With such a long timeframe since the death, coupled with having been submerged, the size and location of the scene was little more than a stab in the dark. To maximize her chance of finding something, she purposely identified an area much larger than normal. This would make things more time-consuming, but it couldn't be helped. Time hadn't made things easy.

"Looks like you're going to need more than just the sheriff's department scouring for evidence." Hollis's comment let Claire know she was closely following her movements.

"Yeah. We don't have the staffing for an area this big. Thankfully, we can always count on enough volunteers to help when we need them."

Hollis chuckled. "Guess it's not like television, huh?"

"You've got that right. Things rarely are."

Claire finally moved to the spot where Hopper had found the skull. The water level was almost a foot below where Claire now stood. "It looks like the water was up a couple of feet right here in the past so the skull had been submerged." Claire looked to Hollis for confirmation.

"Yeah. This was one of the deeper sections of the swamp. The water level was up to where you're standing until the last couple of years. The last few years' lack of rainfall upstream has sucked. Each drought hasn't recovered before the next hits."

Using the crime-scene camera from her kit, Claire captured as many details as possible. Placing the camera back in her bag, she moved leaves carefully to ensure there was nothing of interest above the ground. Finding nothing, she began to sweep away the loose dirt with a latex-gloved hand.

Still nothing.

She moved closer to the flagged spot and repeated the steps methodically until she was inches away. This time when she swept the loose dirt away, she saw a small piece of exposed bone.

"Bingo," she murmured.

"You found something?"

"Yeah, another bone. Looks like I will need to get a team down here. I think there's more to be found." She stood up and pulled out her cell phone. "Damn. You have a signal?"

"No, but I'm not surprised. We're pretty far in the swamp. And you know there are plenty of places even closer to town that don't get a signal."

Hollis was right. With so few people still living in Kalfou Parish there was little incentive for phone services to install more cell towers. "Okay. I'll finish up and then head back to give the sheriff a call. He'll want to know what's going on."

Claire stood and wiped her brow. The Louisiana sun was getting hot and would only intensify throughout the day. "Thanks for being so patient. I'll buy you lunch at Gil's for your help."

Hollis reluctantly shook her head. "I wish I could, but I have a few things I need to get done. I'll have to take a raincheck."

Splash!

A five-foot gator leaped from the water a couple of feet away from her in an attempt to get Hopper's bait, its teeth clacking loudly as it missed the ball of putrid chicken. Claire reflexively jumped backward landing on her backside. Too late, Hollis shouted a warning and began searching frantically for the gator.

"Where did he go?" Claire shouted. "That scared the daylights out of me."

Hollis sounded almost as anxious as Claire. "You and me both. I don't see him, but that bait will draw more. Can we take it down?"

Claire stood with her hands on her knees as she bent forward, taking deep breaths. Her heart was racing, and it took a minute for the adrenaline rush to dissipate. When she spoke, she was breathless as if finishing her morning run. "Yeah. We can take it down. I've already taken my photos. I don't want to have to fight alligators."

Hollis nodded. "You won't get any argument from me. An alligator can jump five or six feet when he wants to. Be careful please."

With Hollis on guard, Claire took down the bait remnants. "God, that stuff stinks." She waved at the flies that stubbornly hovered around her.

"Yeah, unfortunately, the stinkier the better when baiting for gators." Hollis held a hand over her nose and mouth while Claire tossed the bait into the water.

On the way back, Hollis placed a small flag at each turn from the main channel so Claire could find her way back. At the ramp, Hollis stayed on the airboat. "I'll take this back to the station."

"Thanks for all your help, Hollis. As far as Hopper goes, I'll book him for poaching, so I'll need a statement from you."

"You got it. I'll write everything up and drop it off this evening or tomorrow."

Claire headed toward the office, eager to begin the investigation. The idea of solving the puzzle of the skull was more exciting than the mundane tasks that usually filled her day. She hadn't dealt with something like this before and it could be added to her résumé if or when she decided to leave Kalfou Parish. Who knew where this could lead?

CHAPTER THREE

"Hey, Claire," the chief's assistant greeted her as she arrived at the station. "The sheriff said to go in as soon as you get here."

"Morning, Maxine."

She winked at the motherly gray-haired woman who was the longest—serving employee in the Kalfou Parish Sheriff's Department. The fact that the former sheriff had hired a young black woman so many decades ago was tribute to her reputation within the community. Now in her seventies, she still ran the office effortlessly with no interest in retiring. It was common knowledge that it was Maxine who helped Sheriff Willis get hired as a deputy when he came home from his stint in the Army. The elderly woman was the glue that held the department together and if anyone forgot, the sheriff would quickly remind them. More than once, Claire had seen him come down hard on a brash young man who disrespected Maxine.

Claire knocked on the sheriff's door and entered. He didn't look up from his work. "Sit down. Let me finish this and then tell me what you've found."

Claire plopped down in one of the chairs facing the large worn desk and watched as he finished writing something on his notepad. At forty-something, Sheriff James Willis was a consummate lawman. He was rather gruff but rarely impatient if you were upfront and honest with him.

He had been elected as the lead officer of the parish when it wasn't common for a black man to achieve such a position in the deep South. However, his army record coupled with the endorsement of the outgoing sheriff, pushed him to victory over his opponent. At only thirty years of age, many had doubted his ability to handle the job. However, he had proved himself during his first term and he became respected by everyone, proven by his three consecutive election wins.

Finally, he looked up, tossed his despised reading glasses onto the desk and gave Claire his full attention. "Sounds like we may have found that little girl who disappeared years ago."

"Hopefully, we'll find out soon." Claire noticed he looked fatigued though still early morning. She chose not to say anything as it would only irritate him. Instead, she briefed him on Hopper's arrest and the details relating to the skull.

"Hollis caught Hopper baiting for gators this morning. He'd found something and put it in his boat as she approached. When she moved in to make the arrest, she saw the item was a partial skull. That's when she called Lester and got us involved. She took me back to the site. I did a search and near the skull, I found another bone fragment. I think there may be more bones. I went ahead and set up the investigation scene. It's a big area so we could use a few volunteer responders to do a line search."

Sheriff Willis nodded in agreement. "Did you see anything that seemed recent? Undergrowth or leaves disturbed? Maybe something we could theorize to be recent activity?"

"No. I took a lot of photos and I didn't notice anything other than the area where Hopper dug up the skull."

"Any indication this is anything more suspect than the missing girl?"

Claire wriggled in her chair. "Nothing is suspicious at the scene. But I'm interested in how the body got so far into the bayou, particularly a child."

"We have no other outstanding cases for a missing child. Thankfully, we've never had many. My guess is that the coroner may be able to use dental records to show it's her. And DNA confirmation."

"I hope so. Those poor parents..."

"The coroner can probably help us with that. Take him what you have so he can start working with them. I'll go through the original file and pass it to you when you get back."

After a brief pause, Sheriff Willis changed topics. "What do you plan to do with Hopper?"

"Well, I figured I'd make him post bail. It should make him see we're serious about his poaching. Hollis won't be getting her statement to me until this evening or tomorrow morning. I'll talk to him but keep him jailed until she sends them."

He leaned back in his chair. "I've already had Lester book him but nothing else. I figure letting him sit there stewing will be good for him."

"Oh...okay. You're a step ahead of me aren't ya?" She poked at her boss and mentor.

"And don't you forget it," he grunted with a hint of a smile. "Close the door behind you. I have to concentrate on this damned budget."

Claire called the morgue to ensure the coroner could do an initial inspection of the bones. Doctor Avi Wason served tiny Kalfou Parish as well as the slightly more populated adjacent Pierre Parish. Both the hospital and morgue were located in Pierre Parish.

A short time later, she was sitting patiently waiting to see Dr. Avi. She was pleasantly surprised when he came to the door sooner than she had expected.

"Hello, Claire. I understand that you have something for me to inspect." His soft-spoken voice suited the quiet sterile hallways.

As they entered the autopsy room, Claire explained the day's events. "I think there could be more bones there. We'll go back out to search for more. I was hoping you could go ahead and begin looking at the two bones I have. It usually takes a couple of weeks to get DNA back."

"I can do a rudimentary analysis right now. It has been a slow day." He donned the appropriate PPE and gathered a stainless-steel pan for the skull and other bone Claire had collected.

The door opened and Dr Avi's wife, Dr. Siya Wason entered. "Hello, Claire."

Doctor Avi handed his wife a clipboard. "I was just beginning." He began removing the dirt from the skull with a brush. "This appears to be a young person," he said as he took a few measurements. "I wish we had the full mandible and dentition."

He called out the measurements as Dr. Siya wrote them down. His interest lingered on the area where the dome of the skull ended. He directed Dr. Siya where to photograph various places. He pulled a lighted magnifying lens over to aid his inspection. "I will look at the edges at the site of the missing area under the digital dissecting microscope, but I can see nothing conclusive at the moment."

"The few teeth available to us have no dental work but if you notice here—" He pointed to a tooth that was smaller than the others. "The child had not lost all of his or her primary teeth. Without the rest of the jaw, I can only assume the other side is similar. Since the normal age to lose the last primary tooth is twelve to fourteen years, there is a high probability that the person is less than fourteen years old. The range is possibly ten to thirteen years but that is only based on average ages and assumption of identical dentition on the opposite side."

"I should check the National Police Database for Missing Persons for children aged between nine and fourteen?" she inquired.

"I would begin with ten to thirteen and widen the range if you don't find a match," he advised.

He moved the magnifying lens over the partial bone. "This is a left humerus, the bone of the upper arm. Rudimentary observation indicates it to be the correct size to potentially match the cranium for the victim's age. I see no tissue remains.

The head of the humerus is intact but three centimeters below is approximately thirty percent intact." He looked at Claire. "That is the end of the bone that is part of the shoulder joint. I will need to investigate this damaged area more closely."

He moved the bone to show the broken end and refocused. "Hmmm…"

"Do you see anything helpful?" She leaned forward and studied the computer screen.

"Look at this," he said. "This appears very clean most of the way through. It's only the last few millimeters that appears ragged."

"An alligator? You think a gator might have gotten her?"

He shook his head slowly. "No. An alligator's bite is very powerful and of course, it would bite through the bone. However, it's a pressure force paired with tearing. That causes splintering of the bone. Part of this is like a cut from a sharp knife." He looked at his wife.

"Siya, please pull up last year's autopsy from the alligator attack."

While Doctor Siya retrieved the information, Claire stared at the computer monitor trying to make sense of what she was seeing.

"Here it is, Avi."

"Thank you." He found the image he wanted. "I'm sure you remember this."

Claire nodded. A body savaged by a gator with only partial remains was difficult to forget.

"This humerus was bitten and torn from the body by an alligator. See the pitting here and here." He pointed to what looked like smooth dents in a couple of spots along the length of the bone. "Notice how the bone is damaged here indicating a bite, but the real damage occurred at the joint. The arm was ripped from the shoulder socket. An attack may begin with the animal grabbing the limb of the victim but it pulls the victim into the water and rolls and thrashes until the victim drowns. Once the victim becomes still, he rips off large pieces and gulps it down. There isn't a lot of chewing."

He pointed back to the bone lying on the examination table. "In this case, there is nothing but the deep slice below the humeral head. No compression of the bone on either side of a pitted area. Actually, there is no pitting at all. The joint is otherwise in good shape so I can tell it wasn't ripped from the body by an alligator."

He looked directly at Claire now. "Based on this analysis and with so few fragments to work with, my first impression is this is an injury caused by an implement that is very sharp. A blade of some kind is an example of an item capable of creating such an injury. A knife of some kind perhaps—"

A knife wound? She jerked around to stare at him. "What are you saying?"

His eyes stared, unflinching. "It appears that the child's upper left arm was almost completely amputated at some point. I need further inspection, but preliminary findings suggest this as suspicious. At least until I complete the analysis."

* * *

Claire was blindsided by Dr. Avi's findings. Throughout the seven years since the investigation of the missing girl was completed, it was assumed that she had drowned in the bayou or had been killed by an alligator, which would explain why a body was never found.

Was this the little girl? How did the arm sustain such damage?

Back at the office, Claire prepared for Hopper's interrogation. She headed to the holding cells by way of the coffeemaker. She found Hopper lying on the single bed with his eyes closed, the stench of sweat and that godawful bait hitting her in the face.

"You ready to talk, Hopper?" she shouted, jerking him awake.

"It's about damn time," he complained as he slowly sat up, his large frame dwarfing the twin-sized cot. Manual labor at his farm coupled with a hefty beer gut made him physically intimidating.

Acutely aware that he would win in a scuffle, she nonetheless opened the cell confidently. "Hold out your hands," she ordered gruffly and cuffed him. "Now you behave yourself and I'll leave your hands in front. Otherwise, I'll put them behind you. Understand?"

"Yeah, yeah."

They began walking with her hand on his arm, his bulky six-foot-four-inch frame dwarfing her much smaller one. "Where are we headed?"

"First door on your left," she directed. "Same one you had last time you were here."

He grunted but walked docilely to the correct door and waited while she opened it. Then he went to the chair on the opposite side of the table while she took the larger one across from him.

She placed a small recorder on the table as she sat down and turned it on. "Okay, Hopper. You're aware I'm recording the interview and you've already had your rights read to you by Lester. Explain to me what you were doing out there this morning."

"What would it take to get a cup of coffee?" He eyed the Styrofoam cup in her hand.

"Tell you what," she said reasonably. "You show me you're taking this seriously and I'll get you one."

He heaved a sigh to show he wasn't impressed with her bargain. "Fine. I got up this morning and headed to the bayou."

"And why were you going there?"

"To get some fish and maybe see how the gators are looking this year."

Claire didn't bother to hide her disdain. "Hopper, you didn't even bring any bait, except the chicken that you were seen placing on the line above the water. Now unless you were hoping the fish would launch themselves out of the water to hook themselves, you weren't planning on catching one. You were hunting alligators. Your fishing reels weren't wet so you couldn't have even cast out a line to have used any bait. Now if you want to get out of here any time soon, I suggest you get to the truth because I refuse to waste my time listening to your load of crap."

Hopper's shoulder sagged at her words. "What do you wanna know?"

"So you set up bait for an alligator this morning." She paused to see if he would still protest that point. To her relief, he didn't. "Why did you choose that particular spot?"

He shrugged. "Looking for big gators. I've been checking for places nobody else knows about. That's where the big boys are hanging out, I reckon. Where I hung the chicken was about as deep into the swamp as I can go. I figure nobody much will go in so far."

"But gator season isn't until September. Why now?"

"Oh hell. I hunt for good gator spots most of the year. I make most of my money each year selling the meat and hides from the gators. The bigger hides are where the good money is made. Besides, you gotta use one of yer hunting tags no matter if it's a baby gator. All that bureaucratic shit is why all us hunters want big ones."

His words rang true. Claire moved on to the next topic. "Tell me about the skull. How did you find it?"

Hopper grinned, clearly enthused about this topic. "Ain't that lucky? I was just washing the stink off my hands from the chicken and caught sight of it. I dug around it a little bit and got the skull out. Too bad it is missing parts."

"You're saying it was just dumb luck that you found the skull?"

"Of course, it was. Did you think I had a treasure map telling me to look there?"

Claire's eyes flashed her irritation. "It seems suspicious that you have the entire bayou to set up bait and you happen to go to the exact location of the skull. Your boat was just inches away. You're telling me that's a coincidence?"

"Yep, it was just an accident that I found it." His expression changed from dismay to anger. "Now look. I didn't do nothing wrong. I just found the damned thing."

"Why did you take it? What did you plan to do with it?"

Hopper's face reddened and he looked down at his large hands. "I...uh...thought it would be a good trophy for my man cave."

"What?"

"My poker buddies would think it was cool. I mean...come on...It's a real human skull. They'd be freaking jealous of me."

Claire ran her fingers through her hair, clearly exasperated. "Hopper, if you kept it in your man cave, how would we know about the skull? How would we be able to find the person's family? Do you even realize this was once a living, breathing person?"

Her voice grew louder as Hopper slid lower in his chair. In a low voice, he muttered, "I didn't think about that, Ms. Claire."

"Well, you're in deep this time, Hopper. Louisiana Department of Wildlife and Fisheries isn't playing. And your actions don't sound very innocent regarding the skull."

Hopper sunk even lower in his seat. "I—uh want a lawyer, Ms. Claire. Sounds like I'm in deep shit."

Claire led a thoroughly chastened Robert "Hopper" Beaumont back to his holding cell. He sat heavily on the cot and was silent as she removed his handcuffs. All his macho bravado was gone, replaced by worry as the door shut with a solid clang.

CHAPTER FOUR

After lunch Claire found the case file for the missing girl lying on her desk. A note was attached with the sheriff's bold blocky lettering. "LOOK AT IT AND TELL ME WHAT YOU THINK. I NEED YOUR FRESH PERSPECTIVE."

Sheriff Willis and Deputy Sid Rochon had handled the investigation, the two most experienced in the small department. She read the file through once and then took notes as she read it a second time.

The missing child's name was Elaine Shapiro, nicknamed Lanie. The last place seen was the edge of the bayou, feeding bread to something in the water. The witness for this was Constance Vanhoy.

When asked why she didn't warn the girl to stop, Ms. Vanhoy said feeding the wildlife was common. It was after she heard about the missing girl that she wondered if it had been an alligator and reported it.

Those that had seen her prior to Constance were the girl's parents, Frieda and Marvin Shapiro from Shreveport. There was a second child, Eric, who was three years old at the time. The parents put them both down for a nap and Lanie had rebelled. They believed she left the vacation home and went to the area where Constance witnessed her feeding something. The parents agreed that an almost full loaf of bread was gone from the kitchen.

When asked, the parents separately said Lanie was fascinated with the alligators. Neither was surprised that she may have fed them. Both father and mother were visibly upset throughout the interview. Sheriff Willis noted that they seemed genuine in their fear and grief. Neither became a suspect.

Nothing else was found. No other witnesses. No other leads. Even tracker dogs hadn't found anything beyond the area where Constance Vanhoy witnessed her throwing bread into the water.

Claire closed the file.

After lunch, Sheriff Willis was available for Claire to update him. He remained unmoved throughout her summary of both Hopper's interview and the coroner's examination.

But when she explained Dr. Avi's initial findings showed the possibility of foul play, he looked as if he had been struck. "Damn. Someone killed a child during my watch? I've always prided myself on keeping everyone safe."

"You can't blame yourself, sir."

Sheriff Willis ignored her. "I have to make this right. We're taking a group this evening to find any other evidence that may be out there."

His voice changed back to the confident man she knew. "I'm going to call the volunteer fire department and first responders. They will probably be able to put together enough people to search the area. Sid and Lester need to come in to work, too. We'll need their help. Don't want more than ten to twelve of us though. If it gets too big, then we run the risk of contaminating any evidence."

"We're going to need to check in the water. The skull was just inches away from it." Unbidden images of alligator attacks flashed through her mind. She fought a shudder. "I'll need Mr. Henri and his brother Joseph to bring their net for the gators.

It won't be but a few feet from the bank but I'll need the oxygen so I can stay under long enough to be useful. I'll need a bit more than a snorkel."

Claire had once dealt with a drowning victim recovered after a week in the water. After a bit of research, she located the nearest sheriff's department that had their own Public Safety Diver team. She pitched the idea of acquiring her certification for search and rescue and gathering evidence to Sheriff Willis. He not only agreed but became certified as well. Since the bayou was a large part of the parish and it was bordered by the Gulf of Mexico, the decision was an easy one.

Sheriff Willis stopped with the phone halfway to his ear. "Do you need me as well? Should I call Lincoln Parish to send a couple of divers from their team?"

Claire shook her head. "No need to call another team. I'm only using the tank so I don't waste time constantly coming up for air."

"Okay then. But call the Wildlife and Fish guys. Hollis usually works well with us."

"Yeah. Their airboats are a lot easier to use. The drought's making those back channels so shallow I'm not sure about our boats getting there."

She remembered the small pouch from Mr. Henri. "Sheriff, I ran into Mr. Henri on my jog this morning and he wanted me to give this to you." She reached into her pocket and placed the bag in his hand.

"A gris-gris? What the hell for?"

Claire wasn't surprised the sheriff knew what the pouch signified. "Mr. Henri thinks you are in danger from something and made this for you. He was adamant that you keep it with you."

Sheriff Willis stared at it for a moment and then stuffed it in his pocket. Whether he would do as Henri had suggested or keep it out of sight before trashing it later, she didn't know. He picked up the phone. "Let's make those calls."

Less than an hour later, the phone calls were done. Mr. Henri and his brother Joseph were available. The sheriff had found three volunteers able to leave their jobs to help them. This wasn't surprising since all the local volunteer fire departments were trained to assist law enforcement as well as administer first aid. There were almost always a few people that could help.

The sheriff stood up and stretched. "Grab your diving gear and head on out. I'll wait on anybody wanting to follow me."

Claire did as he asked, changing into the wetsuit at the station. Unfortunately, she needed to remove the gris-gris. She immediately missed its small weight around her neck. It couldn't be helped, though. She didn't think it should get wet as it might dilute its power.

Ignoring the slight feeling of dread, she checked her gear. It was ready to go, the tank full. With nothing left to do, she headed down the road. She went by Mr. Henri's and was glad to see both brothers waiting for her. She relaxed at the sight of them. They were wise, experienced, capable men that would do their best to keep her safe.

"Hey there, Claire. What you done got into now?" Mr. Henri loaded an old seine net and an extra pair of shoes into the back of her truck. Joseph did the same before climbing in. After pulling back onto the road, Claire explained the situation.

"We'll keep them gators offa you, Claire. Don't you be worrying about that," Mr. Henri quickly reassured her. "We're glad to help you and the sheriff out."

When they arrived, Hollis and two fellow rangers were waiting at the ramp. Claire directed the two men toward Hollis to put their things on her boat. Claire did the same with her equipment. They would go ahead and set up everything before the others arrived.

The airboat skimmed across the water, just as it had earlier. But she didn't feel peace or tranquility along the way this time. She was anxious and ill at ease. There seemed to be a deeper sense of darkness as she looked into the depth of the trees. She looked toward the sky to focus on something else and saw a huge black crow sitting in the top of a tree. Was this the same damned crow she and Mr. Henri had seen before? As if to answer her, the bird left the tree and moved to another farther ahead, as if it were waiting on them. Three more normal-sized crows followed it.

Claire tried to ignore them but she knew they continued with the boat all the way to the location where the skull had been found. Her sense of foreboding rose even higher.

At the flagged area, Hollis cut the motor and they took a moment to listen to the absolute silence of the swamp. Claire's logic told her it was, of course, quiet because the creatures were hiding from the loud noise invading their domain. But somehow the silence felt stricken.

She attempted to ignore her fear and turned toward the brothers. Her anxiety spiked and she shivered involuntarily.

Mr. Henri stared into the trees, with unseeing eyes. They had turned white as if a thick fog swirled within the iris. His voice was deep and strong, different from Mr. Henri's normally hoarse tones.

"This place cries in pain. Erzulie Dantor, protector of the innocents, is walking among the trees with her baby. She cries tears of blood for the dead child and others to be found in this place...and others yet to come." He closed his eyes and began again. "There is imbalance. Kalfou grows strong while his brother, Papa Legba leans heavily upon his cane. The power of a witch has raised Kalfou up and helps him grow strong."

He slowly turned to them, his eyes regaining their normal deep brown. "It will worsen until balance is restored and Papa Legba can grow strong like Kalfou."

Mr. Henri was a humble man and many in the parish paid him little regard. But he had dedicated his life to the Voodoo gods. He had a depth of understanding that few possessed, and Claire felt it had always made sense to listen to him. His words were chilling.

Hollis, having only lived in Kalfou Parish for a couple of years, looked to Claire. "I'm sorry but I don't understand. What does all that mean?"

Joseph answered as Mr. Henri moved away and began praying. "Bad things have happened here and it stains the land.

The balance of nature has shifted toward Kalfou, the Voodoo god that brings hurt and pain. He has grown strong while Papa Legba has weakened."

"But why has that happened?"

"A Voodoo witch has called to Kalfou and given strength to him."

Hollis shook her head. "I'm sorry but I still don't understand."

As always, Joseph's voice was calm. "Most keepers of Voodoo use spells and potions to help others. But there are some who practice dark magic and use their knowledge to harm others. They are considered witches. A Voodoo witch is doing something with this place where the skull was found. Her actions are making everything unbalanced."

Hollis's expression showed her confusion. "He mentioned someone with a baby?"

Joseph nodded. "One of our gods, Erzulie Dantor, protects women and children. Her presence here is most likely because the skull belonged to a child. Henri will pray to better understand what has happened here and what he can do to right the balance."

Hollis turned to watch Mr. Henri complete his prayer. Moments later, she turned back to Claire. "I thought Kalfou meant crossroads. Are ya'll saying it's a Voodoo god?"

Claire concentrated on Hollis's question, trying to think of something besides her rising anxiety. "I know it's confusing. Kalfou is the god that deals with you when you come to a crossroads in your life. But he is also a trickster, making things unbalanced. Mr. Henri is saying Kalfou has gotten stronger than Papa Legba so things are out of balance. The more powerful Kalfou is, the more things are going in a bad direction."

She looked to Joseph for confirmation. "Is that basically what's happening?"

He smiled and wagged his hand. "Sort of. But close enough, I guess."

Mr. Henri and Joseph began pulling their gear from the boat. Claire did the same, her hands trembling despite her best attempts to remain calm. The silence of the swamp was oppressive, threatening in a way she had never felt before. A sense of dread filled her and she wondered if she was strong enough to overcome her fear.

CHAPTER FIVE

The arrival of the boats carrying the volunteers gave a respite from the quiet, but as soon as the boats' motors stopped, the new arrivals became subdued as well. Everyone spoke in low tones and only when necessary. The atmosphere was cloying.

Deputy Sid Rochon, the oldest member of the Sheriff's Department nodded and winked in greeting to her as everyone gathered around. The sheriff took charge to maintain order before the volunteers began tramping over the area.

"Before you get out, let's go over how we will do this. We certainly appreciate your help, but we also need to preserve any evidence that might be here."

"We'll use a grid pattern to check the area away from where the skull was found—the Sheriff's Department will look after that bit. We're looking for anything different from normal, a manmade item like a cigarette or piece of cloth. Is there a bone or bone fragment? Anything that could be attributed to a human is worth a shoutout to me. Remember. If someone calls out, you all stand still until I give the signal to continue again.

This seems to have happened a long time ago so anything we find may be the only piece of evidence left. We can't afford to ignore something or mess it up by stepping on it." He looked around at each individual. "Got it?"

Sheriff Willis stayed with the volunteers and ensured protocol was followed while Claire worked with Henri, his brother, and Hollis. Joseph pulled out a couple of thick seine nets from their gear. Each was strung between two strong poles, worn smooth from years of use. These nets would serve as a barrier from alligators that might be lurking nearby.

A huge splash echoed in the quiet.

Claire jerked her head up at the sound, her hand automatically going to her hip where her gun usually rested. She saw ripples fanning out near the bank on the other side of the water. Something big had caused that splash.

"Jest a fish," Mr. Henri reassured her. "But there was a gator sliding in the water that scared it." He turned toward the still-rippling water and spoke to it, his words barely a whisper. She understood little of what he said but she caught, "Ou pa pral antre isit la." You will not come here.

Anxiety engulfed her. Mr. Henri only used that phrase during protection rituals when he foresaw someone or something coming to cause harm. Mr. Henri had seen something big enough to invoke the prayer.

She waited nervously as he finished the ritual and wearing a solemn expression, turned to her. "You ain't gonna be harmed today, Claire. You got bigger fish to fry coming your way. I'll be lifting you up to Papa Legba."

With trembling hands, she put on her diving gear, her fear mounting by the second.

What the hell is wrong with me? I've always loved the bayou. I've been swimming before with gators in plain sight.

Mr. Henri placed a hand on her shoulder, his hand burning hot. He stared into her eyes for a long moment, his lips moving but with no sound. He appeared to be praying silently. When finished, he spoke for her ears only. "Kalfou and the witch strengthen your fear. It's not from this natural world. It is of the gods sent here to rouse such fear. Papa Legba is sending Damballah and his wife to be with you. You will soon be needed. No harm will come now. But you must tamp down this fear and enter the water to show Papa Legba you are worthy of his help."

Claire forced a weak smile. "I'm ready when ya'll are." She gathered a bag and a couple of tools and gave a thumbs up. She checked to make sure Hollis was ready with the video camera and then slid beneath the surface.

There was zero visibility. Though she had refrained from wearing fins and tried to slip smoothly into the water, mud stirred all around her. It was impossible to see very far. Despite Mr. Henri's words, she felt like she was suffocating. She was sure there was danger lurking in the water, and she wouldn't be able to see it before it was too late.

"Oh my God, Oh my God," she repeated to herself like a mantra. "I can't see an inch in front of my face. Oh my God."

Claire was unable to draw on her knowledge to think rationally. She could feel her heart racing, her breaths quick and shallow. She closed her eyes tightly, trying to calm herself. She took the time to say a prayer and regulate her breathing as best she could.

But then vertigo hit, and fear became terror.

She heard thrashing in the water, then realized she was the one making the noise. She tumbled in the water, her legs kicking as if fighting off a predator. Bubbles from the air tank swirled around as her breathing accelerated. Her feet kicked up more sediment and the water became thicker and darker brown. There was no up or down, no sunlight penetrating the muddy water to offer a clue.

Her whimpers were muffled and she spat out the mouthpiece. She needed better air. She needed to…

"Get out!" A voice rang in her ear, crystal clear.

The water came alive so close that she was caught in the movement. She heard muffled shouts mixed with unrecognizable noises. Instinctively she put her feet in the opposite direction of the splashes and launched herself out of the water onto the nearby bank. She rolled over into a sitting position ready to defend herself from attack. It took a moment to get out of panic mode and realize what was happening.

The Trahan brothers beat at the water with heavy sticks, just feet from where she had been. They yelled at the top of their voices.

Everyone rushed to see what was causing the commotion. Sheriff Willis ran to her and stood between her and whatever the threat was. Without warning, a shot rang out, the crack of the rifle cutting through all the noise and thrashing.

Then there was silence.

Claire looked around the sheriff's large frame to the largest alligator she had ever seen floating on the water's surface. Mr. Henri and Joseph were staring at each other.

Hollis's shaky voice sounded loud in the silence. "Are you all right, Claire? Mr. Henri and Joseph?"

Claire made no response. She sat with eyes tightly shut, taking deep steady breaths between long pauses, the weight of fear and dread slowly leaving her. She was calming, her heartbeat and breathing steady.

Mr. Henri gave a tiny nod to Joseph and turned toward Hollis, the rifle still in her hands. "We're fine and dandy, ma'am. But I surely don't want you to ever get mad at me. You shot that beast right in the quarter-sized soft spot behind his eyes... That's somethin'."

The others gave weak smiles and nervous titters. Everyone knew it was a miracle that no one had been hurt.

Mr. Henri and Joseph grabbed the reptile's giant head and began pulling it toward shore. It took most of the men to pull it from the water. Lester pulled out a tape measure and the alligator measured just shy of twelve feet. Not a record but still a damned big gator.

"A damn miracle, neither of you were killed." Sid looked at Mr. Henri in amazement. "How in the world did you keep him back?"

Mr. Henri laughed. "We just did what we had to do. We couldn't let that old thing get a hold of Claire."

Hollis spoke up, her nerves still clearly frayed. "It was so close to the surface, that you could see its movement. It made a beeline toward Claire and then Mr. Henri and Joseph jumped in and began beating at it with their sticks."

Joseph shrugged. "It would have gone through the net like it wasn't even there. We had to do somethin'."

Sid hooted. "Well, you sure did something all right. Dang. You two deserve a steak dinner."

The owner of the only diner in the parish, Gil Chevalier spoke. "Hot damn. You two just come by any time and I'll cook it up for you, free of charge."

Mr. Henri and Joseph moved to sit next to Claire. "How're ye doing, Claire?"

Claire took a swig of water from a bottle Joseph handed her. "Much better now. I'm so grateful to you both. It was your yelling to get out, Mr. Henri, that made me move." She looked up when they said nothing and caught them looking at each other. "What's wrong?"

Mr. Henri pursed his lips. "I didn't yell anything, Claire. I mean, I made a lot of noise at the gator, but I didn't say anything. I didn't have time."

"He's right, Claire." Joseph's soft voice echoed his brother's.

"Well, it sure seemed like you yelled for me to get out."

He looked a little sheepish. "I thought it but I didn't say it. I was too busy trying to bang on its big ole head. I done a lot of praying but nothing out loud."

Joseph cleared his throat. "Are you saying you heard Henri?"

"Yeah. I heard him like he was shouting in my ear."

The two men looked at each other but Claire couldn't continue her questions when the sheriff came over to check on them.

"I'll call Lincoln Parish's diving team in the morning." He looked at the men. "Would you be available to help them?"

Claire didn't give them a chance to respond. "I'm going back in now, Sheriff. I'll be fine."

Sheriff Willis's expression showed what he thought of her going back in. "I don't think that's a good idea, Claire."

"I need to. If the volunteers don't see me go back in the water, the entire parish will be buzzing about my incompetence tomorrow. And I feel better now, Sheriff. I can do it."

He stared at her for a moment as he decided. "Okay. But give me a second to put Sid in charge of the line search. I'll be here to watch your back. If anything isn't right, you're to come up immediately. Understand?"

She grinned. "Believe me. There won't be any problem following that order."

His lack of response to her joke indicated his concern as he stood up and headed toward Sid. She returned to the water as soon as the sheriff came back and was almost giddy at how different she felt. As long as she didn't think about the big gator, she could stay on task. The visibility was just as bad, but her claustrophobia had left with the fear.

She felt her way through the darkness. She began in the deepest portion of the netted area and work her way toward the bank. She worked her trowel in the sediment, focusing on her task to the point of almost feeling relaxed. She found several rocks that she cast aside but most of the time she just felt soft mud.

When she came to the surface the sheriff was watching as he had promised.

"I'm finished being underwater. I'll start digging around the first location. It's a few inches above the waterline," she explained.

"All right." His voice deepened as he said, "Claire, getting back in that water after seeing that big gator shows a lot of courage. Nobody's going to be saying anything but praise for you tomorrow."

Claire was touched by his words. "Thank you, Sheriff. That means a lot."

After removing her tank she and the brothers went to the skull's marker while Hollis stood guard, the rifle still in her hand. Claire dug a good foot or so around the first spot while Joseph sifted through the dirt she collected.

By the time the others had completely inspected the wider area, Claire had finished. She had a small collection of bone fragments that may have splintered from the skull to give to Dr. Avi.

They finished up and rode back to the boat ramp. Thoughts of Mr. Henri's prayer, the giant alligator, and hearing Mr. Henri's voice all raced through Claire's mind. The deep groves of cypress trees that lined the banks of the waterway seemed as sinister as they had felt earlier. Childhood stories of ghosts and Cajun fairies came back to haunt her so that she found herself glancing through the trees for balls of light, even as she chastised herself for such foolishness.

At the boat ramp, Mr. Henri patted her arm. "Don't let the fear back inside you, Claire. Kalfou knows he lost back there. He ain't happy about it."

"Thank you both again for what you did." She shivered. "I hate to think what would have happened if you hadn't been there."

The brothers brushed off her thanks and headed to the men talking among themselves as the sheriff and deputies packed up. They were all excited to be associated with the biggest thing to happen to their little parish since Hurricane Lionel.

"You did pretty good today," the sheriff said to Claire. "I'll be putting you in charge of this. You'll keep me informed every step of the way but as long as you stay on top of things, it's yours."

Claire's moment of pride was snatched by Lester's outrage.

"What? I've been on the force longer than her. This should be mine." Everyone's eyes were on Lester.

"Lester," the sheriff warned. "Not here."

"God dammit, Sheriff," he shouted, his face flaming red with rage. "What does she do for you to get this special favor? Everybody knows what she is. She ain't even natural!"

Tears stung Claire's eyes, but she refused to show weakness to Lester…or the others silently watching the drama unfold.

Sheriff Willis stood up to his full height and looked down at Lester. "I'm giving you one more chance. If you want to keep your job, you will shut the hell up right now. If you don't want your job, just open your mouth again."

Lester opened his mouth but then clamped it shut.

Satisfied that Lester was going to keep quiet, the sheriff said, "Sid. Disperse the men and take Lester home. He needs some time to rest before his shift starts again. Then you head on home. It's your day off."

"You got it Sheriff," the older deputy said. "You all take it easy." He gave Claire a sympathetic pat on the arm as he passed.

Lester went with him quietly, but she suspected Sid would be getting an earful the whole way home.

Sheriff Willis waited until it was just the two of them. "I'm sorry that happened, Claire. Lester will be in my office tomorrow for a talk."

When she simply nodded, he wisely changed the subject. "You're in charge of this, Claire. I'll help you as much as you need but it looks like I might be going out on medical leave for a couple of weeks. I'd rather the person that starts it to be the one that finishes it."

"What's going on?" she blurted out before thinking it through. "I mean, if you don't mind my asking."

"The doc says I need an angiogram. I can go back to work after a day or so but I've decided to take some of those vacation days I've accumulated. Then if something else has to be done…" He paused a moment. "Just easier to have you handle things the whole time."

Claire's heart flipped as she listened. With his tendency to push himself too hard, she knew he was probably downplaying the situation. She admired the sheriff. He was a good man and had always treated her with respect. When she was a child he had always taken the time to smile or wave when he saw her. Many had turned their backs on her when gossip concluded she was a lesbian, but the sheriff had never changed.

He continued. "Also, I talked to the sheriff at Lincoln Parish. He owes me a favor and I'm calling it in. Tomorrow you'll be meeting his second-in-command, Undersheriff Jessica Morgan. She's coming to help out while I'm gone. We'll be short-handed plus she worked in Property Crimes Division with the New Orleans Police Department before she moved to her current job. You're taking the lead, but I'll expect you to listen to her advice."

"Okay."

He added, "I'll talk to Sid and Lester in the morning. She will be filling in for me, but mostly just keeping things going so you deputies can do your job without interference. I had expected her job to be mostly the senseless paperwork but now these bones will be adding to your workload, so we'll need her on the roads too."

He checked his watch. "Let's head home and get some rest. It will be sunset soon."

Still smarting from Lester's tirade, Claire was ready to go. Her questions could wait until morning.

As she drove home, she had difficulty concentrating on the road. She felt as if her head were spinning. She was excited about investigating the skull. It would be a first for her and she looked forward to the challenge.

CHAPTER SIX

The moon was a sliver of light in the night sky, unable to illuminate the truck hiding among the live oaks. Here, the black water would normally graze the edges of the dirt path where he sat, but the drought had pulled the shoreline farther into the trees.

The watcher was deep in thought, going through a mental checklist of things to do. He needed his upcoming celebration to go smoothly. Why had the heavens decided it best to have that skull discovered now? The last thing he needed was the Sheriff's Department nosing around the bayou.

The Year of Perfection was upon him—seven times seven. With time so short, more and more sacrifices must be made in preparation of the big celebration. On that day, the world would behold its new Messiah and no longer be in darkness. But until then, he and his people must remain hidden, waiting for the day of his Transfiguration.

Headlights pierced the darkness, having him sit up in anticipation. He needed this shipment badly. The crunch of tires on sand drew near and the lights blinked once before going black. He switched his lights on and off in response. The vehicle crawled toward him. Only when it stopped within a few feet did he get out of the truck.

"We got some," announced the man behind the wheel.

"Some?" Concern poured through his voice. "How much?"

"A bird and a half."

Panic and anger swept over him. "I got only forty-two fucking grams total? I need more than that. I told you—"

The supplier rolled his eyes. "This is all they had ready. My supplier thought I was crazy to want this much. Said it only takes a tiny amount."

"You think I don't know that? You didn't know it existed until I told you."

"Look. You can buy the same amount again in ten days and another bag later."

"There can't be a failure in this. It's too important."

The supplier lit a cigarette and blew smoke into the air. "I understand. You got my money?"

"Of course." He handed a wad of bills to the man. "You get me the full amount in the time I require, no excuses."

The son-of-a bitch grinned, his teeth barely visible. "I'll have it here. That's a promise." Without waiting for a reply he gave a small salute, cranked up, and turned around using only his parking lights.

The watcher got back into his truck, in no hurry to leave. He sat with the windows down and saw the dealer drive out of sight. He held the lightweight package on his lap unwilling to put it to the side. The powder was perfect. Pristine white with the ability to render the partaker subservient using just a minuscule amount. The few people who knew the drug called it "Devil's Breath", but he preferred "God's Breath."

There was nothing diabolical about the powder. It was a sacred tool to use according to his will. The faithful grew more enthused during the ceremonies while the unfaithful became docile, a helpful attribute when discipline was required to show them the error of their ways.

His thoughts turned back to the day and Lester Henderson's temper tantrum. The idiot had made an ass of himself earlier. Sure, he had certainly been useful, but his jealousy and hubris were unacceptable. A plan formed as he stared at the bag of white powder. He couldn't afford for the law to start looking too closely in the swamp. Sheriff Willis was much too smart for his own good. Perhaps Lester's public display had been a sign from the heavens. After all, the timing was perfect. The little deputy had one last job to do. He needed the sheriff out of the way and Lester would help him with that.

He cranked the engine and crept down the road toward Henderson's house. For months, Lester had been sneaking home during his night shift to take a nap for a couple of hours.

The watcher pulled around behind Lester's place. Surrounded by fields and forest, there were no nosy neighbors to worry about. He took what he needed from his shirt pocket, and hand—rolled a thin cigarette, filling it with the white powder instead of tobacco. He headed to the back door, being careful to keep the expensive powder from spilling out.

He knocked and placed one end of the cigarette between his lips. He waved when Lester cracked the door to see who was knocking.

Lester was clearly surprised to see a visitor. "What do you—"

The answer was a blast of air and powder into his face.

"I have something big for you tonight, Lester. It's time for you to show your devotion. How much do you love the Lord, your God? How much do you love me?"

Lester fell to the floor.

CHAPTER SEVEN

Despite her sleepless night, Claire drove to work ahead of schedule. As she traveled by her school and various neighbors' homes, she was reminded of the bullying she had endured as a teenager. Lester's anger had moved her right back to being that young girl, scorned for her feelings toward other girls.

She had mostly remained invisible through school until the rumors began circulating. After that she became a pariah, a target for the bullies. A couple of girls had secretly dated her but never wanted to be seen in public. As humiliating as it was, she had agreed to the terms. After all, the few lovely hours took away some of the isolation.

The memories triggered a sudden rush of loneliness.

As she turned into the tiny parking lot of the Kalfou Parish Sheriff's Department, she literally gave herself a shake. She refused to be cowed down by the past.

She strode to the entrance, a determined glint in her eye, but it fell away as she glanced at Maxine. The strong-minded, ever-cheerful receptionist was upset. "What's wrong?" she asked as she sat down across from her.

Maxine finished wiping her eyes. "I just got word that Sheriff Willis has had an accident on the way into work this morning. He's at the hospital in surgery right now. It's bad Claire...it's bad."

Claire jumped from her chair. "He's going to be okay though, right? Oh my God, why didn't you call me?"

"I got the call about five minutes ago. I haven't called anyone yet. I needed to pull myself together first." She put her glasses back on. "I've known him since he was a boy." Another tear leaked out.

Claire reached out and gave the older woman's shoulder a squeeze. "You go ahead and cry if you need to. I'll head to the hospital now and let you know what's happening. I'll be able to get a signal if you need to dispatch." She started toward the door and turned back, cursing. "Dammit. I almost forgot Hopper."

"Don't worry about him. His lawyer came by last night, and Lester signed everything to let him go."

"Lester did that last night? Without talking to the sheriff, or me as the arresting officer?"

Maxine blew her nose. "According to Sid, Lester said he had been there first, brought Hopper in, and then filled out the complaint, so he had the authority."

From a paper-trail point of view, he was right. But the bastard knew they were keeping Hopper here for as long as they could. Lester was only trying to assert himself after the scene yesterday evening.

Determined to see Sheriff Willis for herself, Claire grabbed her keys and headed toward the door. As she got there, it opened to a tall striking woman. A crisp navy uniform with a shiny gold badge pinned on her breast pocket told Claire this was Jessica Morgan.

Sheriff Willis had forgotten to mention that the woman was drop-dead gorgeous.

She was tall, at least five feet nine, her slim form, feminine perfection with just the right amount of curves to catch the eye. Tawny beige skin matched her lighter shade of hair tied in a loose bun at her neck and hanging in ringlets surrounding her face. Golden highlights brightened the overall effect and emphasized her eyes.

Oh my god those eyes. They're almost the color of amber.

Claire suddenly wished her khaki uniform pants weren't wrinkled from hanging over the chair all night and she had polished the silver badge attached to her own pocket.

The woman appeared oblivious to Claire's stare.

Maxine greeted the stranger. "Sheriff Willis won't be in today. How can we help you?"

The woman hesitated. "Uh…I'm a little confused. I was to meet him this morning."

Claire cleared her throat to get her tongue to function. "You're Jessica Morgan, the undersheriff for Lincoln Parish?" Claire cleared her voice again. "I spoke with Sheriff Willis yesterday. He said you would be coming." She looked at Maxine. "I'll handle this. No worries."

She cleared her throat a third time and hoped it would be the charm. "Sheriff Willis was in an accident this morning and I was just leaving to see him. If you come with me, we can talk along the way."

The woman hesitated a second, then agreed. "I'm ready if you are."

Claire strode over to hold the door for her. She glanced over her shoulder and saw Maxine wiping her face again. "I'll let you know of any changes as soon as I know. I promise."

"Yes. Please do," she responded, worry etched into her face.

Claire headed to the SUV that was her assigned vehicle.

Crap. I forgot to introduce myself.

"Welcome to Kalfou Parish, Ms. Morgan. I'm Deputy Claire Duvall."

"Ahh, you're who I'm here to work with," the tall woman said as she slid onto the passenger seat. "I'm Jessica, but please call me Jess."

They buckled up and Claire headed toward the hospital.

"I'm glad the sheriff has already mentioned our working together." Jess's voice was as smooth as silk.

"Um…Yeah. We talked a little yesterday. You probably know details I don't yet, but you or the sheriff can fill me in." Claire turned to the right at the only stoplight in the entire parish and caught another glimpse of her companion.

"So, what did he tell you?"

Claire cleared her throat. "He said you were on loan from Lincoln Parish as a favor and would be assisting while he's on sick leave. I believe he said you had some investigative experience?"

"Yes. I've been with Lincoln less than a year. Before that, I worked in New Orleans. I got most of my experience there."

"A city girl?" She smiled to remove any sting.

"You got it," was the answer coupled with a flash of white teeth. "Lincoln Parish is giving me a crash course in small-town law enforcement, but you guys are even less than half our size. This will be a learning experience for me."

"Sounds like you will know the procedure and I will know the area. We should work well as a team."

Jess heaved a sigh of relief. "Thanks for being on board about the arrangement. I'm sure it isn't easy when a stranger comes in. But I'm just here to help."

Claire caught a whiff of vanilla as Jess removed her jacket and placed it in the back seat. "The sheriff and I are both happy to have you with us. We've just landed an investigation that's a little irregular for Kalfou."

She explained the skull's discovery and the progress of its investigation, warming to her topic. By the time she finished, she felt much more relaxed with the woman. Claire found her to be friendly and smart with a down-to-earth way of talking.

They parked and headed inside where a receptionist directed them to the third-floor nursing station outside of the recovery unit where Sheriff Willis would go after surgery.

"Hi, Blanche." Claire greeted the gray-haired petite nurse standing at the nurses' desk. "Heard anything yet about the sheriff?"

"Dr. Avi called just minutes ago. The sheriff is out of theater and in recovery."

The woman smiled at Jessica Morgan and held out her hand. "Now who are you, dear? I'm Blanche Rochon. My husband,

Sid, is one of the deputies that works with Claire and the sheriff. Are you here to visit Sheriff Willis?"

Jess smiled and grasped Blanche's hand. "I'm Undersheriff Morgan from Lincoln Parish. I'll be working with the Kalfou department temporarily."

Introductions made, Claire turned to why they were there. "Blanche. How is he? What happened?"

"Lester talked to Sid and told him the sheriff lost control of his car on that bad curve on Deer Haven Road."

"So, Lester knew about it and called Sid?"

"Yes. Afterward, Sid called me hoping I might know something. Sid may be about to retire, but he still thinks the world of Sheriff Willis and is pretty upset."

Claire nodded, equally upset. "How badly hurt is he? What are his injuries?"

"Is this official business?" Blanche asked the question to be able to speak freely without violating the patient's privacy.

"Yes." Claire's response was immediate. She understood Blanche's reasoning.

"There are a few fractured fingers and a rib pierced a lung, so they've dealt with that in surgery. Other than that, it's a lot of cuts and bruises. From what I've heard about the accident, it could have been much worse."

Claire agreed but wondered if it had been luck or the gris-gris that kept him from further harm. Hopefully he was carrying it.

The door opened and in strode Pastor Abel Creech, an imposing figure in his black attire and white collar, typical of the clergy. He was a big man in both height and girth. It was rumored that he had once been a roughneck on an oil rig until he was called to form his small non-denominational church. Claire wished he had stayed there as their encounters were rarely civil.

"I'm here to visit Sheriff Willis," he announced in his usual booming voice.

Blanche's smile was professional but distant. "Why hello Pastor Abel. I was just telling these women that he is in recovery. I expect him to be brought to his room shortly."

He grimaced, his dark brows coming together. "I have a lot to do today. Can you tell me how he's doing? What happened?"

Blanche shook her head negatively. "I'm sorry, Pastor, but I can't pass on details. But there is a fresh pot of coffee in the waiting room. I'll let you know as soon as he can have visitors. It may be a while."

He gave her a disapproving frown that Blanche ignored. "I guess I'll wait but notify me as soon as he gets to his room."

"Of course."

He turned to the two officers and nodded curtly before heading to the waiting room.

"If you girls will excuse me, I need to look in on a patient. I'll call you as soon as I hear something." Claire took this as their cue to leave.

They headed to the waiting room where the pastor sat watching a game show on the TV hanging on the wall. Unfortunately, Claire was very familiar with this room. She had spent a lot of time here with her mother's illness. One breast was removed, then the next, and finally a lung.

The pastor was the first to speak, albeit grudgingly. "Have you heard anything about what happened?"

"Very little," Claire responded cautiously, hoping he wouldn't find a way to embarrass her today.

The door opened and Sid entered the room. "Hello everybody. Sorry to be here due to such a bad situation."

"Hey Sid." Claire moved a hand toward Jessica. "This is Undersheriff Jessica Morgan from Lincoln Parish. She will be working with us for a while. Jess, this is Deputy Sid Rochon."

Sid was as tall as Blanche was short. Both had a quick smile and a caring heart. With a smile that held real warmth, he held out his hand. "Glad to meet you, ma'am. My wife, Blanche, is the nurse you just met. She just told me you ladies were here waiting." He took a seat next to Claire. "Pastor Abel. I hope you're doing well."

The pastor wore a stiff smile but to Claire's eyes it seemed more like a grimace. "I didn't see you at the joint service for all the churches last Sunday. You still attend the Catholic church, don't you?"

"Yes," Sid responded patiently. "It was my turn to work. No biggie."

"Seems like those that want to go to church should be given the chance. Attendance is falling from all the congregations in our little parish. God-fearing people have to work on Sunday as if it's a normal workday." He turned to Claire. "It's just another day for you isn't it, Claire? Perhaps you could work Sundays and let God-fearing people worship as they're commanded."

Claire felt rather than heard the soft intake of breath from Jessica. She really didn't want the woman to witness the embarrassing confrontation that always occurred with Pastor Abel. "Now isn't the time, Pastor." She crossed her arms defensively.

He snorted. "You know the devil is waiting for you, Claire Duvall. You need to come to church and confess your sins to God."

Claire hung on to her temper by a thread. "I tried that before, Pastor, and found it to be an awfully cold place."

"Where you're headed will make you beg for some cold, young lady." He ignored Sid's attempt to calm the situation. "You mark my words—'the abominable shall be cast into the lake which burns with fire and brimstone.'"

"Judge not lest you be judged," Claire promptly snapped back.

Sid jumped up and put his hands toward each of them to calm the quickly escalating conversation. His normally kind eyes stared accusingly at the pastor. "Let's remember why we're here. Let's concentrate on the sheriff. I think we can all get along for another half hour or so."

Claire took a deep cleansing breath. "I'm okay with that."

Outwardly she regained her composure but inside, she was again that hurt little girl, so often attacked because of being different and "unnatural". Not for the first time, she cursed the joke God had played when he let her be born in a tiny town of bigots. Her attraction to women was just as natural as that between a man and woman. God had made her that way. But they would never see that.

After a brief silence, Pastor Abel turned his attention to Jess. "You're here to fill in for the sheriff?"

The door swung open, and Dr. Avi strode in, still in his surgical scrubs. "Good morning, everyone." He came over to stand next to Claire's seat. "Sheriff Willis will be fine. Without any next of kin, he has you, Claire, listed as his emergency contact. He had only filled out the paperwork for this yesterday so you may not have known."

Claire was both surprised and touched. "I didn't know, but I'm not surprised. He would want someone from the department just to keep him up on what's going on." All except the pastor laughed at her joke as everyone knew the sheriff was married to his job.

Dr. Avi turned to Pastor Abel. "You may see him briefly while I speak to Claire."

He waited as the pastor left the room and the others gathered around the doctor. "Are you aware of the procedure he planned to do this week?" His words were directed toward Claire.

"Yes."

"I've spoken to his cardiologist, and we agree it must wait until he heals from today's injuries. It needs to be done soon but this accident will have to take precedence. He will be out of work for a few weeks."

When nobody asked a question, he continued. "When the rib broke, it pierced his right lung, and it collapsed. We placed a tube into his thorax to get it to inflate again. You must understand the sheriff has sustained a lot of trauma which makes the collapsed lung more severe. It also means more time to heal. It can take a while even in the best of circumstances."

"In addition, he sustained two broken fingers on his left hand, along with multiple cuts and bruising. The seat belt undoubtedly saved his life." He held out his hand and when Claire grasped it in a handshake, he placed his other on top and held it. "I will look after him. I promise."

"Thank you, Doctor," she replied. "Everyone from the department, not to mention our town, will be grateful."

He nodded and turned to Sid and shook his hand, adding a few more words of reassurance. When he turned to Jessica, he seemed puzzled. "I don't believe I know you. I am Dr. Avi Wason."

"I'm Jessica Morgan but call me Jess. I'll be helping the department for a few weeks."

"Ahh, well then it appears you have arrived when you are definitely needed. It is a pleasure to meet you."

Claire motioned toward the doctor. "Dr. Wason is also our coroner. We will be working with him regarding the autopsy."

He turned to Claire. "There isn't a lot to do. There is so little to work with, although the bone fragments you found in the mud appear to be part of that missing from the skull."

"When do you think we'll have any results?" Claire asked.

"Soon. I will keep you up to date," he promised. "Now, I must go. Good day to you all."

They barely had time to return to their seats before Blanche stuck her head in the door. "You can see him now."

"The pastor must have been in a hurry to be in and out that fast," Sid mumbled. "The danged jackass."

They laughed, shaking off some of the earlier tension.

Sid looked at the two women. "You go ahead. It will give me time to talk pretty to my wife." He wriggled his eyebrows suggestively.

Claire raised her hands in surrender. "Heaven forbid we stand in the way of true love. We will leave you to it."

They left Sid at the nurses' station and went into the room where Sheriff Willis lay, his eyes closed. Monitors beeped quietly beside the bed. The sheet pulled up to his chin hid most of his injuries, but cuts and scrapes covered much of his head and face and his wrapped hand lay on top of his chest.

"Jesus," Claire whispered.

He opened his eyes and slowly brought them into focus. "Hey." His voice was little more than a whisper.

"Hey." She came over and placed a hand on the safety rail. "Sounds like Dr. Avi did a good job."

"Yeah?" he croaked.

"Yeah. He told us you'll be recovering for a while, but he's fixed everything."

His eyes wandered momentarily and then stuck on Jess. "You Jess?"

"Yes, sir." She stepped forward. "I'm sorry to meet in these circumstances."

"Been...tough...day," he said slowly.

"What happened?" Claire asked. "Was it a deer?"

"Nuh-uh," He widened his eyes as he tried to keep them open. "Run off ...road. 'Nuther truck... came at me."

Claire frowned and looked at Jess. "Did you recognize the truck?"

He gave no answer as he lost the battle to remain awake. His breath deepened, and he slept even when the IV pump alarm began beeping. Before Claire could call the nurses' desk, Blanche bustled in and reset it. Immediately the beeping stopped. She then changed out one of the bags hanging from the IV pole and verified it was dripping correctly. Sheriff Willis didn't stir. She found his wrist and took his pulse. "He will probably sleep for a while now so you might as well come back later."

They turned to leave but the sheriff opened his eyes. "Claire," he called out weakly.

She moved back to the bed. "Yes?"

His eyes fluttered as he fought sleep. "Be careful." His voice dropped to a whisper. "Bastard...on purpose." His eyes shut as the drugs took control.

Claire turned to leave, her mind reeling from the possibility of someone deliberately trying to hurt Sheriff Willis. For whatever reason, her eyes locked onto something lying on his bedside table.

Mr. Henri's gris-gris.

She picked it up and stared at it. Did it do nothing for Sheriff Willis or did it prevent more severe injuries? Was this simply a useless trinket, or something holding power? With a little prayer, she tucked the gris-gris into his hand. She preferred to believe.

CHAPTER EIGHT

When Jess awoke that morning, she had planned her day to be meeting personnel and acclimating herself to their procedures. Instead, she found the Sheriff's Department in a crisis.

The unexpected challenge was a welcome surprise. Of course, she felt sympathy for Sheriff Willis and his staff, but she was also excited to showcase her investigative skills and run the department for an extended period. This would boost her résumé, a necessity to overcome the good ole boy network. It could put her a step closer to becoming sheriff when her boss retired in a couple of years. Being a biracial woman did her no favors in Lincoln Parish, but experience in the tough city of New Orleans and now experience running the Kalfou department could be the thing that got her elected.

The deputy beside her made a sharp turn, the movement catching Jess's attention. Claire was another surprise.

A sweetheart as well as beautiful. Those dark brown eyes coupled with that smile are lethal. But more than just a pretty face. Caring and supportive. That woman, Maxine, was obviously upset, and Claire calmed her down with just a few words. Her concern over the sheriff was genuine, too.

She pulled herself back to the present. Claire had said something to her. "Sorry, what did you say?"

"I asked if you wanted to discuss anything. I mean, you've just arrived and already had a lot thrown your way."

Jess nodded. "Yes. I'm sorting through what Sheriff Willis said. What did he mean? He thinks someone intentionally ran him off the road?"

"It sounds like it."

"Do you know of anyone who's angry with him?"

Claire shook her head. "No more than the usual. I mean, we have the normal DWIs, speeding, breaking and entering…just typical arrests. He's on a morphine drip. I recognized it from when Mom was hospitalized. She began having nightmares that she believed to be real. She even thought the doctors and nurses were trying to kill her. The doctors said that sometimes happens with opioids."

"Maybe…But let's go check out the crash site while it's still relatively untouched. Just in case."

"No problem."

They made a right turn and were soon driving along a country road with nothing but farmland on either side of them.

"Agriculture appears to be king around here," Jess observed as she looked out the SUV's window.

"Yes. We have less than a thousand citizens but lots of farmland and the bayou area to cover. Thankfully, we don't have a lot of crime. It's difficult enough for Sheriff Willis to get enough funding for our small workforce. I would hate to see the squabble over money for a larger one."

Several cane fields later, they saw the sheriff's squad car upside down in an unused field. Although damaged all over, the driver's side appeared to have borne the brunt of it. The distance from the road to the car showed it had probably rolled at least twice.

As they pulled off the road, Jess rolled up her shirt sleeves. "Let's process the scene."

The point of impact was easily recognized from all the debris on the road. Bits of metal, glass, and plastic were scattered around scrambled skid marks.

Claire pointed away from town. "Sheriff Willis would have been coming from this direction toward town. That means the other vehicle would have come this way."

"So those skid marks belong to Sheriff Willis." Jess pointed to his tire marks that preceded the collision. "But the other vehicle has no skid marks until the point of collision. The vehicle didn't brake before colliding with the sheriff."

Claire whistled under her breath. "The skid marks and collision debris are angled toward the field. It looks like the sheriff swerved to avoid the other vehicle, but it came right into his lane to hit him. The collision occurred in the sheriff's lane."

Jess nodded in agreement. "His car hit the ditch causing it to flip."

"Jesus." Claire crossed herself.

The two set to work and began methodically measuring and photographing the skid marks and the debris field. They measured the distance from the road to the squad car. Then they made their way to the wrecked car.

Jess looked at Claire. "We'll need to get the camera and the black box from his car." Any other evidence had been trampled by the numerous first responders who helped get Sheriff Willis out of the car and to the ambulance waiting at the road. Jess started kneeling to look inside the upturned car when Claire threw out an arm and stopped her.

"Be careful. You're about to kneel on a devil's thorn. I assume coming from the city you aren't familiar with it."

Jess looked closely at a yellow-flowered weed. She frowned in confusion. "It doesn't look so terrible."

"Look closer and you'll see spiky burrs that can go through the sole of a shoe or even a bicycle tire. No one has farmed this field in the last couple of years. The stuff is invasive when the conditions are right."

Avoiding the plant, Jess inspected the car's interior. Coffee cups and a map lay strewn among shattered glass from the windshield and both front door windows. However, the dark, almost black blood on the driver's seat and door told its own grim story. The sheriff had been lucky.

They took a few more photos and returned to the SUV. Jess took a moment to remove dirt from her shoes while Claire put away the equipment.

Without realizing it, Jess found herself staring at Claire's ass when she leaned into the back seat. Her uniform pants were not quite form-fitting but tight enough to show it off.

Oh my God. I could bounce a silver dollar on that firm backside. The amazing thing is she doesn't seem to have a clue how hot she is.

Ashamed to be ogling a fellow officer, Jess averted her eyes. "I'm ready to call a tow truck. I'll get the dashcam when the truck gets here and it's easier to get to. The mechanic can remove the black box for us. They will contain the most important information anyway. Everything we've done so far will just back them up as evidence."

Claire pointed to the road where it curved. "I want to take a look at those skid marks up the road a bit. Sheriff Willis said a truck pulled out. It wouldn't surprise me if those marks are where the other vehicle came out and gunned the motor."

Before getting into the vehicle Claire pulled a couple of devil's thorns from the cuff of her pants. "See what I mean? Look at the size of that thorn."

"Ouch." Jess grimaced.

They photographed the skid marks that Claire had pointed out as well as tire tracks in the dirt where a vehicle may have lain in wait. They could be matched to those of any vehicle under suspicion. The location was a good one if you were waiting for a vehicle. There was a long sight line that offered time to get a parked car moving at a decent speed.

They then headed to the sheriff's office while Jess called the tow service listed on a contact sheet from the glove compartment. "I don't suppose there's a Starbucks around here?"

Claire laughed. "Yeah. Good luck with that. Gil's Grill is just ahead. It's the only restaurant here." Gil's came into view. Most of the graveled parking area showed the grill to be a popular place. "I know it doesn't look wonderful, but the food is good."

Based on the unappealing exterior, Jess was skeptical but was willing to try it out. Their steps crunched on the gravel. She opened the door to the sound of jingling bells. Laughter and the mix of both sweet and greasy aromas greeted them.

The dining area was just as small as the outside of the building suggested. Galley-style, it held a line of booths along the windowed wall opposite a worn counter running the length of the room. A narrow aisle separated the booths from the shiny chrome seats stationed along the counter. Silver duct tape repaired the red vinyl seats on several of the booths. Men filled the booths and barstools near the door, their attention centered around a slim man in the middle of them all.

Lester Henderson.

"Shit," Claire murmured.

CHAPTER NINE

The men looked up as the door shut and silence hit the room abruptly. Claire stared at their sheepish expressions, leaving no doubt that she was the focus of the conversation.

"Well, look who just came in." A smirk was plastered across Lester's face.

The awkward silence was broken by the owner, Gil Chevalier. "Come in, ladies. What can I get for you today?" He stood in the kitchen while leaning down to see through the open window that ran down most of the length of the counter.

Claire smiled, grateful for his rescue. "Thanks Gil. We'll take a couple of coffees—"

"At the table back there," Jess finished.

"Coming up." His usual amiable grin was firmly in place.

Jess headed down the aisle with Claire following, their footsteps seeming loud in the silence. Claire held her back ramrod straight as she felt the stares of condemnation and judgment. Sure, she was used to the whispered comments, but she had never become comfortable with it. She wished they had ordered their coffees to go.

They took the booth at the back of the room with Jess facing the men and Claire facing the back wall. Claire leaned forward so as not to be overheard. "I thought we were taking the coffee for the drive back to the station."

"Sorry about that, but I think it might be worthwhile to learn a little about the citizens of Kalfou Parish."

Claire stifled a sigh of resignation and hoped the men kept any disrespect to themselves. Pastor Abel was enough for one morning. She had no desire for another confrontation so quickly.

Gil brought the coffee and a saucer with packs of cream and sugar. A mountain of a man, his white apron barely covered the front of his body. Shoelaces knotted to the apron's strings were tied at his back to keep the apron in place. His huge smile matched his large girth. "What else will you have?"

"You got any of your homemade beignets left?" The tension holding her hostage eased a little at the big man's grin. She even managed to smile as she looked at Jess. "You won't find any better in New Orleans."

"Make that two then." Jess smiled up at Gil. "My name is Jessica Morgan." She reached out a hand and found it engulfed between Gil's own.

"Gil Chevalier, ma'am. Good to meet you, Ms. Morgan. Lester was telling us the sheriff was getting someone to help out. Seems awfully quick since he just got hurt this morning." Gil was unabashedly curious.

"He was calling in a favor before he got hurt. Today was my first scheduled day on the job," Jess explained with a smile.

He nodded in understanding and took a step back. "Let me get those beignets for you."

"You two heard how the sheriff is doing?" Lester's nasal voice cut through the silence, making Clare's tension skyrocket. Lester was apparently itching for a fight.

Claire did her best to appear nonchalant. "We stopped by this morning. He was out of surgery but still sleepy."

"Yeah." To Claire's ears, Lester seemed decidedly smug. "The pastor stopped by. He sure had a lot to say." A couple of the men snickered.

Claire figured that must be why the men were laughing. It was about the pastor's version of their conversation. In spite of herself, Claire reddened in embarrassment.

Lester pushed a little harder. "The pastor gave a little sermon while he was here. You could almost smell the brimstone." He laughed at his own joke.

Jess spoke up, her voice pleasant and confident. "I don't believe we've met. My name is Jessica Morgan. I'll be filling in for Sheriff Willis while he's recovering."

Lester's mouth dropped open. "Huh? Why do we need another goddamn woman on the force? Jesus."

Gil's large form came back down the aisle. "Here you go. Two beignets." He spoke loudly enough to forestall anything more Lester might say. The look he sent Lester as he passed by was filled with warning.

"Thanks Gil." Claire meant it in more ways than one. He had a soft spot for her, and she felt the same way about the warm giant of a man.

Jess turned her attention to the sweet confection in front of her and took a big bite. "Oh man. This is wonderful."

Claire bit into hers but it may as well be sawdust. Lester and the pastor could always infiltrate her armor. Having to deal with them both within just a couple of hours was downright painful.

Gil pulled up a chair at their booth. "If you'll excuse me, I won't bother you but a minute." He had removed the white apron and sat there in his jeans and plaid buttoned shirt, his large frame filling the entire space. Without waiting for a response, he looked at Jess. "First…welcome to Kalfou Parish. Awfully good timing for you to start helping us."

Jess wiped away the powdered sugar from her mouth. "Thank you, Mr. Chevalier. I appreciate that. And based on this beignet, I will be seeing you often." She groaned as she took another bite of the Louisiana pastry. "Where did you learn to make these? They aren't quite the same as the ones in Nawlins."

Gil laughed. "My mama taught me." He turned to Claire. "You said Sheriff Willis was out of surgery? Any news on how well he's doing? I hear it's a miracle he's alive."

"He's stable but sounds like it'll be a while recovering."

Gil nodded. "That was an awful thing. I figure a deer or something must have run out in front of him to make him run off the road like that. They don't call it Deer Haven Road for nothing."

Jess raised her brows. "Are there a lot of deer in that area?"

"Oh yeah. They're all over the place in Kalfou." He turned to Claire. "I hope you're over that gator attack yesterday. I'd be seeing that big boy in my dreams."

"He was a big one all right."

Apparently getting the hint that Claire wasn't very talkative today, he pushed away from the table and stood. "Tell Sheriff Willis, I said to get better quick."

Claire answered for them both. "We will."

Just then Lester stood up and gave a loud belch. "I'm going home to get a little rest before my shift tonight," he announced. "See ya'll later." He pulled a couple of bills from his pocket and headed toward the door.

Jess leaned toward Claire. "Look at his pants, at the ankle."

Claire turned in time to catch a glimpse before he was out of sight. To her surprise, she saw a couple of yellow flowers attached to the fabric. Her eyes moved back to Jess. "Devil's thorn."

Jess gave a slight nod.

Gil stopped by with a coffeepot. Jess didn't give him a chance to speak. "Could you make those to go?"

"Sure." Unperturbed by the change in plans, Gil headed back toward the Styrofoam cups.

They met at the old cash register. Claire was amused to see Jess slip the remaining beignet into a box for later.

Grabbing her coffee, Claire gave a little wave. "See ya, Gil. Catch you gentlemen later." She made sure to make eye contact with each of the men, satisfied to see a few lower their gaze.

They stepped onto the gravel as Lester's car passed by them, spinning gravel and dust in his wake.

As they got into the vehicle, Claire asked, "You think Lester was at the scene? Maybe he heard it over his scanner and went to help out. Lester is a total jerk but pretty harmless."

Jess pulled her seat belt around to click it in place. "I've seen good people do things that were totally out of character. I saw those thorns on his pants and you said they aren't very common. That's all I'm saying."

"Lester absolutely flipped yesterday when Sheriff Willis gave the missing person case to me. But he's a hardhead, nothing more. He talks a good game but doesn't follow through with anything."

Jess sipped her coffee. "It's just an observation. But we have an indication now that he was there. He likely did as you said and went to the scene to help. He knew all about it, but that could have come from his scanner. I hope the sheriff can give better information when he gets the drugs out of his system. Anyway, I want to see where the skull was found." She leaned back, slipped on her sunglasses and pulled down the sunshade. "Onward, to the bayou. Don't spare the horses."

Claire smiled in spite of herself. Jess was smart, intuitive, and possessed a quirky sense of humor, not to mention the fact that she filled out a pair of slacks quite nicely. She felt at ease with her and it seemed that the feeling was reciprocated. It was with some surprise that she realized she looked forward to working closely together. It felt damn good to feel less alone than she had in a long time, too, and it hadn't even been a full day yet.

Jess looked at her. "Bring me up to speed on the missing person case."

CHAPTER TEN

"How much farther?" Jess asked as she slapped the millionth mosquito trying to steal her blood. The heat and deep south humidity made her clothes uncomfortably wet from sweat. Her feet fared no better as they squelched inside the rubber boots Claire had given her. Though uncomfortable, they were proving essential for traversing the mud and standing water through which they currently waded.

"We're getting close," Claire assured her in the kind voice Jess was beginning to associate with her. "Sorry that the flatboat can't get us all the way to the investigation site. It's much easier by airboat but the Wildlife officers needed it. The flatboat is the best they had available."

Jess surreptitiously checked her watch. Had it really only been twenty-five minutes? She forced herself to maintain an even voice, stifling her threatened whine. "No problem."

How the hell did Claire stay so composed in this miserable heat? Jess had grown up in New Orleans, and the heat and humidity were brutal there as well. But damned mosquitos didn't swarm you each time you stepped outside, nor did you slog through muck that smelled like rotten eggs. She checked out the smaller woman leading the way. Damp patches dotted her uniform but she seemed to take it in stride, literally, as she kept up the steady pace Jess found difficult to match.

Another mosquito died under her palm.

Dammit! I even put on repellent!

When the yellow crime scene tape came in view, Claire stopped. "See? We could have come all the way here with the airboat." She reached into her backpack and pulled out two water bottles.

"Ahh...I could kiss you!" Jess was as surprised as Claire when the words tumbled out. "Uh...I didn't mean it like that."

Claire's expression made it obvious she was holding back laughter.

To avoid an awkward silence, Jess began talking, albeit a little faster than normal. "The distance from the car to the skull is too far for her to have walked, if it is the missing the child. And anyway, the mud and water would prohibit from coming through all this. She would stay by the road."

"With the drought, it's only been in the last year or so that the area is accessible by hiking. She couldn't have walked here."

"Okay. So she didn't walk here. Do you think the current may have carried her body to this point?"

Claire pulled out a can of mosquito repellent and motioned for her colleague to turn around. She sprayed the back of Jess's neck. "No. The water is slow but it is moving toward the sea, in the other direction. The missing little girl was last seen near Blue Bay where the swamp empties into the ocean. She would have had to drift against the current to land here. So basically, we can't find a logical way or reason for the girl to get from where she was last seen to where the skull was located. Dr. Avi says the humerus indicates a knife wound with no evidence of an animal attack of any kind."

Claire sorted through possibilities. "Nothing fits."

"Except foul play."

"Except foul play," Claire repeated softly.

Silence settled between them as they considered the implications.

The Louisiana heat gained momentum as noon drew near. Now drenched with sweat, Jess wrapped things up quickly and they began making their way back to the boat. As before, Claire took the lead.

About halfway to the flatboat, it became clear Claire was in better physical shape than Jess. Her steady gait ate up the distance as she sidestepped plants and slogged through puddles. She seemed to be enjoying her walk while Jess was breathing heavily. She swallowed her pride and opened her mouth to call out when she caught a slithering movement near her feet. Instinctively, she screamed, a bloodcurdling sound from deep within as she leaped over the spot where the snake had been and ran toward Claire.

Claire whirled around and drew her sidearm in one smooth movement. She looked around wildly. Meanwhile, Jess grabbed Claire with both arms.

"Snake!" she yelled.

It took a moment for her words to sink in. "Snake?" Claire echoed. "Did it strike you? What type was it?"

Jess took a deep breath to calm herself. However, it did little for her pounding heartbeat. "I don't know what kind."

"Did it strike you?" Claire repeated more firmly, as she put her firearm back in the holster.

Jess began to realize how silly she must look and tried to calm herself. Sadly, her body didn't co-operate. "N-no. I saw it so close and…and panicked." She waited for the inevitable teasing.

Claire didn't laugh or tease. Instead, she gripped Jess's arms and stared into her eyes. "I got you. You're okay."

In Jess's opinion, Claire leaped to an even higher status. She appreciated the fact Claire didn't say the standard, "It's more scared of you than you are of it". The oft-repeated nonsense did nothing to help. She shivered in spite of herself. "I have a phobia of the damned things. I hate 'em."

Claire put a comforting arm around her shoulder. "I promise you, everything's fine. I'm sorry I got too far ahead. I'll do better and walk a little slower so we can stay close. We'll be back at the car soon, okay?"

Jess nodded, embarrassed by her reaction. "Thank you for not laughing at me. Most people just make jokes."

Claire patted her arm for reassurance. "Well, those people are jerks."

Jess agreed wholeheartedly. "You might be surprised at the number of jerks that kick you when you're down."

"I bet I wouldn't," Claire murmured. Her words hung in the air. Their bitterness spoke volumes.

True to her word, Claire slowed down which made the trek longer but less miserable. Still, Jess was immensely glad to see their boat.

Jess found herself enjoying the ride back. The breeze, although hot, was better than no breeze. She never wanted to go into a bayou again without Claire to save her from snakes and alligators. But she had to admit it was a beautiful place. Back at the landing, she found herself wishing the ride had lasted a little longer.

At the SUV, Jess bent to remove the gumboots and when she straightened up once more, gaped at a now shirtless Claire drying off with a small towel. From all the walking, her pants hung lower than usual, making it obvious she did tons of crunches to acquire the cut abs that drew Jess's eyes like a magnet. She jerked away from her thoughts when she realized Claire was speaking to her.

"I have a couple of T-shirts I keep for days like this. Take this one, if you want." She offered Jess another towel and a plain white T-shirt. "Sorry I don't have any pants."

Reluctantly, Jess removed her own shirt, embarrassed for Claire to see her belly. She knew she held no spare pounds and was slim enough, but her body was like an etch-a-sketch next to a master painting. Still, her clothes were saturated and most likely smelly after the day's heat. The T-shirt and towel could only help at this point.

Claire's cell phone rang. "Deputy Claire Duvall." She listened for a second and said, "Jessica Morgan is with me. Let me put you on speakerphone."

The doctor's voice came across clearly. "I performed the usual tests, and this is someone other than the missing girl. I checked the records and she had two primary teeth where our skull has just one in that area of the jaw. In addition, she had a filling whereas our skull has none."

Jess was flabbergasted, her insecurities forgotten. "You're saying we have another missing child?" Children didn't simply disappear in a tiny population like Kalfou Parish without everyone knowing about it. What the hell was going on?

He paused a moment. "That brings me to the crux of the matter. When piecing together the fragments you collected, they form more of the cranial dome. It shows the child experienced a blunt force to the head."

"Pre- or post-mortem?" Jess asked.

"Unfortunately, I cannot say. It would have been destructive enough to kill the child, but I can't pronounce it as the killing blow. The damage to the cranium required a heavy object. The knife marks on the humerus suggest a large, sharp blade. I had an interesting observation on the position of the blade marks. Usually, a cut on the arm is a defensive wound. The victim would likely move his arm up to prevent the blade from cutting the face or body and the arm would be cut instead. However, when you orient the bone as it would be in the body, the cut marks are on the inside of the arm. The location aligns with the position of the brachial artery. Cutting this artery would cause high blood loss and be potentially life-threatening."

"Are you saying either the knife cut or the bashed skull could have killed the child?" Jess had seen brachial artery cuts before, usually associated with heavy-machinery accidents. The victims often died because they couldn't get to the hospital before they bled out.

"Yes, Ms. Morgan. Either of them could have killed the child."

Claire spoke up. "What likely position would the arm have been in for the knife to cut the brachial artery?"

As the doctor hesitated, Jess showed her. "If I lift my arm away from my side, the inside of my arm is vulnerable. The brachial runs along here." She traced a finger along the inside of her arm from her armpit to her elbow.

Claire thought a moment. "What about the type of blade? Maybe a meat cleaver or large butcher's knife? Is that what you're thinking?"

"Perhaps," he said. "But whatever the weapon, the blade was very sharp, and formidable."

"Anything else?" Jess was hoping for something that might lead them to an answer of any kind.

"I will send you my report later this afternoon. I will add the DNA results when I receive them. Feel free to come by and speak with me if you have any questions."

"Thank you, Dr. Avi." Claire looked toward Jess.

"Is there anything else I can do for you?"

"How is the sheriff?"

"He is certainly conscious and lucid. You may visit him whenever you wish."

"Thanks for the update. We'll visit him as soon as we can."

"That will be fine. Good day, ladies."

Claire's voice gave away her frustration. "We were thinking it was the missing girl. Now we basically know nothing about what happened to this child."

Jess responded in what she hoped was a voice of confidence. "I suggest we begin contacting parishes throughout the state for any children between the ages of nine to fifteen that disappeared in the last fifteen years. We'll compare any dental data and DNA. If we can identify the missing child, then we have a face and the chance of getting a background story from the family."

"I can see why the sheriff called you in."

"Thanks." Jess's smile broadened, happy that things were going much more smoothly than she had feared. She stared out the SUV's windows in thought. "You know...let's just say for the moment, that the blunt force trauma was the cause of death.

Our walk today showed it's a darned long way to get from the road to where we found the bones. That would be long time of either carrying a dead body or dragging a live one kicking and screaming, not to mention the water at the crime scene."

"And water in all directions to get to that location, too," Claire reminded her.

"Okay. So, best guess, the child probably arrived here by boat. Dead or alive at that point, we have no idea."

Her stomach chose that moment to growl. "Whoops. I guess that's our clue to grab some lunch. Afterward, we can start getting out the word throughout the state that we may have a missing child of theirs. We can start with the database but if we can narrow it to a couple, I want to talk to them directly." Jess's stomach rumbled again. "How about a working lunch? We can discuss it all while we eat."

Claire started the engine. "Lunch? I suggest you check your watch. But I'm all for an early supper. We can get a takeout and head to the office if you want."

"Sounds good to me."

"Okay, then. Back to Gil's." She laughed at her partner's expression. "I wasn't kidding when I said it's the only place to eat."

"By the way, I was worried we might run across an alligator out there. They seemed to have disappeared."

Claire laughed. "Um, Jess. I saw plenty of gators in the water, on logs, on the banks. I even saw one in a tree. And I certainly wasn't going to mention them or the couple of snakes I saw after I discovered you're terrified of them. I didn't feel like carrying you on my back the rest of the way to the boat."

Jess burst out in laughter. "Oh my God. Of course, you did. I just didn't know what to look for."

Jess was touched to know Claire had taken care of her. She had been excited at the opportunity to help out Kalfou. But she had expected resistance from some of the deputies. Instead, all except Lester had been welcoming, offering any help she might need while showing no sign of territorial posturing. Besides, even if no one else were accommodating, Claire was making it worthwhile. Beautiful, smart, and funny at times, she was an asset professionally. On a personal level, she was charming and sexy as hell, with a toned physique that would still be on her mind as she tried to sleep tonight. Yep, Claire was making this assignment interesting indeed.

CHAPTER ELEVEN

The next morning, Claire arrived at the office a little earlier than usual. To her surprise, Jess and Maxine were already hard at work. "Good morning."

Both women responded with smiles and their own greeting.

Jess went straight to business. "We have five hits from the missing persons database."

Claire's brows rose in surprise. "You've already entered the data and got hits? What time did you get in this morning?"

Maxine wore her expression reserved for mothering recalcitrant deputies. "She was here when I arrived, and I came in at six. Sid said she slept on a cot in one of the holding cells."

Claire whistled. "You didn't get much sleep last night."

Jess waved off their concerns. "I tried the hotel the evening I arrived, and I had several creepy crawly visitors during the night." She shuddered at the memory. "The cot here is much better for getting some rest. Besides, I wanted to talk to Sid and get the shift information entered into the system." Jess leaned back in her chair. "The closest and only hit in Louisiana comes from New Orleans. I think that's the one we need to go after first. Then if we find it doesn't fit, we should expand to the next closest one, Biloxi."

"So, what now? Call their local law enforcement?"

"Yep. And get the DNA analysis."

She handed Claire the database report from New Orleans. "Dakota Grambling. Missing for seven years. Looks like he was taken when he was ten years old. He left home on his bike to go to a friend's house. The last time seen was riding through a park." Claire looked up from the file. "Seven years. That would put the body below water for most of that time."

Jess refilled her cup with fresh coffee and poured one for Claire too. "The dental records match. The age fits the suggested range Dr. Avi came up with based on the cranial sutures and teeth."

"New Orleans is two hundred and fifty miles from here. Seems like a long way to transport a child, dead or alive. Any possible scenarios as to why a missing child from the other end of the state would show up here?"

Jess stifled a yawn. "I only know what's in the report. I think we need to talk to the detectives who were involved at the time. On our end, we need to look at anyone with a criminal record, particularly regarding violent crimes that was in the area seven years ago."

Claire's eyes grew wide. "We were still trying to get over Hurricane Lionel back then. Some people were still in transition. That doesn't take into account the construction work which brought in lots of strangers. This could be difficult to get a handle on."

Jess nodded in agreement. "The perpetrator could potentially have moved to a different parish. But still bring the body here because he was familiar with the bayou."

Claire thought a moment. "Sid, Maxine, and the sheriff would be the best departmental resources. They were all on the force during that timeframe."

Through the open door, Maxine called out, "I'll start searching through records as soon as I finish this report."

Jess picked up a pen. "Sid called. The sheriff wants to meet with us around eight-thirty. Sounds like the sheriff can talk this morning. Afterward, we can reach out to the New Orleans Police to ask about the missing boy."

Two hours and an empty coffeepot later, they drove to the hospital where they were allowed to visit with little grumbling about the early time. They found Sheriff Willis eating breakfast while Sid and Blanche kept him company.

"Looks like this is where the party is," Claire announced as she walked in. "You look much better today, Sheriff. Blanche must be taking great care of you."

"I would be doing fine if they let me have some redeye gravy and a sausage biscuit." He set his apple juice down on the cart. "And some strong coffee."

"Nice to see you looking better, Sheriff Willis." Jess took the vacant seat next to his bed.

"I'll go check on my other patients," Blanche said as she moved to the door.

He pushed the tray away, his food only half eaten. "Now you're all here, let's start with the skull found in the bayou."

Jess explained yesterday's events ending with the database findings.

"If the DNA evidence supports the missing person information, you may be taking a trip to New Orleans," the sheriff said when she finished. "Meet the officer in charge of the case. Get a feel for the place where the boy lived, where he was abducted. Maybe the parents know someone from here or something like that."

"That could be worth the trip all right," Jess mused. "I'll keep you up on the status."

Sheriff Willis ran a hand over the back of his neck. "I was too groggy to make much sense yesterday. I want to talk to you now that I'm awake." He looked at Sid. "I don't know if you are aware of what's going on, Sid. But I expect you to keep it to yourself."

"No problem," the older man agreed solemnly.

Sheriff Willis turned to Jess. There was no confusion in his eyes. "The bastard did it on purpose. He was coming in the other lane and then turned right in front of me. He had to swerve hard to hit me like that."

"Sheriff—"

"I tell you it was deliberate." He schooled his features into the stern glare normally reserved for criminals and turned to Claire. "You be careful out there."

Jess saved Claire from answering. "Can you tell us exactly what happened yesterday morning?"

The sheriff took a moment to gather his thoughts before speaking. "I got ready for work like I always do. I left at my usual time, about five-thirty. That lets me get to work and have time to talk to the night shift for a while."

He gave Jess a minute to catch up in writing her notes. "Everything was normal until I rounded the curve and into that straightaway. A truck parked on the side of the road pulled out and headed toward me. When he got close, he swerved to hit me head on, but I swerved as well. The truck ended up hitting the side of my car and pushing me off the road. The impact took me past the ditch and into the field with the car upside down. I got beat up a bit but was able to call 911. They arrived and got me out."

"What about the truck?"

"I would recognize the truck anywhere. It belongs to my deputy, Lester Henderson."

The sheriff's pronouncement startled them all.

Sid couldn't believe it. "Lester...are you sure? It must have looked like him or something."

Jess watched as the sheriff argued that he knew what he saw. "Okay, let's all take a breath and sort it out." Her voice rang with authority and everyone made an effort to calm down. "Let's give Sheriff Willis the chance to explain. Sheriff, what identifies the person as Lester Henderson?"

"First of all, he drives a black Chevrolet half-ton pickup with a dent in the front passenger door where he hit a deer last winter. It's also got one of those brush grills that protects the front when off-roading. The body style of the truck that hit me fits the 2008 that Lester owns. No one in the parish matches all that exactly except for Lester."

"Tell me about the driver."

"I didn't see the driver for more than a couple of seconds, but I saw him well enough to know he wore one of those full-face knit things that you pull over your head when it's cold. It was black or at least a dark color."

"Anything else that he or she wore?"

He thought a moment. "More black. I'm guessing a black T-shirt or something? I don't remember any colors except black."

"Sheriff, I need to ask this because, as you well know, this is a serious charge." Jess let her words sink in. "Are you sure the collision was deliberate? Is it possible it was an accident? It would still be hit-and-run but what you're describing is vehicular assault or possibly even attempted murder."

"I know. But I'm telling you what I saw."

She turned to Sid. "You and Lester have been on night shift this week. Has Lester said anything or acted differently?"

Sid nodded slowly. "Yes. Last night was real strange. Lester was on pins and needles all night. Any little sound would make him jump. He usually comes in and talks a lot. Last night, he just came in and did what he had to do before heading out. I bet he didn't say three words even when I tried to make small talk."

"What about the night before?"

"Well, he was kinda upset about Claire getting the go-ahead to investigate the skull. He felt disrespected and said the same old stuff he usually says when it comes to Claire." Sid looked embarrassed and said, "Sorry Claire."

She shrugged. "It's nothing I haven't heard from him myself."

"I can write it all out if you need me to. It would give me a chance to remember it and make sure it's in order."

"I would appreciate that, Sid." Jess turned to the sheriff. "We will check into this, of course."

The door opened and Blanche strode in briskly. "James Willis, you are getting yourself agitated. Your visitors are going to have to go outside."

Reluctantly, they allowed themselves to be shooed into the hall as they waved goodbye.

Sid headed home to get some sleep while Jess and Claire stopped by Dr. Avi's office to pick up his coroner's report. It would be days before any DNA evidence would arrive and Jess hoped it would match up nicely with the information from the National Police Database for Missing Persons.

They split up responsibilities with Jess driving to the mechanic's shop and picking up the black box and dash cam from the wrecked squad car while Claire went to obtain the search warrant for Lester Henderson's property.

The warrant took some time, and the sun was high overhead when she walked out of the courthouse. Going after Lester held no triumph for Claire. She couldn't stand the guy, but until now she had never known him to be a real troublemaker.

Sid once told Claire his thoughts on why Lester was such a jerk to her. Lester had been raised by his grandmother. While his dad spent most of his time drunk and sleeping away the day, his grandmother had been the caregiver. Sid believed that anything good out of Lester came from her, but all his anger and hatred came from his dad. Lester's family was extremely poor and some of the local kids made fun of him. When Lester begged Sheriff Willis for a job, he hired him partly because he wanted to be a deputy so badly and partly to keep him from becoming a drunk like his dad. Lester thought Sheriff Willis hung the moon. Then Claire came onto the force and Lester lost the sheriff's attention. Sid reasoned that Lester was jealous of her.

Claire had often thought about that conversation, how she and Lester had things in common. They both were unable to fit in with many in the parish and had paid a price. But while Claire had followed her mom's example and braved the whispers, Lester had done to her what others had done to him.

Did Lester deliberately hurt Sheriff Willis because of her? The thought sickened her.

CHAPTER TWELVE

Jess wasted no time. As soon as they had the search warrant, they got ready to go to Lester's home.

Jess brought Claire up to speed on the camera. "I watched the dash cam footage and it's just as Sheriff Willis said. The truck, the mask, everything matches. I haven't begun tabulating the data from the black box yet. I'll work on that after we finish the search."

She was adamant they put on their bulletproof vests. It may have been overkill, but Lester had already proven he could be violent. Coupled with his animosity toward Claire, she decided it best to be safe.

"Let me go to the house and do the talking," Jess instructed as they neared Lester's home. "Stay with me but be quiet. He seems fixated on you in a negative way. I don't want to incite him."

"I'll follow your lead. That's his house up ahead."

The place was in disrepair. Weeds fought for dominance over the trash in the yard. One of the front windows was cracked and patched with duct tape. Much of the siding beneath the front porch canopy was missing. Claire hadn't driven out this way in a while and was surprised by the changes to the once-pretty house. She wondered what was going on in his life to cause this downward spiral.

Jess knocked firmly on the front door while Claire stood at the corner of the small porch. She could see down the side of the house if he chose to run.

"Open the door, Lester. This is Jessica Morgan." There was no answer, so Jess pounded on the door once again. "Open up. We're here to talk to you, Lester."

Claire peered through the broken window. There sprawled on the couch in an undershirt and boxers was Lester. He seemed to be asleep, but how could the man sleep through all that pounding? "I can see him on his couch. He is either asleep or something is wrong."

Jess pounded on the door once again. Lester did not move.

"Wait a minute. We're such a small community most people don't bother locking the door when they're home." Unfortunately, it was locked but when Claire ran her hand across the top of the door's molding she found the key. She opened the door and stood back for Jess to enter first. They hurried to Lester where Jess felt his neck for a pulse.

"Steady and strong."

"Oh my God. What has he done?" Claire pointed to the coffee table. It looked like fifty or more pills lying spilled out.

Jess picked up the empty prescription bottle. "Eszopiclone. For the treatment of insomnia."

After several failed attempts to wake Lester, Claire began counting the pills and found only half of the prescription remaining. Jess continued trying to wake him. Finally Lester opened his eyes. "Lester. How many pills did you take?"

His eyes widened as he tried to focus. "Dunno." His speech was slurred.

"Why?" Jess tapped his cheek a couple of times.

He said nothing and didn't respond to anything else she said.

Meanwhile, Claire called an ambulance. They had no way of knowing how many pills he had taken. Jess monitored his condition, which appeared to be stable. Claire brought in evidence bags and gathered the pills.

Soon, the ambulance siren could be heard in the distance. Jess explained the situation to the EMTs. All agreed that it was best to take him to the hospital, especially since Lester remained somewhat non-responsive. Within minutes, Lester was loaded onto a gurney and placed inside the ambulance. Jess gave her contact information to the EMT with directions to call if needed. Then the ambulance headed to the hospital while Jess and Claire stayed behind to complete their search.

They first headed out back toward the dilapidated shed that once sported a coat of red paint. Now weathered gray, traces of red still clung to the wood giving the appearance of unhealed wounds. A board lying in a cradle held the double doors in place. Claire lifted it and the doors swung open to illuminate Lester's pickup.

The sunshine exposed the twisted brush guard on the front of the truck. She knelt down to take a closer look. She knew the guard was something Lester and his buddies had made themselves. It actually replaced the truck's front bumper as well as extending upward in front of the grill and lights. All the joints had been welded or bolted with heavy-duty hardware. The guard had minimized damage to the front of the truck but the guard itself would have to be replaced. Streaks of white paint marred the guard's black surface, and the front of the truck's grill and surrounding metal was smashed. Claire would bet money the white paint matched the sheriff's car.

While Claire inspected the outside of the truck, Jess checked its interior. She opened the door on the driver's side and found a black ski mask matching Sheriff Willis's description exactly.

Almost in unison, they called out, "Guess what I found."

"Damn. I've worked with Lester for several years and would have never thought he could do real harm to someone."

"The evidence doesn't lie," Jess replied as she placed the mask in a bag. "Call for a tow truck, please."

They entered the house once again. It verged on a hoarding situation. Every room was filled with half-eaten takeout, dirty laundry, and just plain trash. Wearing latex gloves, they searched the living room and worked their way through the kitchen and bathroom.

In the bedroom, right beside the bed, Jess spotted the pants Lester had worn at the diner. She lifted them gingerly and was rewarded with a glimpse of the devil's thorns attached to the cuff. Beneath the pants was a black T-shirt, just as Sheriff Willis had described.

It was obvious Lester had no intention of hiding anything. Everything was sitting in the open, almost as if they were waiting to be found. She photographed it all and bagged the clothes as evidence. The rest of the house showed nothing.

After checking the rest of the home and then assisting the tow-truck driver, they headed to the hospital to check on Lester.

After a long wait, a doctor came out to bring them up to speed on Lester's condition. "Mr. Henderson didn't take an amount that would appear life-threatening, but more than a normal dose. We've pumped out his stomach and are keeping him overnight for observation."

Jess crossed her arms over her chest. Claire recognized the gesture as a power move. "It's imperative that you alert us as soon as he can be released. He's under arrest. We want him for questioning."

"Of course. I'll pass along the information."

Jess offered a curt nod. "We will place a deputy to ensure he stays put."

The doctor's brows raised at her words, but he said nothing. They left to find their car. Along the way, Jess called the sheriff of Pierre Parish and got assurance that they would post someone at the door of Lester's room.

As they drove back to Kalfou Parish, Jess called the sheriff to explain the situation. After disconnecting the call, she looked at Claire. "He's still pressing charges."

"Wow. Sheriff Willis must be furious. Lester has screwed up big time."

They drove back to the office and began trudging through the paperwork from the crash scene and Lester's place.

"Jess?" Maxine came to the door. "There is a man on the phone from New Orleans Police Department. Do you want me to take a message?"

"Send it through to me, please. I've been waiting for the call." Moments later, the phone rang and Jess picked up. "Hello. Undersheriff Jessica Morgan speaking."

"Morgan? This is Detective Darren Johnson with New Orleans PD. I am calling in reference to the missing boy."

"I'm glad to hear from you. Please be aware Deputy Claire Duvall is with me and you're on speakerphone."

"I received your information on the skull you found. We ran Robert Beaumont through the database and got a few hits but nothing suggesting he was involved in the death of a child."

"What about the boy? Did your investigation find anything that might point to a suspect?"

"I wasn't on the force at the time. I inherited the case when the lead investigator retired. Right now, I have the same information I've just sent you."

Jess leaned toward the speakerphone. "We just sent off the DNA evidence yesterday and it could take at least a week. Do the parents still live in New Orleans?"

"They moved to another neighborhood but are still in the city."

"Detective, the skull's location indicates the perpetrator probably knew the bayou well. I would like to be present when you speak with the parents. I am interested if they are familiar with the bayou or if they have any type of connection with someone from the area."

"All right. When can you head this way?"

"If the DNA evidence confirms the bones belong to their son, we'll set up a time immediately. My original call was to alert you to the potential break in your case and see if there were any known connections to Kalfou Parish."

The sound of shuffled papers came from Detective Johnson's side of the conversation. "There was nothing in the file about a connection to Kalfou. We can ask the parents but I agree with waiting on the DNA results. They've waited almost seven years. Another week or so won't matter."

"I will contact you as soon as we get the DNA report."

They signed off and went about their normal duties for the remainder of the day.

* * *

The next morning Jess checked Lester out of the hospital and placed him under arrest. As they passed Claire's desk en route to a cell, she was surprised to feel a pang of sympathy for him. "How ya feeling?"

"Piss off." He barely glanced in her direction.

She heaved a sigh. Lester was back to normal.

He refused to answer any questions until his lawyer could be present, so hours passed before they brought him to the interrogation room. Jess and Claire sat across from Lester and his lawyer. Claire would take notes while Jess took on the role of interrogator.

The lawyer was the first to speak. "My client is willing to talk with you in return for charges reduced to hit and run."

Jess stared at Lester for a long moment before answering. "I can't do anything unless I understand what happened."

The lawyer placed his hand over Lester's to remind him to be quiet. "My client will speak through me."

Jess snorted. "You know as well as I do, an innocent man will talk to clear himself. I want to hear what happened in your own words, Lester. Help us understand what happened and why."

The lawyer leaned over and whispered something to him. Lester nodded in agreement. "My client will explain himself, but at any time we reserve the right to stop."

Again, Jess ignored him and spoke to Lester. "Tell me what happened."

"I don't know," he blurted out. "I can't remember."

"Start from the beginning and tell us what you do know."

Lester's hand shook slightly as he began to speak. "I went home about four-thirty in the morning to take a break. I...I must have fallen asleep because I woke up with my scanner alarm going off. When I got to the crash, I realized it was Sheriff Willis. I helped the EMTs until they finished. Then I went home instead of heading back to the station. I figured I'd fill out the paper during my shift."

Jess frowned. "You were off duty from four-thirty until shift change?"

Lester wouldn't meet her eyes. "Not exactly."

"What do you mean? Were you doing your job or were you not?"

Lester wriggled in his chair. "Look. It sounds crazy but this is the truth. Just minutes after going home I heard a knock on the door. I remember opening it but I don't remember anything afterward until I woke up to my scanner alarm."

"Who was knocking on your door? How can you remember the knock but nothing after the door opened?"

He ran a hand through his hair. "I know it sounds crazy but it's the truth. I was kind of freaked out because I've blacked out like this before."

Jess shook her head, obviously not believing him. "How did your truck hit Sheriff Willis's car?"

Lester leaned forward. "I'm telling God's honest truth. I don't remember. When I got some breakfast at Gil's, I saw my pickup had all that damage. I was shocked. I didn't notice it until I was talking to everybody and glanced out the window. I didn't know how it got there." His voice rose. "I still don't know what happened."

"What about the pants you wore that day?"

Lester looked puzzled. "What about them?"

Jess pulled them from a bin she had under the table. "We obtained these from your home during our search. See these spurs? They come from a plant prevalent in the area where Sheriff Willis's car landed after being hit."

He stared silently at them and his lawyer spoke up. "Devil's thorn, I presume?" At her nod, he continued. "Farmers spray to get it out of their fields. This is very common."

Jess ignored him and turned her attention back to Lester. "How did these get on your pants, Lester?"

"I have no idea. I didn't even know they were there. But I was on the scene when the EMTs arrived…in the field, I mean. Is that where they came from?"

Jess ignored his question. "If you were on the scene, why didn't you call Maxine to report it?"

Lester heaved a sigh. "She wasn't at work yet." He stared at Claire, his thin lips set in a firm line. "You know Sheriff Willis always comes in early."

"But you didn't leave a message?"

"I was sleepy and wanted to go home. I decided to go straight home. I went to Gil's after I'd had a nap. I woke up hungry."

Jess wrote a few notes in her notebook. "Hmm… You're in trouble, Lester. Both Deputy Duvall and I saw devil's thorn on the pants you were wearing while at Gil's. We will need to corroborate your story about helping the EMTs at the scene, as we only have your word for that. We also saw you drive off from Gil's in your pickup. It's damaged. The sheriff's description of the vehicle that hit him matches yours, and the paint on the brush shield matches the squad car Sheriff Willis was driving that morning. We also have the dash cam that has pictures of a truck with your same customized grill veering straight into the sheriff's lane."

Lester slammed a fist on the table. "I tell you I don't know anything."

His lawyer put a hand on his shoulder and spoke to Jess. "Let's pretend that all you say is true. That similar paint is on Lester's pickup. Maybe you should begin looking into the person that stole Lester's truck? You can't place my client at the scene until after the crash. While he slept, someone stole his truck and then put it back after hitting the sheriff. He has also just mentioned that he was being a good citizen and trying to assist the sheriff and EMTs at the scene of the accident."

Jess pulled out the bag containing the ski mask. "This was found during the search of your home, Lester."

Lester opened his mouth to speak but his lawyer placed a hand on his arm to stop him. "I believe my client has said all he should say at this time."

Jess attempted a few more questions, but Lester refused to answer on the advisement of his attorney. Claire escorted Lester back to his cell and, for the first time since she had met him, Lester spoke to her without malice.

"Honest. I don't remember anything. Me and the sheriff don't always see eye to eye, but I would never want to hurt him."

Claire didn't know what to say, so she just closed the door and said, "Call me if you need to talk."

CHAPTER THIRTEEN

Back at the station, Jess launched into deciphering data from the black box while Claire took her routine tour of the parish. Between the investigation, the absence of Sheriff Willis and now Lester, normal operations were slipping through the cracks.

Jess sent the completed paperwork for Lester's arrest to Maxine to be placed in his arrest file.

When Claire stuck her head in the doorway, Jess glanced at the clock and was shocked to see it was lunchtime. "I'm gonna check things on the western end of the parish and then stop by Gil's on the way back. You want anything?"

Maxine stopped stapling papers. "I brought the fixings for a tomato sandwich, fresh from my garden. I'll share if you want."

Claire shuddered. "Thanks, but I'm not a fan."

Maxine groaned in sympathy. "Bless your heart. That simply isn't southern. How can you say you're a southerner and not love tomato sandwiches?"

Claire turned to Jess and winked. "What about you? Wanna nice lunch or would you rather eat a tomato and mayonnaise sandwich with soggy bread and tomato juice dripping everywhere?"

Jess joined in the fun and made a show of deciding. "Although tempting, I think I'll head to Gil's with you. As they pulled onto the street, she said, "I hope you don't mind my turning this into a lunch rather than a carryout to the office. I thought we could talk and clear our heads at the same time."

"No problem. It's nice to leave the paperwork sometimes. I enjoyed following my normal routine this morning."

Jess hoped that wasn't the only reason. She stared at the countryside as she tried to come up with a conversation. She finally gave up and went back to business. "The black box data corroborates the skid marks at the scene. Sheriff Willis braked several seconds ahead of the collision. He was only driving forty-five miles per hour, so his speed had decreased dramatically before the truck collided with him."

Claire's fingers tapped on the steering wheel. "I don't get what would make Lester try to hurt Sheriff Willis. I know he was mad the night before, but I can't fathom him trying to hurt or even kill the sheriff."

Jess didn't know Lester well enough to comment. Instead, she changed the subject. "Lester's attorney called. He's sending someone over to evaluate Lester's mental health. He wants to see what might trigger his blackouts."

"Do you believe Lester's story of blacking out and not remembering anything?"

"Not really. And I want someone that isn't hired by the defense counsel to evaluate Lester. Does the department have someone that performs mental evaluations?"

"There is a list of expert witnesses the department uses. Maxine will have it. It will mean driving him to Baton Rouge."

They pulled into Gil's parking lot, dust billowing behind the SUV as they parked. They really needed some rain.

"Hey, ladies," several men said in greeting. They had no chance to sit down before the questions began. Little happened in this small community and the skull was big news. Added to that was the hit-and-run of the popular sheriff with a deputy being held as a suspect.

"How is the sheriff?"

"Have you talked to the parents of that little girl yet?"

"What the hell was Lester thinking doing something like that?"

"Are you gals sure you can handle all this? Seems like everything's gone to hell since the sheriff got hurt."

They ordered their meals and fielded the questions with answers too vague to be informative but still maintained rapport with the community. Finally, after their food had arrived, the barrage settled, and they were able to talk quietly.

A woman, rather than Gil, brought their meals. Jess smiled but got no response. The woman barely spoke even to take their order.

"Who was that? She isn't as cheerful as Gil."

Claire shook her head. "No. That's Gil's wife, Cammie. She and their son, Chris, always seem to be frazzled, or just plain unhappy to be here. I think Gil is the energy behind this place." She took a sip of her sweet tea. "Did you get caught up on the paperwork this morning?"

Jess rolled her eyes. "Not even close. I'm sure Sheriff Willis meant to have things more organized before he went out on leave, plus we had planned to give me several days to learn where everything is but, he didn't plan the accident."

"I'm sure it's a pain trying to just walk into another person's job. Your best resource is Maxine. Lean on her as much as you need." She waited while Chris filled their tea glasses. Then, "I'm hoping things will calm down and go back to normal as quickly as possible. Of course, this mess with Lester is going to hang over us but…"

Jess sipped her tea. "With two of you out of commission, the workforce is cut in half. This must be like an avalanche for the department."

"Can you imagine what it would have been without you? With only Sid and me? And Sid is supposed to retire next month."

"Do you think he would be willing to stay longer?"

Claire thought about it. "He would probably be happy to work part-time. By the way, where are you staying while you're helping us out? As you've seen, the hotel off the highway is terrible."

Jess was embarrassed to admit her predicament. "I'm staying at the office. I'm using the shower kept for the overnight prisoners, but I'll soon be running out of clothes."

"Yeah. We're not exactly a tourist hotspot."

"I had thought driving home was the best option. After all, it's just over an hour from here and I was only supposed to fill in for Sheriff Willis for a couple of weeks. I didn't expect the time to be extended or for things to be so hectic. I spoke with Maxine, and she couldn't come up with anything either."

Claire swallowed a french fry before answering. "People only come if they're visiting family or camping during hunting season." She was quiet for a moment. "Darn, Jess. I have an extra bedroom at my house. You can crash there. It's nothing fancy but it's clean and close by."

Jess bit her lip. "I don't know, Claire. I hate to be an imposition. I can do as I planned and drive home."

"First of all, you wouldn't be imposing. Second, it's an easy solution and you can get a lot more rest at night driving ten minutes rather than an hour to get home."

Jess opened her mouth to respond but was interrupted when their radios went off simultaneously.

Maxine's voice came over the air. "Officers Morgan and Duvall, we have a call from LDWF requesting a return call asap." There was a brief pause. "Advise 10-61."

They needed to call Louisiana Wildlife as soon as possible on a private line? What the hell? Jess squeezed the button and replied. "10-4 dispatch."

Claire told Jess to keep eating and headed outside with her cell phone in hand.

Jess watched the many curious stares following her. Yep. This was a small town, all right…like an ornery version of Mayberry. She saw Claire with the phone to her ear talking briefly before coming back inside. She didn't sit down again.

"Let's get our stuff together. We need to go." She spoke so quietly Jess barely heard her. I'll explain outside." After heading out the door, Claire made a beeline to the SUV with Jess following closely behind.

As they were buckling up their seat belts, Jess asked, "What's up?"

"Hollis found more."

"More bones?"

"No." Her voice shook a little. "More bodies."

CHAPTER FOURTEEN

"Bodies? What? Did she say how many bodies?" Jess asked as they drove down the road.

"No. But she was pretty creeped out which is rare for Hollis."

"Damn. This puts us into a different world."

Claire glanced at Jess's stricken face. "What do you mean?"

Jess took a heavy breath. "Multiple bodies indicate a serial killer."

Claire instinctively threw on the brakes. Thankfully, no one was on the road at the moment. "What? We have a serial killer?"

Jess placed a calming hand on her arm. "I shouldn't have said it. The last thing I want to do is throw you off your game. Right now, I need you to focus on the task at hand. One thing at a time."

Claire kept her eyes on Jess. She took a couple of calming breaths. "Thanks. Sorry."

"Don't be sorry. This is overwhelming. But we'll get through it. Okay?" She looked into her side mirror. "We have a car coming. We can pull off the road if you need some more time."

Claire shook her head and touched the accelerator.

Jess kept up small talk until they turned into the parking area for the boat ramp. Hollis and her fellow officer were waiting. Both wore grim expressions. There would be no easygoing banter today.

Claire made the introductions. "This is Jess Morgan, filling in for Sheriff Willis. Jess, this is Hollis St. Martin, and Tomas Alvarez." As they exchanged handshakes, Claire thought Hollis looked a little green around the gills. "What did you find, Hollis?"

Hollis grimaced. "Tomas and I were checking water depth in a few of the channels and we smelled decay, something seriously putrid. We checked for evidence of poaching but instead, found what could only be thought of as multiple graves. Some were buried shallow and left parts exposed with varying degrees of decomposition." She shuddered at the memory. "As soon as we realized what we were seeing we went back where we could get a phone signal and called you. Based on their location, they were buried, not submerged. I don't think they were ever underwater."

Jess pulled out her phone. "We will need to get the coroner here."

Hollis still looked nauseous. "You're going to need as many hands as possible."

Claire reluctantly offered to call Sid. The poor man was losing sleep these last couple of days.

As they waited for them to arrive, Hollis gave a description of the graves' locations. "The main group is just beyond Alligator Alley, where Hopper found the skull. It's on a piece of land that forms a peninsula."

"How close to the skull?"

Hollis thought a moment. "A little less than a half mile by water."

"And by land?"

"Less but there is a lot of standing water." She glanced at Claire, no doubt thinking of the gator attack a few days ago.

Claire pulled out her kit and Hollis said, "You won't have enough flags and maybe not enough bags either."

Claire responded, "It's a full one. I refilled everything since—"

"It won't be enough, if you're planning on flagging everything individually." Hollis held firm.

Claire stopped in her tracks as she envisioned the scene awaiting them.

Sid was the first to arrive. As he shut his truck door, Claire called out, "Hey Sid. You got a scene kit with you?"

"Yeah."

"Better bring it with you."

"What's going on?" As always, Sid was calm and unhurried. They explained and he gave a whistle. "I've been on the force over forty years and never seen anything like what you're describing."

"I haven't seen anything like this and hope to never see it again," Hollis wiped sweat from her brow.

Keen to begin, Jess, Claire, and Tomas navigated to the crime scene to set up the search perimeter. Sid and Hollis waited for the doctors. They smelled the site long before they saw it, and Tomas, his face the color of a tomato, gagged several times. The three of them stepped onto land where the smell drew them to the exact location.

The area took Claire's breath away, literally. Six mounds lay in a haphazard fashion, a couple showing more of the body exposed than covered. The stench of death hung in the thick humid air so strongly you could taste it. The southern sun was at its hottest, adding another misery to the mix. It took a moment for Claire to understand the loud noise she was hearing: a sort of buzz.

Then she realized it was the sound of swarming insects. The knowledge chilled her to the bone.

Jess automatically assumed command of the crime scene for which Claire was secretly grateful. She was totally overwhelmed by the extent of death surrounding them.

They had just completed the task of placing crime scene tape around the area when the sound of the airboat coming their way told them of the doctors' arrival. The boat pulled to the bank. "Oh, my goodness," Dr. Siya Wason exclaimed. "The smell is overpowering."

"Breathe through your mouth," Jess advised. "Claire has some menthol to dab under your nose. It helps a little."

After donning the white Tyvek contamination suits and shoes they began their grisly task. Tomas and Hollis took the boats and moved along the winding waterways to check for other cadavers, neither of them wanting to stay in this terrible place.

At the first mound, Claire snapped photos as Dr. Avi unearthed a body with just a few swipes of his gloved hands, the sand and leaves barely covering it. The left arm was missing from near the elbow. The remaining stump was torn and jagged, as if an animal had made a meal of the rotting flesh.

Flies buzzed around it sounding like a swarm of bees. The entire corpse was covered in maggots and flies. Bone was exposed as the flesh had been devoured. Behind her, Sid made a retching noise that pushed Claire to do the same. She somehow squashed the urge down despite the horrendous odor of death and rotting flesh, grateful for the mentholatum on her upper lip.

The naked body lay on its back with arms splayed out. Flesh still remained on most of this one but appeared to be breaking down. As Dr. Avi touched the arm the skin slid away easily, exposing rotting muscle and sinew. Feasting maggots writhing within the cavity were as repulsive as the smell enveloping the area.

The female victim's long black hair was matted with fluid that was most likely blood. Dr. Avi began his inspection and some of the hair came away in his hands. He gently probed the back of the head. His gloved hand sank into the cranial cavity, making a squelching noise that was simply too much for poor Sid. He tried to put some distance between himself and the others but the sound of his retching was too much for Jess as she joined him in his misery. Claire's eyes watered and she squinched them tightly as she fought back the bile that rose into her mouth. The mentholatum was no longer working, just another scent added to the sickening potpourri.

Dr. Avi carefully probed the side of the head as the others silently watched. Liquified flesh slid along the skull. The movement disturbed maggots and they streamed out of her mouth.

Claire's gut clenched. She whirled away but had no time to do any more as she lost her recently eaten lunch. Miserable, she knew this scene would haunt her for a long time. She turned back to the gruesome task just as Dr. Avi gagged, making her do the same again. He took a moment to compose himself before continuing to gather a sample of the maggots into a vial.

There was a slight tremble in his voice when he said, "It appears that there was a hole in the cranium in the approximate place as the child's." His features had taken on a gray pallor.

Claire looked toward Jess who, although obviously nauseated, indicated she was ready to begin her inspection. She spoke aloud as Claire took notes.

The woman appeared to be Asian, surprising since that demographic in Louisiana was uncommon. However, that was almost lost on them as her mouth was twisted into a silent scream. The moment she died was frozen in time and the utter terror and, perhaps, anger at her predicament stared at them through eye sockets bereft of flesh.

The flesh on the tip of her nose was gone exposing her sinus cavity. The body was nude except for a ring encircling a finger on the one remaining hand. They finished with this corpse and Claire suffered a moment of horror at the realization that there were five more bodies. Claire wasn't sure she could finish this job.

Jess moved to the next corpse to assist the doctors leaving Claire and Sid to bag and tag this one. The two began the grisly process of picking up the body and placing it inside the bag. Try as they might, pieces of flesh fell to the ground as they slipped it inside the body bag. They used another smaller pouch to scoop up the earth around it in case there was something important beneath it.

Then they moved to assist with the next body. This one was a young male, probably not a full-grown man yet. This corpse was much more decomposed than the woman. Just as before, this one had a hole in its skull but maggots had eaten much of the brain matter and facial muscles, leaving the face oddly flat.

After taking photos, they began bagging the body which agitated the insects. The swarming flies were almost more than Claire could bear. The noise was absurdly loud. They buzzed furiously before alighting on her face. Shaking her head violently offered only a moment of relief and she was on the verge of screaming. She couldn't open her eyes or hear anything above the noise of the swarm. Blind and deaf, she ground to a halt, fighting panic as the swarm seemed to focus on her now.

She gave up and hunkered on the ground, her hands over her ears. Eyes closed, she still knew that it was Jess's hands that drew her upward into a hug and guided her a few feet away. Jess swatted her hand lightly against Claire's body and limbs to get the more stubborn flies to leave.

"You okay?"

Claire opened her eyes and saw Jess's sympathetic face close to her own. She nearly burst into tears but held them at bay. Jess kept her in a hug as she tried to gain full control of herself. Another hand came to rest on her back in a gesture of comfort. Sid had left the body behind as well.

"Whew. It's about the worst thing I've ever seen." He pulled a handkerchief from his pocket and wiped sweat from his face. "The bodies are bad enough but those maggots and flies are unbearable."

Dr. Avi walked over with his arms around his wife. Tears and her disheveled appearance showed she was also having difficulty. He kept his arm around Dr. Siya even as Jess's arms dropped to her sides. Claire felt the loss.

"Let us take a few minutes to re-evaluate our strategy," he suggested "Perhaps we can simply bag the bodies and do the evaluation in my office? I realize it isn't as thorough as my original intention but—"

Jess interrupted. "I agree." They would bag the bodies for further analysis at the morgue.

They remained at a distance as a brief respite from the flies. After a good ten minutes they decided to try once again. They managed to bag three more bodies that were in a similar state of putrefaction. The remaining two were farther along in the decomposition process and the insects weren't as overwhelming.

By now, Tomas and Hollis had returned. They had found three more bodies at a location close by. The group split into two groups. Sid and Tomas loaded the six body bags into an airboat and would assist in the transport to the morgue.

It was evident the corpses in the new site had been there longer than the others as they were much more decomposed. The smell of death hung in the air but it wasn't nearly as ghastly as the other site. The maggots, flies, and other insects had finished most of their work, leaving behind almost fleshless bones. A couple of sunken areas in the soil suggested the bodies might once have been buried. However, scavenging animals had found them, ripping them to pieces and dragging bones away. This made it difficult to decide which bones belonged to a single body. The investigation ground to a crawl as only the two doctors could make sense of organizing the remains. The group attacked the problem by the doctors working with the remains while the officers circled the area to locate anything left behind by the predators.

Claire shuddered when she found what remained of one particularly ravaged skeleton. The rib cage was crushed and the large pelvic bone was broken into several pieces. A closer look showed the same damage to several vertebrae and the one remaining femur.

An alligator was the only bayou predator she could think of that would have enough crushing power to break the heavier bones. Macabre thoughts of the beasts tearing the bodies apart and then gulping down large chunks of what had once been someone's son or daughter flashed through her mind. How many times had she seen an alligator eat its prey?

After today, she would never be able to stomach seeing it again.

* * *

After several painstaking hours, all the corpses were bagged and tagged. They included both black and white, male and female, of varying ages. The skulls that were mostly intact all showed damage like that of the original found in the swamp.

Hollis and Tomas returned and helped load the bodies and the equipment. Hollis reported to the doctors. "There wasn't enough room for all the bodies in the emergency vehicles so they're currently taking the first four."

"That's fine," Dr. Avi said. "Siya and I will go to the hospital and ensure they are taken care of this evening. But we will wait until tomorrow to begin the evaluation. We need time to cleanse our minds of this place."

"Of course," Jess agreed. "I know this must be overwhelming for you. But I would be remiss if I didn't explain the need to expedite the autopsies. These bodies point to a serial killer. Everyone is in danger until this maniac is put away."

Dr. Avi nodded in agreement. "Can I now assume there are no more cadavers to be exhumed from the bayou? Or should I expect more?"

Everyone was momentarily stunned as his words sank in. They hung in the air as they rode back through the swamp. Even though Hollis sped through the black water as fast as safely possible, the stink escaped the bagged bodies. Claire wondered if a long hot shower would erase the stench any more than sleep would allow her to escape the day's horrors.

After beaching the boat at the landing, Hollis said, "Tomorrow, Tomas and I will scour every inch that we can. And we will continue to be on the lookout as the water continues to drop because of the drought."

"That's something that is different," Claire thought aloud. "The child's bones were underwater until the drought. All those today were buried. There was no water there when he disposed of them. That gives us an idea of the timeframe in which they were killed."

The ambulances returned and loaded the rest of the body bags. The Wasons left and the group dispersed.

Jess looked at Claire, her words barely audible. "Is your offer to stay with you still good?"

CHAPTER FIFTEEN

It was late when they pulled into Claire's driveway. She had lived in the small vinyl-sided cottage her entire life, but it became just a house instead of a home the night her mother died. Together, they had updated the exterior to give it a more modern appearance. But since her mother's death, Claire had made none of the improvements they had discussed over the years, just necessary maintenance. She had no plans to leave, but she didn't want to stay either. So, why bother?

She drifted along as she waited for something…anything… to give her inspiration to move. Jessica Morgan's presence was pushing Claire to think about the future and what she wanted from life.

She unlocked the door, tossing the keys onto the tray that had served that purpose for as long as she could remember. "Sorry for the mess. I haven't had much time this week."

Jess dismissed her words with a wave of her hand. "I'm soon going to run out of clean uniforms if I don't do laundry in the next few days. And I certainly know the week you've had."

An awkward silence fell between them. "Let me give you the nickel tour," Claire offered as she headed away from the living area. "Your bathroom is here," she pointed out as they walked down the hall to the bedrooms. "My room is here, in case you need anything. You can have this room." She opened the door and flipped the light switch. "It's not big but it's clean."

"This will be fine. Thank you for letting me stay. The cell cots aren't the most comfortable."

"True. By the way, I'll drive my truck tomorrow morning. You can take the department's SUV."

"Why?"

"I told Sid to work a half shift and I would take the back half of his. He lost sleep by helping us out today and I'm a lot younger than him."

"Damn, I should have thought of that. I can—"

"Nope," Claire interrupted. "Remember? You have been going on a couple of hours' sleep for the last few days. It's my turn."

Jess had to agree with her. Such a tiny group of officers was making things tough on all of them. "Okay. But the next overtime is on me."

"Right." Unsure what else to do, Claire backed out the door saying, "Would you like something to eat? I can rustle up something."

"No thanks. I'm wiped out. I want to shower until I can't remember the smells from today and go to sleep."

Claire was relieved as she had no idea what she might have that was edible at the moment. "Good night then. I'll see you in the morning."

She closed the door behind her and headed to her bathroom for a long hot shower. She needed to feel the cleansing water running over her skin. She stepped beneath the spray, letting the hot water wash away some of the fatigue. She washed her hair twice and scrubbed until her skin was pink before she reluctantly turned the water off.

She hadn't had a chance to do laundry and found no clean pajamas. Too weary to bother searching for anything, she slid under the covers, naked, and fell asleep.

* * *

Claire knew nothing until she awoke to Jess shaking her. "What?" Her eyes felt like they were filled with sand and opening them was difficult. Then she realized her alarm was blaring. "Ah, dammit. I'm sorry Jess." She rolled over and slapped the clock.

Blessed silence.

She sat up and moved her legs over the side of the bed. "Go back to sleep. I'm up now."

"Okay then. I'll see you in a few hours." Jess's voice was a little breathless.

Claire stumbled to the bathroom, her eyelids not wanting to stay open. It was only when she looked in the mirror that she realized she was naked.

Ah, Jesus! I'm naked in front of my boss.

Three a.m. was darned early but poor Sid needed the break. She was soon out the door. She found Sid in the office, talking to Lester in his cell.

"Morning."

"Morning, Claire," Sid said with a yawn.

For once, Lester kept his mouth shut.

"I'm going to make some coffee. You guys want some?"

"You talking to me?" Lester looked up in surprise.

"Yeah."

"Sure," he said in return.

"Sid?" She looked over and caught him in the midst of another enormous yawn.

"No. I need to head on home. Long hours aren't as easy at my age." He stood up and stretched. "I'll see you both later. Thanks for coming in so early, Claire."

"No problem, Sid. And I appreciate your responding so quickly when we called yesterday." She rinsed a cup while she waited for the coffee to percolate. "I hope you had the good sense to stay in the office tonight and not out on patrol."

"I came straight here and showered. Then slept a few hours. I didn't want to go home smelling like I did." He stared down at his feet. "You know, that was about the worst thing I've ever had to do in all my years of policing. Whoever is doing that mess is sick and needs to be put down like a rabid dog. Know what I mean?"

"Yeah. I do."

"I know you and Jess will be going to see the sheriff, but uh…would appreciate it if you didn't say much about yesterday in front of Blanche." He finally met her gaze. "I don't plan on saying much either. She ought not have to know about that kind of thing."

"I understand, Sid. I'll tell Jess so she won't say anything either."

"Thank you." He patted her shoulder. "I'll see you later."

"Okay, Sid. Take care."

"Yep." His footsteps clicked down the hall.

Claire turned back to the coffee and made two cups. She walked down the hall to the holding cell and handed one to Lester. "Watch it. It's hot."

He took it from her and pulled it slowly between the bars and took a sip. "Thanks," he muttered grudgingly.

Silence descended on the room as neither of them knew what to say.

Claire finished her cup in record time and announced, "I need to head out and make my rounds. I'll cut the lights way down so you can get some sleep."

Lester hung his head and moved back from the cell's bars. He said nothing, just sat on his cot while she cut the lights and walked out. He was a broken man, no longer full of rage, just regret and the fear of what lay ahead.

CHAPTER SIXTEEN

Sunset colors of coral and pink were long gone when the ritual began. The bold glow of a bonfire kept the darkness at bay, the moon little more than a quarter of its strength. Intricate rhythms of Voodoo drummers called to him, asking for his presence, as other followers danced around the fire. As usual, everyone was dressed in white, a sign of purity and holiness. Many had removed their shoes. After all, their Messiah walked among them. It was holy ground.

Some followers began chanting in unknown languages, accompanied by yips and trills, signaling the dancers' rising fervor. A few enraptured souls called out, begging their Christ to join them.

The door to the house opened, his body silhouetted from the light behind. Every motion stilled and all grew silent as he stood there. No dancing, singing, or beating of the drums, as if all held their breath at his approach. He drank in their sign of respect. He deserved it.

He closed the door and strode toward the firelight.

Their Lord was ready to begin.

He stopped at the altar, where a young woman lay, eyes open but with no hint of fright, thanks to the God's Breath his disciples had used. Her arms were outstretched, her wrists bound with leather strips. Her ankles were strapped down similarly, placing her in a horizontal version of the cross. The wooden surface had been carved to make channels that drained blood to the table's edge.

He stepped onto the altar's raised platform. It allowed his followers a better view of him performing the sacrifice, but just as importantly, it allowed him to see his followers. He tolerated nothing but their total focus on him during the rituals. Just a frown from him and one of his apostles would seek out the recalcitrant follower and show him the error of his ways.

Tonight, he held the full attention of the large crowd. Apparently, sending his apostles to the homes of any recalcitrant locals had worked. He recognized several chastened faces among those that lived within Kalfou Parish.

Good. They should feel chastened. When so many followers traveled long distances to get here, those blessed to live so close should never miss an opportunity to commune with their master.

As he began the service, he smiled magnanimously. "Today is a day of celebration," he announced. "The day of the second coming is soon upon us. Rejoice in this season of prayer and glory in my presence. Soon, my brothers, I will wield the sword of God against those that deny me. Soon, my sisters, I will heal the wounds of injustice and corruption. Soon, my children, I shall rise up and take over the kingdoms of heaven and earth. I will cast my judgment upon the wicked while you, my faithful, will be embraced. Well done, my good and faithful servants. Well done."

The crowd clapped and shouted while drums resumed their cadence. Many moved to the rhythm, the beat rising in volume and speed. Several dancers swooned in the presence of their Messiah.

He kept a watchful eye for anyone not participating to his satisfaction. These were his most devout followers and yet, they still carried so much baggage from their old religions. Didn't they understand there was no one religion with all the answers? Only he held the true answers.

He had studied and prepared for his divine place from the time of his mother's prophecy. She had seen him as the new age of God arriving to a misguided world. Between her sight into the future and his divine nature, they had seen that Voodoo and Catholicism should merge. After all, the Voodoo loa and Catholic saints were shades of the same spirits.

More followers arrived through the wooded section to the south where the bayou emptied into the ocean. Arriving by boat, these followers had only recently come to the United States from the Caribbean. His spirits lifted at seeing those early believers that had traveled so far to follow him.

To the delight of the crowd, he joined in the dance, reveling in their devotion. He smiled and stomped to the drums. Their Savior kept a watchful eye on the sacrificial table even though it prevented him from complete immersion in the praise and worship being offered to him.

I didn't have enough God's Breath to keep her compliant for the usual amount of time. I need her to be a willing participant. I must have more God's Breath.

Ready or not, it was time to begin the ceremony. The crowd stilled once more. He patted the woman gently. He knew the women and children liked it when he did that.

He lifted high a large smooth stone, its gray surface marbled by a vein of red. He paused long enough to ensure he had their attention, then announced, "This is the rock of ages, holy with the blood of Christ. Only I, the cornerstone of my Church, can absolve your sins. It is only right that I use this hallowed stone to perform the sacrifice that cleanses you."

The rock crashed down savagely on the young woman's skull, the sound of crunching bone mingled with the thud of the rock. Blood splattered and flowed onto the table.

He inhaled deeply, the blood's coppery smell an aphrodisiac. He picked up the knife and, as dispassionately as a butcher, carved a large chunk of muscle from one of her thighs. His blade found the femoral artery and blood sprayed coating the victim, the altar, and their Savior. His smile was of unadulterated joy.

Peter, his disciple, placed the mass of cut flesh on an ornate silver tray and quickly carried it inside the house.

With the leather strap holding her arm in place, he swiped the knife across her inner arm. The knife sliced deep into the flesh, severing the brachial artery and striking the bone. Blood flowed along the channels cut into the altar table and filled the chalices as he held them. With each slowing beat of her heart, its diminishing pulse became a visual display of her death.

Their Christ bowed his head and began praying silently. Just as Peter arrived with the flesh which had been pulverized, the Savior spoke in a loud voice, "Come, come. Bring the little children to me and do not hinder them for such as these belongs my kingdom."

All eyes remained on him. "My children. Today I have provided us with an offering for our future. Today our children will drink my blood and eat my body that they may have everlasting life. See that you do not suffer one of these little ones to come to me for theirs is the Kingdom of God."

He paused a moment and then placed the chalices on the table and picked up a knife again. Raising it high for all to see, he said, "This is my blood that is shed for you. Drink of it and pray to me that you may be saved."

Parents formed a line to his right and began passing by him with their youngsters. Each child drank from the cup, and if they resisted, then the father or mother dipped a finger into the drink and spread it over the child's mouth. For each child he murmured, "This is my blood that you drink. Behold the King of Kings." He then placed a small piece of flesh on their tongue. "This is my body. It was given for you. Remember this and believe in me."

Lines formed behind the families as the others patiently waited for their turn to partake of their Messiah. After receiving their blessing from the blood and flesh, each person passed the blood-covered altar. Some swiped each hand through the pool of red before smearing it on their clothes and face. Some simply traced a finger through it and drew a cross on their forehead. The amount wasn't as important as having at least something to show their devotion to their God.

The music resumed and people began to dance again. Rum was brought out and circulated among the followers. As people began to feel the effects of the alcohol, they opened themselves up to the spirits that were surely present at such a wondrous ceremony.

People grew more frenzied in their worship. Many went back to the altar and ran their hands through the blood and smeared it all over themselves. The chance to revel in the blood of the Lord was enthralling. As the last of them sipped from the cup, Peter and John poured the remaining blood onto themselves, a symbol of their close relationship with their Lord. The followers cheered.

Snakes were brought out to be passed among them. They were handled gently and lovingly as they symbolized God's strength and sanctity. The Bible spoke of handling snakes without dying in the days before the Messiah returned. As their Messiah now walked among them, snakes were a part of every service.

The crowd didn't disperse until the morning sun rose high enough for them to make their way through the bayou. They all knew the Kingdom was at hand. The countdown had begun and soon their Lord would assume the Throne.

Afterward, no one saw the woman's kidnapper carry her body into the swamp, blood covering both of them. He located the new burial site that he had recently found. It accommodated the one requirement he demanded. It must face east with enough room between the trees to see the rising sun, symbolic of the biblical reference to Jesus coming again from the eastern sky. As he dug between the tree roots and vegetation, he thought about his first victim so long ago.

He hadn't bothered with burying the child. Instead, he had counted on the alligators to take care of the body. It hadn't occurred to him until later that the sacrificial lamb might be found when processing a gator. Fortunately, that foolish oversight on his part had not happened. And now, after all these years, Hopper Beaumont had found the first lamb. He wondered about the divine timing for the boy to be found just weeks before his Transfiguration ceremony.

He lifted the woman's body and placed it in the shallow grave, flesh jarringly absent from her legs and arms, exposing the white bone. He chuckled as he remembered how clumsily he had prepared that first sacrifice. The boy's thin arm had very little flesh. He had almost amputated it. He still hated to work with a young sacrificial lamb. They were so small to feed so many.

CHAPTER SEVENTEEN

The next week was a whirlwind of activity for Claire. With only three active officers, everyone worked long hours as they tried to keep up with everything that needed their attention.

Jess contacted the Lincoln Parish sheriff to request volunteers for overtime. Sheriff Willis did the same thing with Cameron Parish. Between the two of them, they had a steady influx of deputies working from four to eight hours each day, mostly cruising the roads to maintain the law's presence.

At home, the two women quickly fell into a routine and found they got along quite well. Jess was a considerate houseguest and Claire looked forward to their time shared away from work. It had been years since Claire had lived a normal life. Her mother's fight with cancer and subsequent death had left her dreading coming home. Sharing a joke or conversation was something she had missed.

The more time she spent with Jess, the more her feelings for her grew. She admired and respected the professional Jess, but away from her role as undersheriff, she let down her guard and allowed Claire to see the real Jess Morgan. Smart and kind, she laughed often, and Claire found herself laughing along with her. She loved that Jess hummed without realizing it when she cooked, and she snored a little when she slept. Claire moved from a big crush on the woman to a friendship that was heading toward more serious feelings. She had no idea how Jess felt about it all and knew nothing of her personal life. Hell, she wasn't sure if Jess was even a lesbian.

Although still in the hospital, Sheriff Willis was keenly aware of his team's struggle with the workload and was determined to help. After much arguing, he convinced Dr. Avi to let him work two hours each day from his hospital bed. Between his help and the deputies cruising the roads, Jess and Claire were able to work on the case with minimal disruption.

Doctors Avi and Siya worked long hours to get their reports available as quickly as possible. Sheriff Willis called in every favor he could to get DNA expedited for the nine new victims. But even the sheriff couldn't get them in less than a week. Analyzing DNA was a complex protracted process.

Claire's office phone rang late one evening. "Hello?"

A quiet voice came over the line. "This is Avi Wason. I have received the DNA results from victim number one. You should receive the documents in the next few minutes."

She was delighted but managed to contain her excitement. "That's great, Dr. Avi. Did it match the missing child in New Orleans?"

"Yes, it did."

"Is there anything in the report that deserves extra attention?"

"There is nothing that warrants undue attention. But please give me a call if you need to discuss anything."

She went in search of Jess and found her at the copier. "The DNA on victim one is a match with Dakota Grambling. The results are coming right now."

Jess removed the papers from the machine. "Great. Want to go over the report from New Orleans police right now?"

"Jess," Maxine called out. "Sheriff Willis is on line one."

Jess looked at Claire. "Come on in. He's probably asking about the DNA results. He's called about them already."

"You got anything on the DNA?" The sheriff didn't bother with a greeting.

"Dr. Avi just called," Jess answered. "We haven't had time to review it yet. By the way—Claire is with me. I have you on speakerphone."

She began going through the report aloud. "The victim's name is Dakota Grambling. Caucasian. The boy went missing seven years ago at age ten. He was last seen on his bike as he cut through a nearby park."

There was a pause as they digested this new information. Claire broke the silence. "His picture and his height and weight stats seem small for a ten-year-old. I wonder if the perp thought he was younger."

Jess checked the report. "His birthday was just a couple of days prior to the kidnapping so he was barely ten."

Claire used her cell phone to call up a satellite image of the park where the boy was taken. "Damn. It's an empty lot now. I can probably locate an older photo but it will take a little time."

"Wouldn't NOPD have pictures?" The sheriff's voice sounded tired today.

"Yes. I just wanted to get as much information as possible."

The sheriff cleared his throat. "Seems like a trip to New Orleans is in order. I want both of you to go. Jess, you're familiar with the city and the police department. Claire knows Kalfou Parish like the back of her hand. After the meeting, I want to know how Kalfou Parish fits with the kidnapping and death of a little boy in New Orleans. Between the two of you, all the bases will be covered."

Jess agreed. "I'll call the NOPD and see when we can meet."

The sheriff disconnected as Blanche was heard in the background scolding him for overdoing it.

Jess left a message with the NOPD explaining their findings about Dakota Grambling. With that task accomplished, she moved to the large whiteboard mounted on a wall of the office. In front of it was a conference table, scarred from years of use. The few chairs around the table matched it in blemishes.

She pulled out a marker and wrote, "Dakota Grambling." Then, item by item, they discussed the report and listed anything that might be pertinent. "We finally have our first big batch of information."

"Jess?" Maxine called from her desk. "Line one for you."

"Thanks." She picked up her phone. "Hello? Detective Johnson? Jessica Morgan." She gave the detective a summary of what they knew before requesting a meeting with the NOPD as well as a meeting with the parents.

She listened for a moment. Then, "Got it. I look forward to meeting up with you."

"The parents can meet with us at nine o'clock, Saturday morning. We will meet with Detective Johnson, hit the park where he was abducted and then interview the parents. Since it's such a long drive, we will have to go up Friday evening. I hope that's okay with you."

Claire chuckled. "I'm fine with it, but you do realize that Friday is tomorrow, right?"

Jess's eyes widened. "Today is Thursday, already? Damn. All these long hours are beginning to run together."

Jess asked Maxine to make reservations for them as Claire headed out the door to a suspected shoplifting call at the local hardware store. Life in the small parish continued as normal and needed the Sheriff's Department no matter how horrendous the murders.

Friday didn't slow its demands, so it wasn't until they were in the car, on their way to New Orleans, that they had time to catch up with each other.

Claire's excitement couldn't be contained. "How long did you work there? Are you happy to go back?"

"Actually, I grew up in the suburbs. But I worked in the police department in the property crimes division for four years before moving to Lincoln Parish."

"That makes you a has-been local, but you'll still know the best restaurants to hit."

Jess laughed. "I can probably find a couple. Have you been there much?"

"A few times." Claire was a little embarrassed to admit it. She felt rather lacking compared to Jess's more sophisticated life. "But to visit family. I didn't see much of the normal tourist attractions."

"You need a taste of the Big Easy." Jess changed topics. "By the way, you have no idea how much better I feel since I get a full night's rest now. Thank you so much for letting me stay with you."

"No problem. I'm enjoying having you. It's been kind of lonely at times in the last couple of years."

A silence permeated the air for a moment. Then Jess began in a serious tone. "Claire. Have you ever thought about moving somewhere else?"

Claire looked at her in surprise. "Why do you ask?"

"Well, I've witnessed a lot of prejudice here. Pastor Abel and Lester seem to take great pleasure in hurting you." She smiled. "I gave the good pastor a ticket for speeding yesterday, by the way. He called me a heathen since I stopped him on his way to do God's Work."

Claire laughed. "Yep. That's Pastor Abel. You're on his shit list now."

"I believe I was on his shit list, anyway."

Claire's smile faded a bit. "You're probably right. He spews hate toward anyone that isn't the same as him. And my being a lesbian is particularly heinous in his eyes."

Jess snorted. "I've never understood why people choose homosexuality as something to be so angry about. There is so much evil in the world, with hate at the center of it all. But they are all fucked up about who I love? It's ludicrous."

Wait! Claire thought. *"Who I love"? Is she saying…?*

Surprise must have registered on her face as Jess's kind smile turned into laughter. "What? Oh wait. I hope I didn't say anything out of line to you. I thought since you've been open with me about being gay, I assumed you realized I am as well."

Claire shook her head. "I had no idea. Between Lester and Pastor Abel, no one is allowed to forget I'm gay. You've only been here a short time and you've already heard them condemn me. I haven't got the option to be open or not about my sexuality."

Jess reached out a hand but then withdrew it without touching Claire. "I've not dealt with the amount of bigotry and animosity that you receive, Claire. I've always been able to just be myself most of the time. I wish you could know the freedom of being yourself without judgment."

This time, without hesitation, Jess covered Claire's hand with her own. "I want you to think about moving at some point. There will always be prejudice, but I've found Kalfou Parish to be worse than anywhere I've lived before."

Claire was intensely aware of the warmth of Jess's hand, her strength and compassion conveyed in the simple gesture. It made her feel safe to discuss things she normally kept private. "Have you dealt with the hate very often?"

Jess shook her head. "I haven't dated anyone since I moved to Lincoln Parish so I can't say how the rural area would be. But New Orleans is much more enlightened." She squeezed Claire's hand. "I wish you could have grown up in a more progressive area. You don't deserve the garbage they spew at you."

Claire cleared her throat. "It has been challenging at times. During school it was awful. But Pastor Abel is the worst single individual I've had the misfortune to encounter. And it seems like so many people have gotten more belligerent. I don't really know why. It's like they have become ultra right-wing religious freaks lately. I've broken up several fights in the last few months and most started with arguments about religion." Claire was quiet a moment as Jess smoothly took a sharp left turn onto the next road. "I must admit I've thought about moving quite a lot in the last couple of years but haven't pursued anything. I've kind of been in limbo since Mom died. With the increasing 'hate thy neighbor' attitude of so many, I'm beginning to think about it more often."

"Well, just remember you have options. You don't have to be a punching bag for anyone."

The countryside flashed by alternating between trees and bayou to fields of sugar cane and dilapidated homes. Early evening, the sun was still above the line of trees. It wouldn't be dark for a few hours. Jess flipped on the headlights. "Lester is going to be transferred on Monday. He is refusing to ask for bail until his trial."

"Why? He can't afford it?"

"I think he is scared to get out. He keeps saying he wants to stay. He won't even discuss it with his lawyer."

"Wow." Claire was puzzled at his choice. "Lester hasn't been the same SOB since all this happened. He talks to Sid a lot and still says he doesn't remember anything. It's like he really did black out or something."

"This morning, I questioned him while Sid was there." She looked over at Claire. "I would have asked you to join us since you have been involved with the case. But I was hoping Sid could keep him calm."

"While I get him upset…" Claire rolled her eyes. "You made the right call. Seeing me is enough to upset him."

"Well, as you know, Lester has admitted that he went home to sleep for a couple of hours. Apparently, he does that a lot on night shift. He still swears someone knocked on his door. He answered, saw someone with a funny sort of cigarette, and the next thing he knows, he is waking up from a hazy dream. But he says he can't remember anything else.

"He still claims he doesn't remember running Sheriff Willis off the road?" Disbelief was evident in Claire's voice.

"That's what he says."

"Does he remember who was knocking?"

"He doesn't know. He said it has happened several times in the past. But all he ever remembers is a tall dark figure with a cigarette."

"What in the world is he talking about?" Claire couldn't decide whether he was lying or using drugs.

Jess shrugged. "Something is screwy. He talks about blackouts and a tall stranger. He would rather sit in jail than be released on bail. None of those things seem to be rational. I've got a psychiatric evaluation scheduled for him. I'm hoping it will give us something that explains what's going on with him."

A car pulling onto the highway with squealing tires turned their attention away from Lester. Jess shook her head in exasperation. That idiot drives worse than my brother."

"You have a brother?"

Jess nodded. "Yeah."

A wistful note crept into Claire's voice. "That's nice. I always wished I had siblings."

"Well...I have a mixed bag when it comes to family. I also have two cousins who came to live with us when I was a teenager. It ended up being four of us kids." Jess winked at her. "I can stop talking about them now. I just—"

"No. You're fine. Honestly." Claire turned back to Jess. "I'd love to hear about them."

Jess took her at her word and regaled Claire with her childhood stories until the sun no longer cast shadows. Claire was still missing sleep most nights while helping out on night shift in Lester's absence, so she drifted off to the rich sound of Jess's voice. Her last thoughts were how she wished to be a part of something as beautiful as what Jess had.

CHAPTER EIGHTEEN

"We're here."

Momentarily disoriented, Claire's eyes fluttered open. She sat up to the sights and sounds of downtown New Orleans. Locals and tourists intermingled on the streets, making the area buzz with excitement. She could hear a street musician playing a trumpet nearby, but the throngs kept him hidden. Their hotel sat in the heart of the French Quarter, amid restaurants ranging from fast food to renowned cuisine. Cajun fare was promised in most of the buildings, the aromas reminding Claire that she hadn't eaten since lunch.

As if reading her mind, Jess said, "I know it's late, but why don't we get settled in our rooms and then, get something to eat. That is, if you feel up to it."

"That's a great idea," Claire enthused. "Sorry I slept so much of the way, but I'm raring to go, now. Besides, I'm starving."

"Well unless you want something specific, I can recommend a couple of restaurants," she offered as they handed the car over to the valet.

"I'll put my taste buds in your capable hands," Claire quipped as they walked into the hotel's lobby with their bags. Pictures of the bayous shared walls with photos of New Orleans architecture. Pamphlets for ghost tours, museums, and discount stores promised something for everyone in the Big Easy.

"Room 364. Here are your keys," the woman behind the counter said. "I hope you enjoy your stay."

Claire frowned in confusion at the key in her hand. "I believe there is a misunderstanding. We should have two rooms."

"Oh dear. Well, let me double check…" The woman stared at the computer for a moment. "The reservation was made for two queen beds in one room."

"Well, we need to get a second room," Jess explained patiently. "No problem."

"I'm so sorry, ma'am," the woman said. "But we have a softball tournament going on. The hotel is fully booked."

Jess looked at Claire. "I'm fine with it if you're okay."

Claire shrugged. "Okay with me. Maxine was probably trying to save money."

Their room was located on the top floor of the three-story hotel and had two windows overlooking busy Dauphine Street. Beyond the windows was a private balcony sporting the traditional New Orleans wrought-iron railing. Claire headed straight out to it and peered down at the sea of tourists and locals mingling below.

A few minutes later she returned and fell onto the nearest bed. "Wow. This room is perfect. Close to the hustle and bustle but still above it all."

Jess laughed at her open excitement. "I believe you have staked your claim over there so I'll take the bed closest to the bathroom."

"I can take either bed," Claire offered apologetically.

Jess waved her off. "Take that one Claire. I'm used to the city. I want you to get the most from the trip as possible. I'll close the door soon to keep the room cool but I want to hear the street for a while. I love the sound of it all. This is home to me. There is nothing else like it."

"You're a lucky woman." Claire swept an arm toward their room. "Right now, we're both lucky women. Just look at this place. It must have cost a fortune. I hope Maxine doesn't get in trouble for this."

"I doubt it," Jess said and stepped away. "If you trust me to select the restaurant, I'll call for reservations."

"Feel free." She continued to stare at a world she hadn't seen before. Her two trips to New Orleans had been to stay in an elderly aunt's home, both times for a family funeral. This was her first visit as a typical tourist, at least when she wasn't interviewing the parents about their little boy's death.

She concentrated on ridding herself of negative thoughts. She was in New Orleans, and she planned to make the most of it. The city buzzed with an energy that rivaled the fast-flowing current of the Mississippi's dark water.

"We have a reservation at The Rowdy Gator in an hour. It's not far so we can stay here for a bit or just start walking and see what we find along the way."

Claire turned and was startled to see Jess standing in her bra and panties as she changed into a colorful blouse and white shorts. She looked like a supermodel. Her throat went dry, and she gave a little cough. "Uh…let's walk." Though it lasted only a moment, Claire knew the vision of Jess's near-naked body was tattooed on her brain. "Whew. It's hot in here. Are you hot?"

Jess smiled as she jostled the shorts up her body and fastened them. Her breasts jiggled a little as she adjusted them. "No. I'm fine but close the balcony door if it's too hot already."

Claire moved to her suitcase and mumbled, "I hope I have something to wear that's okay for the city."

Jess laughed. "You'll see just about anything imaginable where we're going. Jeans and T-shirts are always the norm. But I'm not kidding when I say, anything goes."

Claire held up a pair of khaki shorts and a blouse still sporting the sales tag. "Is this okay?"

Jess glanced over and did a double take. "Oh god, yes. That blue is perfect for you."

Claire laid the clothes on her bed and stripped down to her underwear. She heard a gasp from the other side of the room. She recognized the sound as she had made it moments before as she watched Jess dress.

Without thinking it through, she turned nonchalantly and walked past Jess on her way to the sink. She was keenly aware of Jess's eyes following every move she made as she removed the ponytail and brushed her hair into a mane that hung below her shoulders. Her normal self-doubt and inhibition fell away as she knew Jess hadn't torn her eyes away yet.

She headed back to her clothes but never made it. As she passed her, Jess reached out and touched her shoulder.

"Claire," she began hesitantly. "You're beautiful. I—"

Claire raised her eyes to stare into those amber depths and saw longing in them...something she had hoped to see since they had first met. She leaned toward her instinctively. That small movement broke all constraint and Jess drew her into a long, desperate kiss.

Jess's body was satin-smooth, her firm muscles without an ounce of extra flesh. Her lips, soft and warm, invited Claire to tease them with her tongue, an action that drew a moan from her while pulling Claire tighter against her.

Their embrace tightened until they melded into one, each clinging to the other. They remained that way for a long moment, only pulling away when both were desperate for breath.

"My God," Jess breathed against Claire's forehead. "You're as sexy as you are beautiful." She pressed gossamer kisses over her face.

"Unh..." Claire could barely speak. Jess literally took her breath away. "You're amazing."

They moved together once more, this time gently, sweetly, taking their time and savoring the moment. Finally, Claire leaned back to look into those beautiful amber eyes. "I wanted to do that the first morning we met."

Jess grinned and planted a soft kiss on her lips. "I have more restraint. I waited until you at least introduced yourself." She kissed her again. "Of course, I was nervous with it being my first day. I might have been a little preoccupied."

Without warning, New Orleans zydeco music echoed through the room and Jess moved away to grab her cell phone. "It's time to go or we'll miss our reservation." Her voice was thick.

Claire almost said they could call for room service, but Jess's stomach chose that moment to growl.

"It sounds like we should go now," she teased. "But don't think this is over."

Jess winked at her. "Not by a long shot."

The temperature still hovered near ninety degrees but a slight breeze kept the humidity at bay, perfect for a stroll to the restaurant. Enthusiasm filled the air. Letting the good times roll, people were embracing that N'awlins exuberance unique to the grand ole city.

Claire felt almost weightless without the contempt of her hometown, finding herself smiling for no apparent reason as she weaved her way through the crowd. She felt a rush of warmth when Jess reached for her hand and cradled it in her own. She didn't care that Jess was most likely just keeping them together in the crowd. It felt good to do what came naturally without worry.

Then, when Jess brought their entwined hands up for a gentle kiss and squeeze, she knew Jess had more in mind than preventing them from becoming separated.

The thought stopped her in her tracks causing a man to take a quick sidestep around her to avoid a mishap. Jess arched an eyebrow and gave her hand a gentle squeeze but didn't surrender it. Instead, she leaned forward and kissed her.

Right in the middle of the street, with throngs of people milling around them, they kissed. No one stared in disgust or even acknowledged them at all.

It was magnificent.

They had timed their arrival at The Rowdy Gator perfectly. Claire was glad they had made reservations as the entrance was swamped with those waiting for seating. The aroma of grilled steak mixed with Cajun spices as they headed inside. "Sweet Home Alabama" blared out of speakers set strategically throughout the bar and entrance and the crowd was living up to its rambunctious name.

However, the two of them had eyes only for each other, the noise just background that added to their excitement.

Everything was perfect but barbecued crawfish and oysters on the half shell sat on the table barely touched. It was difficult to eat while thinking about ravishing the beautiful woman sitting across from you. They were ravenous but not for food. They left the restaurant hand in hand and traversed the distance to the hotel in record time.

Back in their room, Jess took the lead as she quickly stripped Claire of her clothes before doing the same for herself. There was an unmistakable hunger in her eyes that matched Claire's. Jess's panties had barely landed where she tossed them before she had pulled Claire into a tight embrace.

The heat of her skin was tempered by the breeze from the ceiling fan, the difference heightening the sensual caresses Jess trailed down her back to her bottom. She cupped the firm cheeks in her palms and forged their bodies tightly together.

Claire moaned at the feel of silky skin tracing down the length of her body. Any movement caused the clipped triangle of bristly hair between Jess's legs to brush against Claire's belly. The combination of sensations had her ready to burst.

When she began using her tongue to play with Claire's lip, an animalistic sound erupted from the younger woman, and they tumbled onto the bed with legs entwined. Jess landed on top and used her position to her advantage. Jess trailed kisses from Claire's throat down to her breast, drawing maddeningly close to her pebbled nipples.

Claire groaned and writhed under the torture. Jess snickered but kept up the torment until Claire thought she would explode. Finally, she drew a pert nipple into her mouth shooting a surge of lust straight to her core.

Jess wasted no time in finding the small nub between Claire's legs, her fingers and tongue flicking the sensitive flesh until Claire's heart pulsated in rhythm.

Claire inhaled the vanilla scent that was Jess and felt like she could never get enough of it.

It was at that moment that Claire crested the edge and crashed in a climax harder than she had ever experienced. She clung to Jess as she groaned aloud, her body jerking uncontrollably. When she finally quieted, Jess held her, stroking her hair, murmuring words of reassurance that made Claire feel more loved than she had ever been before.

When she began to stroke Jess's silky skin, Jess stopped her hand. "This is your night. I want to hold you."

Claire settled for a long gentle kiss. Exhausted, she didn't move when Jess threw an arm and leg over her, covering her like a warm sexy blanket.

Claire's breathing evened out in sleep and Jess joined her minutes later, still holding her.

CHAPTER NINETEEN

Sunlight shone through the window illuminating the room, its light erasing the warm colors of sunrise. Claire stirred and opened her eyes, blinking at the brightness of morning. She started to roll over but was reluctant to lose the warmth of their bodies nested together snugly.

Thoughts of the night came flooding back and her heart raced at the memory. Jess had been amazing—sweet and sexy as hell. She seemed to know everything Claire wanted, every movement performed with tenderness and love.

Thinking of her guilty trysts in the past, Claire hoped the morning didn't bring awkward silence or excuses for why last night had been a terrible idea.

Oh God. Please don't let her have regrets. I couldn't stand it.

"Morning." Jess's voice was husky from sleep.

Claire went all gooey inside at the sexy timbre of her voice. However, anything that might have been said was forestalled as Jess's cell phone chose that moment to ring.

Jess groaned as she moved the phone to her ear. "Hello?"

She listened for a long moment. "So when do you want to meet?"

Another long pause.

"I guess we have no other choice. We'll see you then."

She placed it back on the side table. "That was Johnson. The meeting's been moved from this morning to five this evening. The parents want the original detective that worked on the case to be there, which is understandable. The guy's retired and refuses to miss his golf game today. Apparently, it's a championship match. He won't be available until late."

"What?"

"I know. But we're at his mercy. At least he's willing to meet with us. Johnson said it took a bit of talking to get him to agree to the meeting at all. So, we now have the day to ourselves." A broad grin enveloped Jess's face and she pulled Claire more firmly against her.

Claire nestled into the crook of her arm. "What do you want to do while we wait?"

Jess's eyes held a hint of mischief. "We still need to check out the area where he was kidnapped but right now…" She leaned down to kiss Claire until they both were breathless. "I can think of better things to do."

"Mm…." was the best Claire could manage after that scorching kiss. She rolled over and wrapped Jess in a hug, their naked bodies entwined.

"You feel wonderful," Jess murmured in her ear before nuzzling her neck. "You have no idea how many times I've wanted to hold you like this."

"Mmm…" Claire murmured once again. She trailed kisses down Jess's slender throat and moved down to her breast. Her tongue flicked the pert nipple that hardened immediately.

"Mmm…" This time it was Jess unable to find words. Claire snickered at her.

"You're laughing at me? I would get my revenge, but I don't want you to stop."

"Don't worry, I won't." Claire teased right back before moving to the other breast and giving it the same attention.

Slowly, she traced her hand downward to the nest of curls as she continued teasing her with her tongue.

Jess moaned, her voice filled with need. Claire shifted to look into those beautiful amber eyes before kissing her with a passion that surprised them both.

"Are you ready for me?" she asked after taking a deep breath.

"Oh God, yes!"

Claire didn't try to hide the smirk at Jess's words. She wanted to please Jess in every way possible, and it was wonderful to have her respond so passionately. She trailed kisses down along her throat, down her abdomen, and still further until she reached the inside of her thigh. She kissed the velvet skin.

The answering tremor made her confidence soar. She kissed the other thigh just a breath away from the bundle of dark curls. She trailed a finger along the soft skin where thigh and body merged, then planted a kiss there as well. Jess responded with a groan.

Gently she traced her hand across the engorged nub hidden among the curls and was rewarded with moisture that showed Jess was ready for her. She flicked it with her tongue and Jess gave a reflexive jerk but pushed down toward her a little more.

Claire began to flick steadily with her tongue. Jess's body moved in rhythm with her. As Jess's movements grew stronger Claire thrust one and then another finger, her tongue still lapping at the swollen clit.

"Ahh…" Jess's cry had no words. She gripped the sheets in desperation, her hips rocking uncontrollably. Her breath quickened and her muscles tightened around Claire's fingers as the first wave of her climax swept over her. Wave after wave rocked her body, clenching with each crest.

When she grew still, Claire kissed the soft thigh she had gripped so tightly. Then she made her way upward to lie next to Jess. She cradled her in her arms, inhaling the scent of her hair, vanilla and sandalwood mixed with something warm and comforting that she knew was simply Jess.

Claire laid a hand on Jess's stomach. "You're so beautiful."

Jess grimaced. "I wish my body was in shape like yours."

Claire rose to an elbow to better look at her. "What? You're the most beautiful person I've ever seen. The first week I worked with you I was tongue tied because of it."

Jess put her hand on top of Claire's where it still rested on Jess's smooth stomach. "I feel the same way about you. You're gorgeous, you're in wonderful shape, and you're just as perfect on the inside. But I don't think you know it."

Claire leaned down to kiss Jess gently. "Want me to make love to you again?"

Jess groaned. "Give me a few minutes and I'll return the favor. You've just worn me out."

"Don't worry about me. I'm just enjoying holding you." She glanced at the clock. "Dammit. We'd better get going if we're going to see the park ahead of our meeting."

Jess checked the time as well. "Ugh. You're right of course."

Reluctantly, they left the comfortable bed to begin their day. Normally, Claire could shower and get ready in record time, but she usually didn't have a partner with her who couldn't keep her hands to herself. Light caresses and playful kisses slowed them considerably and the late morning sun was hot when they emerged from the hotel.

Dressed in lightweight slacks and cool shirts rather than their uniforms was a nice treat on a hot day. Jess knew from experience that the detectives for NOPD usually wore plainclothes rather than uniforms. Claire was glad for the chance to blend into the crowd.

Jess didn't veer from Dauphine Street even though some of the eclectic shops and venues could be heard nearby. Architecture in this area had a different feel to it and Claire understood a little better why people believed ghosts inhabited much of New Orleans. Signs in multiple places proclaimed the Voodoo temple was just blocks away making her wonder if Jess was about to take her into one of those cheesy tourist traps where they pretended to read your palm or sold small dolls made of corn shucks with a pin sticking out of their chest.

"Here it is," Jess announced, and Claire's mouth dropped open. It was indeed one of those cheesy tourist traps.

Claire read the sign aloud. "Madam Bonet, seer of the future and the past, palm readings available. Voodoo ceremonies coming soon."

Jess grinned at her disbelief. "Come on. Relax."

Claire reluctantly followed, certain that this was a waste of time. The door opened into a room that looked like it had been decorated by a Voodoo hippie on an acid trip. Tie-dye and bold colors were everywhere. Containers marked as sage, rosemary, Epsom salts, and a host of dried plants sat on shelves for purchase. Small bags that touted good health sat next to a box that read, "Don't let a Voodoo hex get you down. Buy a gris gris. It's great great." Pictures of famous spiritual advisors hung next to Voodoo priestesses. Taxidermied chickens, snakes, and other animals rounded out the salute to the weird and taboo.

Jess went to the counter where an ancient cash register sat on an old oak countertop. She tapped a bell several times.

"Welcome. My name is Madam Bonet. How can I help you this morning?" The hanging beads parted.

Whatever Claire was expecting, it certainly wasn't a young woman sporting white hair with rainbow stripes and wearing a boho style dress and tennis shoes. "This is a Voodoo priestess?" she thought and almost snorted out loud.

Jess raised a brow at the young woman. "Madam Bonet?"

The woman's features broke into an enormous grin. "Jess? Come here and give me a hug."

As Claire stood there confused, the two embraced. Jess knew this person? Did that mean she was a customer? Judging by the extended hug she was on more familiar terms than that. She felt an unexpected stab of jealousy.

Jess pulled away from the woman but kept an arm around her as she turned to Claire. "Let me introduce you two. Claire, this is my cousin Jazz. Remember I mentioned my two cousins that came to live with us? Well Jasmine is one of them." She hugged the smaller woman again before moving to stand by Claire.

Her cousin? Claire stepped forward as relief washed over her. "Hello," she said as Jess put an arm around her shoulders.

Jazz's smile broadened as she noted the gesture. "Hello, Claire. It's so nice to meet you." She gave Claire a fierce hug while talking to Jess. "Darn it. I have an appointment arriving any time now, but we can talk until he arrives."

"That's okay. I couldn't visit the city without stopping by and checking on you. I'd ask you out to dinner but our plans changed and we may be tied up until late."

Jazz shrugged. "I have something else I have to attend this evening anyway."

Jess patted her shoulder. "We'll catch you another time."

Jazz moved behind the counter and brought out some bottled water for each of them. "Jess? So how do you like the shop? It's pretty rad, huh?"

"It looks great. Mom says you already have an established client base." Jess's proud smile was almost as brilliant as Jazz's.

"It's getting there. Of course, most of it is just in fun, but I have a few regulars." She shot a mischievous smile at her cousin. "One of my regular clients is Monica Langston. Remember her? She certainly remembers you. Very fondly, I might add."

For the first time, Claire saw Jess squirm in embarrassment. "You're killing me, Jazz."

Jazz chuckled but her reply was lost as the bell on the entry door jingled merrily announcing the arrival of a rotund gentleman in shorts, sandals, and black knee-high socks, an outfit marking him as a stereotypical tourist. He gave a blissful sigh as he stepped into the air conditioning.

Jazz smiled and offered him a bottled water. "Be with you in a second. Come back to room two with me so you can get comfortable." She looked at Jess. "Be right back."

While Jazz was getting her client settled, Claire wandered around the room, beginning with a wall of posters and photos of famous occult figures including Madame Marie Leveau, the famous High Priestess of New Orleans. However, it was the picture next to it that caught her eye. "Who is this? I feel like I've seen her before."

Jazz returned in time to hear the question. "Oh, she was one of those people with fifteen minutes of fame. Her name was

Celeste Marie Dios. Look her up on the internet if you're really interested. She was crazy as hell."

Jess wrapped the younger woman in a hug. "Glad I got to see you, Jazz. I've missed you."

Jazz grinned. "Glad you got to see me, too." She pulled back and hugged Claire more gently, but warmly nonetheless. "I'm so sorry I have an appointment and another afterward, but it's been great to see you, Jess. And to meet you, Claire. Please don't wait so long to come back."

Jazz turned to leave but then turned back around. "Hold on to her, Jess. She's a keeper." With a wink and a grin, she disappeared behind the beaded curtain.

Face flushed red, Jess moved as if to give chase but decided against it. "Run while you can," Jess shouted to her back.

Jazz's giggle was cut off as the door clicked behind her.

Jess looked down at Claire. "You just had a reading."

"What?"

"When Jazz hugged you, she was gaining insight from her touch. She reads people through touch."

Claire frowned. "You mean, she actually has a psychic gift?"

"Yeah. She read you and liked what she saw. That's why she said, 'you're a keeper'."

Claire was skeptical but chose to be diplomatic. "Well, I can say that was the first time I've ever had a reading."

"Really? I'm surprised."

Claire shrugged. "Mom had a hangup about it. She always worried I would find out things related to my dad. She didn't want that."

Jess didn't respond but simply squeezed her hand. "You want a cab or take our time walking back? It's pretty far but there are a lot of interesting things between here and the restaurant I've chosen for lunch."

"I haven't had my run today. I'm all for walking. That is, if you can keep up."

"Did you just challenge me?" Jess bent down and kissed Claire until she was breathless. "Now. Still think you can walk?"

"I—I can barely stand."

CHAPTER TWENTY

After enjoying lunch at a quaint bistro, Jess and Claire drove to Dakota Grambling's home address. They planned to check the distance from his home to the park where he was abducted. They were surprised that the park was almost visible from the family's driveway. However, the area marked as the location where he was taken was currently out of sight from any of the neighboring houses. They traversed the area and even spoke to a couple of elderly women gardening in one of the homes surrounding the lot.

The area had become rather transitory nowadays. Most places were now rented to students at the nearby college. Even the two women would soon be moving. One was going to live with her daughter while the other had chosen an assisted living community.

Both remembered the boy's kidnapping. It was on everyone's mind and many worried that more children might be abducted. They were fond of the Grambling family. The father was the coach of Dakota's little league baseball team and the mother was a Sunday school teacher at their church. The parents had been devastated by the loss of their son. Unfortunately, neither woman had any more information.

All in all, it felt like a disappointing start to their investigation. Claire hoped their meeting with the NOPD detectives would be more productive.

They met with Detective Johnson and former detective Ben Neely at a small café near the college, its shady terrace giving them privacy. The younger man was dressed in a snazzy pale blue suit and tie, perfect for his ebony skin. Judging by the pale white skin where sunglasses would rest, Ben Neely was enjoying his retirement outdoors, likely spending time on the golf course based on the local club emblem on his polo shirt.

"Hello," the younger man greeted them. "I'm Detective Johnson but call me Darren. And this is former detective Ben Neely."

"I'm Undersheriff Jessica Morgan and this is Deputy Claire Duvall." She looked at the younger man. "Thank you so much for taking time to meet with us. Both of you," she added for the older man's benefit.

They ordered drinks and then got down to business.

Jess first summarized all they knew about the skull, the autopsy and DNA results. Darren Johnson pulled out a rather thin file that illustrated how little they had from their investigation.

"In this picture you can see the park. The photo was taken from the boy's driveway." Ben Neely pointed to the lower right quadrant of the 8x10 photo, then trailed his hand to the opposite corner. "The bike located here belonged to the boy, so this is the probable point of the abduction."

Jess nodded. "We visited the park...or rather the empty lot earlier today. There are still a few trees on this section. Currently, there are no houses or buildings of any kind within sight of the trees."

"There wasn't back then, either," Neely growled. "They had scheduled an expansion of the small field into a full-sized baseball field for local leagues to use but enthusiasm slipped after Dakota was taken."

Darren jumped in. "The FBI was involved since it was considered a kidnapping, but obviously, they never found him. I've contacted them to let them know he has been identified," He handed a manila envelope to Jess. "I'm sure they will be contacting you. I have a packet here with all the information in it along with all of this." He waved his hand over the items on the table.

"The information you sent us said there were eyewitnesses?" Jess asked.

Ben cleared his throat. "Yes. Some kids were playing in the park about the time of the abduction. They said a dark pickup truck stopped, a man got out of it, and jerked the boy inside. They heard the boy crying and the man said…" He looked down at the report. "…your father has need of you."

He frowned in concentration. "I always thought it was odd, ya know? I would think a guy would say something like 'your dad needs you' but all three kids swore he said it that way."

"Your father has need of you," Claire repeated under her breath.

The retired officer nodded. "Yeah. We leaned hard on the dad at first but he had an alibi for the entire evening. He worked evening shift, and you can't enter or leave the place without swiping a card reader. He swiped out at midnight. I always figure the abductor didn't speak English well and got it wrong."

"Is it possible the guy said, 'The father has need of you'? As in a priest needs you?" Claire wondered aloud.

Ben shook his head. "We checked that out too. The family is Baptist which doesn't have priests. But we still checked their pastor and got nowhere."

Jess took a swallow of water and said, "The guy may have tried to tell the victim his father needed him in order to get him to go willingly."

"Probably," Ben agreed, "but it didn't work if you believe those kids. They say he was kicking and crying until the guy did something. Then the victim just slumped in his arms."

"The guy hit the boy?" Claire looked up from the photo.

"According to the kids, he pulled out a cigarette while the kid was screaming, leaned over and said something to him. And then he slumped over."

They continued their conversation, only stopping when the time became crunched to meet the parents on time. They left Jess's SUV at the café and took Johnson's larger vehicle so they could continue the discussion while driving.

Dakota Grambling's parents had moved, but it was in the same general area. Claire suspected they had relocated to reduce some of their pain. Living in the same home with memories of her mother was sometimes difficult. She couldn't imagine what they had gone through, and she knew this visit would be difficult for them.

They pulled into the driveway of a typical brick ranch style that varied from its neighbor only by the shade of the brick. The four of them headed solemnly to the door, their footsteps crunching on the sidewalk.

The door opened before they could knock, the couple standing together. Their drawn features made them look older than expected.

"W—would you like a glass of iced tea?" Ms. Grambling pointed to a group of glasses filled with ice sitting by a tall pitcher.

Normally they would have declined but since she had already gone to such trouble, they accepted her hospitality. Claire glanced around the living area and noticed pictures of smiling children including a young Dakota. The photos also showed a girl, a sister maybe, that had transitioned between snapshots into a young woman with a baby of her own.

When all had settled down, there was an awkward pause until Ben Neely spoke. "It's been quite a while, Mr. and Ms. Grambling. You went through quite a lot during that horrific time. To be honest, I hate to bring back such bad memories, but I think we owe it to you to update you on your son."

Ms. Grambling reached for her husband's hand and clung to it. In reflex, he held her hand between both of his, a simple sign of support.

Mr. Grambling answered, his voice hopeful even now. "We appreciate any new information you might have."

"These officers are from Kalfou Parish, on the west side of the state. Some…evidence was found and both dental and DNA results confirm it to be your son, Dakota. Unfortunately, we must change the status from missing to probable homicide."

Ms. Grambling made a sound of deep painful grief. Her husband clutched her tightly against him. She reached for a tissue and dabbed her eyes while Mr. Grambling cleared his throat several times. Ben gave them time to process the information before continuing.

"We are hoping you can help us understand why your son might have been taken to Kalfou Bayou. Does the name mean anything to you? We think the perpetrator was familiar with that area."

Mr. Grambling shook his head. "We've only heard the name. We've never been there."

His wife simply shook her head in reply.

Darren spoke up. "How did you hear about Kalfou Bayou? What was the context?"

Mr. Grambling shrugged. "On the news like you do for weather reporting, stuff like that. Of course, there was the devastation from one of the hurricanes but it was a long time ago. To be honest, I thought the parish had sort of fallen off the map so to speak after Storm Lionel."

Ms. Grambling, her eyes bright with tears, said, "Can someone tell me what happened to my little boy?"

The officers swapped uncomfortable glances before Jess answered. "Ms. Grambling, the autopsy report showed it was a blunt force trauma to his head." She paused as the mother groaned and began crying softly. "The nature of the trauma makes me believe it was over quickly."

"Do you have any leads on the person that did this?" Mr. Grambling asked while hugging his wife to his chest.

"Nothing yet," Jess admitted. "But I'll make sure you're notified when we capture the perpetrator."

Mr. Grambling sighed heavily. "I know you mean well, and Mr. Neely you tried your best, but the bastard seems to have baffled ya'll entirely. Never a shred of evidence that led anywhere. We would love to receive a phone call saying this monster is in custody, but we won't be waiting by the phone." He bent his head down to hug his wife tightly and to hide his own tears.

Jess leaned forward and asked, "Mr. Grambling, can you tell us about anyone that could have a reason for taking Dakota?"

The couple both thought about it for a long moment. "We don't know anyone. We're sorry, but we've been asked that question a thousand times. We can't think of anyone that would want to harm our family."

With nothing else left to say, everyone stood. "Thank you for your time. We promise to keep you posted," Darren said as they moved toward the door.

The officers walked to the vehicle, their somber mood spoke to the grief they had just witnessed. It was silent on the drive to pick up Jess's SUV, each lost in their own thoughts.

Jess and Claire had already packed their luggage and immediately headed west toward Kalfou Parish. Sid couldn't handle the parish by himself and until they returned, he was the sole deputy on duty. It might be midnight or later when they arrived but could at least give him some much-deserved time off the next day.

They hadn't left the city limits when Jess's phone rang. It was Dr. Avi.

"Officer Morgan?"

"Yes. I'm here with Officer Duvall on speakerphone."

"I have acquired some information on the bodies recently found. I assumed you wanted it as soon as possible." The doctor's voice was calm and professional as always. "We have sent off dental records on all of the victims and the autopsy reports are ready. I am expecting the DNA sooner rather than later due to the heightened criticality with the large number of victims."

"Thank you, Dr. Avi. That's a lot of work in a short time."

"All part of the job. I will send the report electronically as soon as we hang up. Have a good evening."

The drive home was a long one with no more answers than before.

CHAPTER TWENTY-ONE

Claire woke up with the unfamiliar feel of a warm body next to her own. As she became more awake, she remembered the weekend and rolled over, content to enjoy Jess's embrace.

Her time with Jess had been perfect. Even after the long drive home and the knowledge that work would likely be hectic, they had dropped their bags on the floor and headed to Claire's bed where they made love until they were too exhausted to continue.

Soon after, Jess fell asleep with her head on Claire's shoulder, but sleep hadn't come for Claire until later. With the soft whisper of Jess's breath against neck, Claire had remained wide awake, worried about things to come.

I think I love her. How am I going to deal with it if she isn't serious about the relationship?

Doubt overshadowed the pleasure of Jess's embrace, and she got up to start the coffeemaker, anything to still her negative thoughts.

With a steaming mug in her hand, she went to sit in the chaise lounge on her patio to clear her mind. She cruised the internet for something mundane when a hair-color advertisement reminded her of Jess's cousin. Her rainbow hair was striking as much as her quirky personality. She suspected no one forgot Jazz.

She looked up Madame Bonet's Voodoo and Palm Reading services. The website was similar to Jazz herself, whimsical and eclectic sharing equal time with the mystical and macabre. Her hair was purple in the picture. She claimed to be a seer of both the past and the future with a keen interest in Voodoo.

The picture was taken in that absurdly decorated shop. Behind her was the wall that housed so many of the famous spiritualists and soothsayers of the past. The familiar picture of the woman hung behind Jazz's shoulder. On a whim, Claire googled "Celeste Marie Dios".

"Whatcha doing, sexy?" Jess's voice at the door startled her.

She shook her head ruefully as Jess snickered at her expense. "Good morning."

Jess came out with her coffee. "You're a little jumpy this morning aren't ya?"

She plopped down on Claire's lap, effectively trapping her. Claire was perfectly satisfied to have Jess sit on her.

Jess bent down to kiss Claire, gently. "Mmm…good morning."

Claire was struck by the way her body reacted to even a simple kiss. She had awakened a desire in her that was difficult to keep in check. She could barely think as Jess traced kisses along Claire's neck and downward toward her breast…where she blew a raspberry on the soft skin.

Claire laughed in spite of herself, if for no other reason than the mischievous look in Jess's eyes as she teased her.

Then the hurt of past rejection rose up causing doubt to set in once more. How many times had she had liaisons kept as dirty little secrets because no one wanted to be seen publicly with her? How many times had she been left devastated when the same person that had made love the night before was the first to make cruel remarks while hanging out with their friends?

Could the same thing happen with Jess? Would she forget about this when things became inconvenient? Claire was uncertain about so much of this budding relationship, but one thing was for sure—she didn't want to go back to what had been. "What happens now?" she blurted out.

"What?" Confusion spread across Jess's face.

"Is this just a fling for you or will we try and continue a relationship?" She couldn't look at Jess, and instead kept her head bowed.

"You think this was…" Disbelief was evident in Jess's voice. "…that you are someone I would just play with and then toss aside?" It was clear Jess was hurt. "Claire. This weekend was special to me. I thought you knew that."

Jess cupped Claire's cheek and forced her to see the sincerity in her eyes. "I think you're amazing, Claire. I certainly want to explore a relationship with you. I've wanted to since the day I met you. I have been fighting to stay professional, but it's been a losing battle. Hell, I've even moved into your home. I'm sure I could have found different arrangements if I'd tried."

Claire leaned into Jess's arms. "I feel the same way. I just don't want my life to go back to the way it was before."

Jess wrapped her arms around her. "We just need to relax and see where things take us. Okay?"

Claire nodded but blurted out without thinking, "Who is Monica Langston?"

Jess's brows rose to her hairline at the name. Her face flushed a dark red as she muttered, "I'm going to kill Jazz."

She heaved a deep sigh. "Monica was one of my less successful relationships." She glanced at Claire. "All was going well, or at least I thought it was. Monica surprised me with a trip to a new club. We arrived and I saw the name "Bottom's Up" making me think it was a bar. But when we went inside, it was an S&M club. It turns out, she was becoming bored with our relationship, and she wanted to spice things up a bit."

Claire remained silent, her only response was a raised brow. Jess sighed and kept talking. "We tried a few things with each of us taking turns as who was top and who was bottom. I told her I was ready to leave. It ended up that I left, and she stayed."

She shrugged. "That was the end of that."

Claire felt foolish for her outburst. "Why was Jazz teasing you?"

Jess's face flushed. "Monica told her all about it. Jazz hasn't let me forget it."

"Have you had lots of relationships?"

"I wouldn't say lots. I've had my share. But remember, New Orleans is an easier place to be yourself than here." Jess leaned down for a long kiss. "I haven't been in a relationship since Monica so I'm not stepping out on someone for a quick fling with you. I promise to be respectful of your feelings, Claire. I would never hurt you purposely."

"I care for you, Jess. I don't want to get hurt."

"And I don't want to hurt you either." Jess kissed her firmly. "I've fallen for you, gorgeous. I've been wanting to make love to you long before this weekend came on the horizon."

"Knowing Maxine, she did it on purpose."

Jess snorted. "She needs a raise. Her matchmaking skills are wonderful." She placed a blistering kiss on Claire's lips, chasing away the doubt.

When they finally pulled away to catch their breath, Jess noticed Claire's cell phone. "Did you find out where you've seen that woman's picture? The one in Jazz's shop?"

"I had just logged on when you startled me." She read aloud. "Celeste Marie Johnston grew up in Haiti, the daughter of missionaries."

"Makes sense when you think about her name," Jess said. "Celeste Marie. Isn't that Heavenly Mother?"

"So you're more than a pretty face huh?" Claire teased. "You're also a trivia queen?"

Jess snorted. "Hey, I went to mass each week. I'm no heathen."

"At the age of sixteen, her parents sent her back to Louisiana where she brought intimate knowledge of Voodoo Hoodoo from the locals in Haiti. She married sixty-year-old Etienne Chevalier and bore a son."

Claire paused a moment. "Wow. According to the dates, she married within a month of arriving in Louisiana and gave birth a month later. She didn't mess around did she?"

"Well, actually. Yes, she did," Jess smirked. "She most definitely messed around."

Claire rolled her eyes but laughed in spite of herself. "That's not what I meant, smartass. She did things quickly...okay?"

"I agree, she did things quickly. She was a fast woman as my grandma used to say."

She ignored Jess's teasing and continued reading, "...a high priestess of great influence in the Voodoo religion, but her husband was a devout Catholic. Celeste mingled Catholicism into her rituals and ceremonies with a novel approach. This appealed to many people and she gained followers throughout the southern area of the state. In 1972, Etienne Chevalier died under mysterious circumstances. Leaving her three-year-old son in the care of Etienne's aunt, Celeste moved to New Orleans, where her abilities and knowledge of Voodoo were high in demand from both locals and tourists.

"Celeste was known for precognition, defined as the ability to foresee the future. She had an apparent talent to make her clients believe in her abilities and became a successful woman of means. However, she wanted to rise to a higher and more significant fame for her predictions. She claimed to foresee the resignation of Richard Nixon, among other global matters. But she overstepped a societal threshold around 1977-1978 when she predicted the Second Coming of Christ to arrive in the year 2018."

"What? That's this year. Wonder what makes this year special to her?"

Claire continued reading. "This proved disastrous for her professionally, and her name became one of censure and derision. Her faithful clients disappeared leaving her with only tourists to entertain. She moved back to Haiti with her son in 1978 where she changed her name to Celeste Marie Dios."

She looked up from her phone. "That's pretty much everything worth mentioning from the Wikipedia article. They don't say anything about what happened when she returned to Haiti. I guess she had her brief stint in New Orleans and that was the end of it."

"Any clue as to where you have previously seen her or her photo?"

"No. It made me curious, that's all. I was surprised to run across something I recognized in Jazz's shop."

Jess grinned. "Not expecting to see something familiar in her shop of sorcery?"

"Well," Claire didn't want to offend Jess. "It took me by surprise. No biggie."

At that moment, Claire's phone rang. Sid was reaching out for help at a domestic dispute. The two of them scrambled to get dressed and gather their things. The demands of the parish were back with a vengeance.

CHAPTER TWENTY-TWO

They spent Sunday catching up with items left from before their trip. Monday morning proved to be even more hectic. The Sherriff's Department was swamped with calls requesting an officer. Claire went on patrol and didn't return until late morning to check in with Maxine to start her normal routine. By the time she had settled at her desk, Maxine had poured a hot cup of coffee for her, which Claire gratefully accepted.

"Word has gotten out that the Sheriff's Department is shorthanded. Look at all these tickets. They are running riot out there. It would normally take a week for this many traffic violations."

Jess interrupted the conversation as she came in. "Do you have time to sort through Dr. Avi's reports? Maxine printed them out for us."

"Sure," Claire replied, trying not to think about the mountain of paperwork awaiting her. "By the way—I got ya'll a snack while putting gas in the car." She reached inside the bag and pulled out a MoonPie and a candy bar.

Maxine groaned. "You always know when I start dieting."

"Oh. "Claire moved to take away the snacks. "I'll just—"

"Don't you dare," Maxine fussed as she grabbed the MoonPie, an old-fashioned southern chocolate and cream treat. "You know this is my weakness." She turned to Jess with a sheepish grin. "That is, unless you would like it."

Jess looked at the MoonPie and grimaced. "I know it's heresy, but I don't like them. I'll be happy to take the candy bar."

Claire made a production of reaching in and bringing forth the brand of chocolate she had noticed Jess munching on several times in the past. "You mean, something like this?"

Jess moaned in pleasure. "You're an angel." She unwrapped it and took a big bite. "Sheer bliss."   Her voice was muffled because of the chocolate. "Are you ready to start?"

"I'll get my stuff and meet you in your office."

Minutes later they sat at the conference table that filled most of the sheriff's office.

"Thanks again for the chocolate. I was craving one of these."

Claire grinned at her as she handed Jess a copy of the printed report from Dr. Avi. "I'm glad I've found your weakness."

They sifted through each victim's information while Jess entered it all onto a spreadsheet. The coroner had sent the dental records to the missing persons database along with anything that could be used for identification. Several victims had been identified already.

"It looks like New Orleans, Abbeville, and Thibodaux have matched dental records," Jess remarked.

"That's amazing. It usually takes the State Bureau longer than three weeks for lab results."

Jess didn't look up from the report. "Yeah. It just shows how high profile the case is becoming. The Feds will soon be pressuring us if nothing breaks." She tossed her report onto the table and moved to update the whiteboard.

Claire whistled. "You know, most perps go after a certain look or a certain age group or sex. But these are all over the map. Men, women, teens, down to Dakota at ten years of age. Asian, black, white, and Latino. It's like the modus operandi is to be as varied as possible."

Jess finished writing and looked at the report. "The oldest is a seventy-year-old male. Mmm…The cities I just mentioned are all in Louisiana," she observed. "They're a wide range in population though."

"Damn, this guy doesn't care who or where he attacks." Claire's frustration showed in her voice.

"So maybe the perp is more interested in the killing than the victim. Let's go over his method."

Claire flipped back through the report. "All were killed by blunt cranial trauma. Dr. Avi believes it's possibly the same instrument because the damage is always the same. All victims are hit on the same side of the head with enough force to crush the skull in one blow. Plus, those corpses in good enough shape to inspect the skin showed ligature marks on hands and feet."

Claire flipped through a couple of papers. "All bodies with limbs still attached show smooth cuts with large portions of skin and muscle missing. Umm…Two have knife marks on the humerus and one body has the marks on a femur. The marks are present within the area of missing flesh. The location of the marks on the humerus pair with the brachial artery. The cut would have resulted in large amounts of blood loss, possibly life-threatening. Marks on the femur match the femoral artery that would also result in high blood loss and could be life-threatening."

"So, a blade of some kind cut either the leg or arm in a way that would induce major blood loss and potential death." Jess reiterated the findings.

"If the cuts were made pre-mortem," Claire reminded her.

"Right." Jess raised the pen toward the board. "How many victims show that?"

"Missing flesh? Um…six. The remainder were too decayed."

"Did you find a map so we can see where the bodies were buried?"

Claire stood up. "Let me check with Maxine. She was going to print one for me." She returned in a few minutes, the map in hand. "She had it ready. She also told me the officer from Cameron Parish has called in sick."

Jess made a face. "Let's hope we have a slow day then."

Claire placed the map on the whiteboard and circled the relevant areas with a highlighter.

"How accurate is this satellite image?" Jess asked. "Is it recent enough to include changes from the drought?"

"For the most part. It was done a couple of months ago."

"Dakota Grambling's bones were found way over here while the other two groups were here and here. They're much closer together."

"We know that Dakota was found further inland in the deepest section of the bayou and had no indication of having been buried," Claire reminded her. "The graves were in an area rarely flooded due to a slight elevation."

"They died after the drought began too. Nothing indicates they would be submerged at any point." She looked to Claire for agreement.

"You're right," she said and then frowned as she stared at the map. "How do they even get to that area?"

"What do you mean?"

"Well, Dakota's remains could be reached via boat with little problem when his body was dumped. Didn't even need an airboat." She pointed to the burial sites. "But these bodies were buried after the drought began so getting there without an airboat would be difficult. Of course, the perp could have his own airboat but they're expensive so only a few locals own one. I guess we could check that out. It might narrow our search. But even our own department doesn't have one. That's why we keep having to catch rides from Hollis."

Jess studied the map again. "These shacks along the bigger channels of water...do you know all the owners?"

Claire looked closer. "I would need to study it better before I could say for sure. But I could pull up the parish records. It will just take some time."

Jess nodded. "Do that. We need a name for every owner out there and whether it's a local or not."

Claire studied the burial sites more closely. "You can't see a damned thing because of all the trees," she complained. "It would be easy to hide a lot of things in an area this large and with that thick canopy. But you must have a way to get in and out."

"Claire, we need to look farther into the bayou. I think a helicopter might be good. Who knows? Maybe the drought is unearthing areas we should know about and investigate."

"That's a good idea. The flight might point us to a specific area of the bayou, narrow it down, and then check those areas on foot. Jess, we have a guy in the parish who made a small landing strip at his place. He has a helicopter."

"Good. I think we should concentrate on the area between these two burial sites and find out what is there. Hopefully, we can gain information from above." She checked her watch. "Let's take a break while I see about renting the helicopter. Do you think you could find the names of the owners of those properties in the next hour? I want us to lay all of this out on the conference table and begin figuring out what the hell connects all of these victims."

Claire had no more than stood up when Maxine sent her out on a call. On the way back, another call came in. A glance at her watch showed the afternoon beginning to slip away.

She called Jess. "In an hour I've got an appointment with a landlord for a couple of evictions. Unless you need me to cancel, I'll be tied up until late this evening."

"Go ahead. Do you need my help with anything? Maxine said you're getting slammed today."

"Nothing I can't handle."

Jess snorted. "In other words, you're too proud to ask. When I talk with Sheriff Willis, we'll try to come up with a game plan. By the way, I spoke with the owner of the helicopter. He's out sick and will be a few days before he can fly. Sounds like we have more time to sort through the information."

The sun had set when Claire pulled into her driveway. Supper had been a honeybun on her way home. Jess was sitting on the couch and sipping a glass of tea, Dr. Avi's reports lying open on the coffee table.

"You've had a long day. You must be exhausted."

Claire didn't disagree. "What time did you get away?"

"Oh, I beat you home by an hour. There's lasagna on the stovetop. It's not homemade but it was at least quick. A salad is in the fridge."

"You won't hear me complaining. It's great to come home to something already cooked."

Jess smiled. "How do you feel about some more brainstorming?"

Seeing Jess had shaken the weariness from Claire, just happy to be home talking with her. "Sure. Let me change and I'll be right back."

She hurriedly slipped into pajamas and returned to the living room to a small table set up with food and iced tea. "God, this is nice," she sighed as she sat down. "I was exhausted when I got home but this makes it all better."

"If you're tired, I can stay in the guest room tonight."

"No." Claire startled herself with how loudly she responded.

Jess held up her hands in surrender. "I won't. I just wanted to make sure you're comfortable."

Claire shook her head. "I prefer you sleep with me, please."

"I wouldn't want it any other way."

Mollified, Claire picked up her fork and dug in as Jess brought her up to speed. "I added more information Dr. Avi sent this afternoon and added where our victims lived to the map." She held up the map of Louisiana. "Every city is easily accessed by Interstate Ten. Kalfou Parish seems to be pretty much in the middle of them all."

"Wow." Claire stared at the map. "I mean, it makes sense, but to see it right in front of you makes it more real."

Jess used the sort command on her spreadsheet and the nine victims were placed with Dakota at the top of the list. "Now they're in order of the time of their disappearance."

"Jess, if we don't look at Dakota Grambling, there is almost a pattern. It just looks like we don't have all the data to make it concrete."

Jess squinted as if that would help her see a pattern. "I don't see anything."

"Well, the couple that were taken together makes it look a little screwy as do the victims with no information. The data is showing about every four months and then skips to eight. If you insert one of those unidentified victims in, then it looks like each one goes missing about every four months."

"Damn, you're right," Jess exclaimed. "She wrote a note on the spreadsheet. I wonder what is significant about four months."

Claire sipped her tea as she studied the map. "All the identified victims lived within Louisiana. Does he realize the FBI is less likely to get involved if the victims aren't transported across state lines?

"Maybe." Jess shrugged. "He has avoided detection for a long time."

After staring at the data with no more ideas, Jess put the pages back in the file and turned off the laptop. "By the way, after you were called away, Maxine helped me find many of the property owners out in the bayou. Apparently, her sister is friends with someone in the zoning department."

Claire stifled a yawn. "That would be Stella Miller. She is the only employee of the zoning department."

Knowing another long day loomed ahead, they called it a night and went to bed. Claire fell asleep within minutes, her head resting on Jess's shoulder.

A perfect fit.

* * *

The next morning started off just as busily, so Jess and Claire tackled the tasks separately which made it manageable. Things had leveled off by noon, so Claire headed back to the office with a quick stop at Gil's to pick up lunch for Jess and Maxine.

As usual, the small restaurant was hopping. There were no tables left so Claire sat on a tall, vinyl-covered stool at the counter as she waited for her food. Without Gil, the service was slower, and the quality of the food would be questionable but she was hungry. The restaurant was abuzz with the news of more bodies discovered in the bayou. Their gruesome state made the gossip more enticing even as they sat eating their noonday meal. Several people called out questions while others made comments about the ineptitude of the sheriff and his deputies.

After repeating "No comment" several times, most left her alone, allowing her to pretend interest in the menu posted above the window separating the kitchen from the dining area.

A head swept past the large window of the kitchen passthrough. Claire snickered to herself as she recognized it was Gil's wife, Cammie. It struck Claire as funny that Cammie was barely tall enough to be seen while Gil had to stoop down to look through the window when placing the food on the counter that acted as a windowsill.

One of the local teenagers was trying to waitress and got Claire her iced tea so she could sip on it as she waited. The newbie and Cammie were busy but doing a pretty good job of handling the crowd.

Claire watched absently as Cammie tossed a couple of frozen burgers on the grill making it sizzle. As the flames died down, Cammie stacked the burger and placed it in a to-go box before stepping away to find a bag. Claire noticed a picture hanging on the wall next to the grill. It was the same woman that she had seen at Jazz's but just a different photograph.

That's where I've seen the woman. Maybe she was more famous than I realized. What was her name? Celeste?

Cammie came out of the kitchen and called out, "Claire?"

She rose and walked over to the cash register pulling out her wallet. "How are you, Cammie?"

The smaller woman took the time to wipe sweat from her brow and rub her hand on her grease-stained apron. "I'll be glad when Gil gets back. He is getting supplies but with just me it's almost too much to handle. My help over there is too new to be much use." She pointed in the direction of the teen taking an order.

Curious about the portrait hanging in the kitchen she tried to make small talk. "I guess Chris must be busy today. He could have been a great help to you with this crowd."

Cammie's impatience at Claire deciding to have conversation was evident. "Chris is with Gil."

Not to be put off, she waited until Cammie took her money. "I noticed the picture you have on the wall near the grill. She seems familiar."

Cammie looked over her shoulder. "Oh, that's Gil's mama."

Claire studied the photo as best she could. "That must be it. She looks like Gil."

Cammie nodded as she slammed the cash register door shut. "Yes. He favors her a lot." The transaction completed she had no more time for idle chitchat. "Come back to see us. Thank you." She turned and left without bothering to get a reply.

Claire was shocked. Of course, there was nothing wrong with one's mother being an eccentric. Knowing Gil to be a solid, down-to-earth man, he was probably embarrassed about his mother's notoriety. She made a mental note to ask Gil about his mother the next time she saw him. But for now, she had another long afternoon in front of her.

CHAPTER TWENTY-THREE

The whirr of the helicopter blades made talking impossible, so Claire and the pilot remained silent. After days of waiting, she was glad to be in the air. Unfortunately, Jess had remained behind. There was simply too much to be done by too few people. Claire had better knowledge of the area so she would go with the helicopter while Jess remained available for calls.

Below, the town gave way to fields and trees, the chopper seemingly mere feet above the tall cypress. They headed toward the section of the bayou connecting the two burial sites. Armed with a copy of the map and a corresponding list of plot owners, Claire was amazed at the synchronicity between the satellite image and the earth beneath them.

They passed above the area where Dakota Grambling's skull was found. The records showed it to be government land, the closest private parcel belonged to Pastor Abel Creech. She grimaced at the thought of speaking with him. But he may have noticed something suspicious that could help them find this killer.

The larger burial site, where the six bodies were found, was also government land with the closest private landowner being Arnold Beaumont. Arnold loved to hunt as much as his son, Hopper, and kept a cabin somewhere beneath the canopy of trees.

The forest below grew thicker until there was no glimpse of water or sand. She wished she could see what was hidden by the canopy but it was simply too thick.

Suddenly, she sat up straight and shouted into her helmet's microphone. "Look at the trees below us. The color has changed and the trees are denser than before."

"Yeah?" It was obvious the pilot had no clue what she meant.

"Cypress grow in the water. The color change is because it's other trees beside cypress. I think it's so thick because it's land rather than water down there. Let's circle the perimeter of that color change. I'm looking for possible paths or trails into the denser canopy."

The area was large. It would be nearly impossible to scour the entire area on foot. An entire community could be there and no one would ever know.

Then she saw it. "Look. Right there, at the edge of the darker trees. Do you see that patch of land just before it goes back into the canopy again? There's a trail or path."

The pilot gave Claire the coordinates for the land below as she wrote them on her notepad. They slowly swept the area until they found a trail exiting the bayou and wandering along the tree line until it eventually came out among a couple of fields of sugar cane. Once again, he gave its coordinates as she wrote them.

They turned toward home, Claire running their findings through her head. After landing and a quick conversation with the pilot about payment, she climbed into the SUV and drove toward the office.

Her phone buzzed. It was Sheriff Willis. "I was checking to see if you have an update from New Orleans."

"We didn't have much luck there, but I just took a field trip via helicopter. We found a trail leading to an unused area of the bayou near where the first six bodies were found. We need to check it out from the ground. I'm heading back to the office right now."

"I need to meet with you as soon as you can. Grab Jess if you can and come over here."

Claire bit her lip as she wondered what could be wrong. "Sure. Is something wrong?"

"We will talk when you get here," he replied cryptically and hung up.

Claire called into the office and explained the sheriff's conversation. Jess was standing at the front door when Claire swung by.

Blanche Rochon waved them through to Sheriff Willis's room, her usual smile missing. They were surprised to find Sid in one of the chairs.

"Hi, Sid," Claire ventured. "What's up?"

He grinned but it quickly disappeared. "Lester's been talking a lot. I wanted the sheriff to hear it first. Now that he has, I'll let him explain." He looked at Jess and added, "I meant no disrespect by talking to the sheriff first, ma'am."

Jess smiled reassuringly. "No offense taken, Sid. Now what has Lester been saying?"

The sheriff sat a little higher in the bed. "We all wondered why Lester wanted to stay in jail even when his lawyer got his bail reduced. Apparently, Lester is scared to leave. He thinks someone might come after him and hurt him, or even kill him."

"Lester admitted to Sid that drug shipments have been coming into Louisiana via Kalfou. They've been arriving in conjunction with Lester's night-shift schedule. No fear of arrest and he gets a cut."

Claire pushed aside her thoughts as Jess began speaking. "How are they coming in? How often are they coming?"

"Well, that's part of why they like it here. They have the option to come by land or the bayou. They change it a lot to make it more difficult to track them. He said it started out as about once every three or four months. Now it's become monthly."

"When was the last shipment?"

"About three weeks ago, so it's about time for another shipment."

Sid looked at the sheriff. "I'm on night shift. I'm guessing I need to stake out his place?"

"Yes," the sheriff and Jess answered together.

Silence fell on the group as they digested this information.

Sheriff Willis sighed deeply. "Lester's been involved with them for close to three years. He caught them one night and they invited him to join them. He figured the money made it worthwhile. He doesn't know how long they had been here before he caught them."

His voice turned bitter. "I tried to give Lester a chance to make something of himself. He didn't have much of a chance growing up, and I wanted to give him a leg up in the world." He stopped talking and put a hand to his temple.

"You okay?" Claire asked quietly and placed a hand on his arm.

She was a little surprised when he didn't shake off her hand. "Yeah, yeah. I guess I'm just disappointed…and goddamn mad."

"Did Lester give more details?" Jess looked at Sid. "The type of drugs? The group he has been working with?"

"Lester says it's sometimes just cocaine, and sometimes other stuff he has never heard of before," Sid replied. "He didn't have any names of the dealers, but he said some of them have accents. The way Lester described it, sounds like maybe Caribbean."

"Caribbean?" Claire exclaimed. "Why enter here? Why not come in at Florida?"

"Why come in where there is lots of security when you can come to a small place with only four law enforcement officers?" Sheriff Willis looked up at her. "Not to mention one is retiring, another is crooked, and one is a very young woman."

He saw her frown. "I mean no offense, Claire. They only see a young face. They have no idea you're a fine officer. When they began four years ago, you were barely out of the academy. And some people still see the woman first, and then the officer. It's not right, and it's not fair, but it still happens."

Unfortunately, he was correct. During her first two years on the force, Claire had had more skirmishes while making arrests than all three men put together. Thankfully, most of the locals left her alone as they realized she could and would enforce the law as stringently as the sheriff.

Jess spoke up. "Has Lester said where their entry point is in the bayou? The main channel?"

Sid shook his head. "He has no idea. He only knows the boat comes in from the ocean and a truck goes into the bayou to meet it. Then they head out to god knows where. He has no idea if it changes from shipment to shipment or if it stays the same. He has been too scared to ask any questions."

"How do they contact him?"

"A piece of duct tape is stuck on inside of his screen door at the back porch a couple of days before it happens."

Claire spoke up. "Does he know who in the parish is receiving the drugs? And where he or she is selling them?"

Sid shook his head. "Lester hasn't heard a peep about that."

Jess looked at him. "Do you believe him?"

Sid bit his lip. "I agree Lester has lied to all of us, but I do believe him about this. It's like he's trying to face up to his mistake. He's been doing a lot of thinking while he's been in jail."

The sheriff pounded his leg with a fist. "We have nine bodies and a skull from as far back as seven years, a deputy who tried to kill me, or at least hurt me, and drug shipments arriving through our parish. The place has gone to hell and I didn't have a clue." He looked around at the small group, his entire workforce. "I think we give a whole new meaning to 'thin blue line.' We're about as thin as it comes."

Claire asked, "What are our options? Any way we can get more help?"

Jess spoke up. "One option is to stay as we are with volunteers coming from the other two parishes' sheriff's departments. Another option is to ask for the FBI to take over."

The sheriff looked at Jess. "And I have two potential candidates coming in tomorrow for interviews. That was one of the reasons I wanted to talk to you."

"Oh yeah?"

He nodded. "I know we're barely making it, even with your help. I got two hits on the job posting to replace Sid. One is brand new out of the academy. Another wanted to leave the bigger city and move to a smaller community. You can't get much smaller than us."

Jess bit her lip. "If he is wanting less excitement, he may turn tail and run when he sees what we have going on."

The sheriff took her comment seriously. "He might very well do that. But we're sinking right now. I'm hiring both of them if they're any good at all." He looked at all of them. "I want you all to know how much I appreciate what you're doing. I've talked to Dr. Avi and told him I'm going back to work tomorrow. I'll do any interviews to keep Jess freed up."

All of them tried to talk at once, telling him to take care of himself. He simply waved their comments away.

"Doc Avi is releasing me tomorrow. I'm not about to go home and just lay around while hell is falling on the three of you. I'm healed up enough to sit behind my desk and ride in the squad car. I won't be having the angiogram or any other damned procedure until we get all of this shit settled."

"Who is going to look after you at home?" Claire was clearly worried about him.

He snorted. "I can look after myself. The darn chest tube's been out for days and I'm breathing close to normal. I'm getting stronger and my hand has stopped throbbing. Nothing prevents me from going back. I promised the doc to sit back and watch if there are any bad guys to beat up."

Claire threw her hands in the air. "If you're determined to do this, then you're staying with me and Jess." She didn't think about the possibility their relationship was best kept quiet. She was too worried about the man she had come to respect as she would have a father.

"I can go to my home. I'm not getting between you two."

It didn't dawn on Claire he wasn't surprised by her revelation. "If you don't, then I'm coming to stay with you."

They argued back and forth until finally Sid raised his hands and thundered, "Both of you, hush." They fell silent, shocked at their old friend raising his voice to them. He looked at first Claire and then the sheriff. "You're coming home with me. Claire is right. You need to be with somebody for a bit, but Claire and Jess also need their time together. Me and Blanche have a spare room and she knows how to care for you if you need it."

The sheriff opened his mouth to speak but Sid ignored him. "I heard what Dr. Avi said when you bullied him into letting you go back to work. Blanche is worried about you, and she won't have a problem with you staying with us. If you head home, we'll all be spreading ourselves thin by trying to take care of you. This way, it works better for everyone."

Sheriff Willis started to argue but grabbed his healing ribs instead. After taking a couple of deep breaths, he said, "Damned ribs still hurt like a son of a bitch sometimes. All right. I'll do it. Thank you."

Before they were dismissed, Claire spoke up. "Now that it's settled, I have some updates for you. I flew over the bayou this morning to check for anything out of the ordinary. We flew over both burial sites and they are on the edge of government land. I also found an area that looks like it's handling some traffic. Based on your information from Lester, I wonder if it may be associated with the trucks going in and out to access the water."

Sheriff Willis grunted. "Good find. Needs to be checked out. Any idea who owns the land with the burial sites and the trail?"

"I didn't get a chance yet, but I have the map and paperwork with me." Claire pulled out the papers. Using the coordinates from the pilot, she searched for the owner on the corresponding paper. "Looks like Pastor Abel owns land near Dakota Grambling's site. The other two grave sites are also close to the other side of Pastor Abel's property."

"Shit!" The sheriff spoke for them all. "I'm going to give the pastor a call."

Jess quirked a brow. "What about that trail entrance you found?"

After a long moment of searching, Claire looked at Jess in disbelief. "It belongs to Lester Henderson."

CHAPTER TWENTY-FOUR

It was evening when everyone left the hospital. Sheriff Willis didn't try to hide his frustration with his inability to be discharged that very day. Thankfully, Blanche was able to keep him in by threatening to hide his clothes.

Jess and Claire went home. Although neither of them planned to stop working, the idea of brainstorming in their comfortable pajamas rather than a full uniform was too good to resist. After taking a long hot shower and piling an assortment of snacks on the coffee table, they settled down to work.

"Let's go over Dr. Avi's reports to get us started." Jess handed a copy to Claire and gave her a few minutes to read it. When Claire looked up, Jess was ready to begin. "Let's start with the blood pooling on the bodies."

Claire checked the reports. "The victims have lividity on the back of their bodies. I don't see a single one that didn't have it. Either they were killed on their back or placed on their backs soon after. It can develop pretty quickly, particularly in the heat."

Claire's forehead wrinkled in thought. "Okay. The report mentioned some of them had ligature marks on their wrists and hands. Maybe he kidnaps them and ties them up. Then kills them as they are lying on the ground."

Jess typed in the possibility. Then added, "It might indicate the perp ties them to better see their faces as he kills them?"

Claire gave Jess a chance to finish typing before adding to the list. "Next is stone particles in the hair and around the skull damage." She shuffled papers to check information on all the victims. "Cotton fibers were found in multiple places but most were found at the cuts to the arms and legs. Dr. Avi says the cotton fibers are always white but the abductions that had an eyewitness had the victim wearing colored clothes, not white and mostly not cotton."

Jess thought a moment. "Maybe the perp dresses the victim in something that is made of a white cotton fabric?"

Claire squinted her eyes in thought. "Seems like a lot of trouble and time to make someone strip, then redress. To do that, the killer must be really sure that no one will hear them."

Stifling a yawn, Jess kept her eyes glued to the laptop. "If I were to categorize the method, I would call it ritualistic. Right?"

"Yes."

"Okay, so each victim is abducted from a seemingly random location. They are dressed in a white cotton garment. Their hands and feet are tied at some point prior to death. They're killed with blunt force associated with a stone, they lie flat out for long enough to have blood pool on the skin of their backs, those that are not too decomposed have large chunks of their leg and or arms muscles hacked out, and they are eventually buried or tossed in the water. All particularly horrible."

Claire poured another round of soft drinks. "Well, only Dakota Grambling was in the water, and he was presumably the first victim. Or at least the first of those we've found. It looks like the perp changed his method of disposal of the bodies. There is a long time between Dakota and the next body. Or maybe Dr. Avi's thought is right and there are more victims elsewhere in the bayou."

Jess stood up. "Let's do an experiment. Lie on the floor for me, Claire."

While Claire got into place, Jess grabbed her notepad. "The killer apparently has a rock or something that he bashes in their skulls. Dr. Avi's report says whatever it was appears to be somewhere between ten to thirteen inches in diameter. He believes it to be round in order to get the skull caved in consistently. A flat rock or one with angles should show something different in a couple of the victims."

They tried numerous positions using Claire as the victim. Each position was either awkward so it would be difficult to maintain the consistent accuracy of the killer's blow to the head, or it required someone very strong to overcome the awkward position.

The least awkward position that was repeatable for Jess was with Claire lying on the kitchen table. "I can hit the target area of the front of the skull without kneeling and being able to maintain my balance lets me hold greater weight and still be consistent."

Claire sat up. "So the killer is most likely a large strong man."

Jess stepped between Claire's knees as her legs dangled from the table. She kissed the side of her neck. "Let's step back a moment and recap. The blood pooling tells us the victim is always on their back either at death or soon thereafter. The ligature marks say their hands and feet are tied. The position of the strike says it's probably a large man."

"Say this guy is totally about the ritual," Claire unsuccessfully tried to stifle a yawn. "He doesn't swerve from it. He will abduct any race, age, or sex. It's just all about the ritual for him."

"Right." Jess took her hand and pulled her from the table. "Come on. It's time to go to bed. We're both tired."

Lying in Jess's arms, Claire listened to the heart beneath her ear. Jess was beautiful both inside and out. She was everything Claire had ever dreamed of. She just hoped Jess felt the same way about her…

CHAPTER TWENTY-FIVE

The next morning, Claire woke to the sound of the shower running. She stumbled toward the kitchen following the scent of freshly brewed coffee, reason nine hundred and ninety-nine to keep Jess.

She poured a cup and opened the patio door onto the screened porch to greet the fresh morning air and the sounds of birds chirping in the morning light. She watched the antics of a few squirrels as they chased one another among the trees. A smile spread across her features at the lack of tension in her neck and shoulders. She savored the peace.

She squeaked in surprise when two arms entwined themselves around her. Warm breath fanned her cheek as a kiss landed just beneath her ear.

"Good morning," Jess murmured. "I love the way you're greeting the world this morning."

Claire turned her head to kiss her. "I'm communing with nature. What better way than naked?"

"Hmm…" Jess nibbled on her ear. "I like you best without clothes so seeing you like this as I come for some coffee is quite a treat." Jess captured her lips in a searing kiss that left Claire hanging on to her when they finally came up for air. "I'm not a whiz in the kitchen but I can make a mean breakfast. Do you want something?"

Claire shook her head. "You're welcome to whatever is in the cabinet but I'm not much for breakfast."

"Then I'll have some cereal while you shower."

"Mm'kay," Claire agreed before kissing Jess once again. "I'll be ready soon."

They arrived at the office early enough to speak with Sid before his shift ended.

"Morning ya'll. It was a long boring night at Lester's. No drug dealers, no strangers, nothing but crickets and mosquitos. I'll try again tonight." He gathered up his belongings. "I'll skedaddle and get Sheriff Willis. He's already called fussing at me to pick him up. I guess you just can't keep a good man down."

Claire winked at him. "Sounds like you're going to have your hands full. Don't let him bully you."

Sid laughed. "Have you met my wife? She's the sweetest woman in the world but when she is looking after someone that's sick, she becomes a drill sergeant. I reckon she can handle him all right."

Claire touched his arm. "You two will be the best medicine for him. Just make sure your gun is loaded when you pick him up. You might need to shoot him to make him listen to you."

"I'll tell him you said that." He turned to Jess. "He swears he's coming to work this morning."

Jess spoke up. "If he does, I'll drop him at your house later so you can grab some sleep."

Sid thanked her and headed out the door, whistling as he so often did.

Claire and Jess began the routine of starting their day and had barely completed the normal items when the sheriff walked through the door. His skin was ashen and his stride rather tentative, but his pride and determination were present and in full force. "Maxine? The coffee sure smells good," he hinted, his voice already tired.

The woman jumped up from her seat and gently wrapped him in a hug. "It's so great to see you, James. But you shouldn't be here until you're feeling better," she enthused and scolded at the same time.

He ignored the reprimand. "I'm glad to be back." He looked around. "Jess must be taking care of things. Not as much piled up to be reviewed as usual. Ya'll might elect a new sheriff next time."

Jess shook her head. "Oh no. You are and will always be the sheriff. A day doesn't go by that people don't ask how you're doing."

He sat down behind his desk, a slight tremble to his hands as he picked up the coffee cup Maxine had placed in front of him. "Have I missed anything since we talked yesterday?"

The officers updated him on their theory regarding a ritualistic killing. He was receptive to their ideas but disappointed there was still no suspect. He turned to the subject of Lester Henderson.

"I haven't been face-to-face with the son of a bitch since he ran me off the road. I want to talk to him and see what's going on." He focused on Jess. "I want you to come with me. I need a second person with me and, unfortunately, he gets riled with Claire."

He turned to Claire. "If things take a turn and I want him to get more emotional, I'll bring you in so don't leave unless you're called to an incident."

"Do you mind if I stay in the viewing room for the interrogation?"

"Not at all. I want you to be involved."

Jess went to fetch Lester while Claire walked with the sheriff to the interrogation room. She made sure everything was ready as the sheriff wanted a camera and recording of the interview.

Lester arrived looking sheepish. He kept his head down and barely glanced at the sheriff.

The sheriff was the first to speak. "Lester. We have a lot to talk about, don't ya think?" Sheriff Willis stared hard at him while Lester squirmed in his seat, still saying nothing. "You're in some deep shit, Lester. You ran me off the road. You have been working with a group of drug smugglers. What the hell were you thinking?"

Lester stared at his cuffed hands in his lap. "I swear I don't remember anything about running you off the road, Sheriff. I swear it." He finally looked up at the large man across from him.

"But you did," Sheriff Willis insisted. "I saw you with my own eyes. Now how the hell do you not remember that?"

Lester gulped and shook his head. "I dunno, but I honestly can't remember. I've had blackouts several times in the last few months."

"Have you blacked out since you've been in jail? I haven't heard of it happening so why should we believe you? Seems awfully convenient to me that you black out only when you've gotten in trouble."

Tears shone in Lester's eyes. "I have no idea. I just know it's the truth."

The sheriff remained silent for a moment. "So you don't deny that you ran me off the road. You just say you don't remember doing it."

Lester took a deep breath. "Sid told me about all the evidence you have that proves my truck was involved. But it must have been the drug runners using my truck to make it seem like me."

Sheriff Willis snorted. "Why would any drug runners want to kill me? I didn't even realize they're in my parish until you told Sid." He shook his head in frustration. "But you had just gone on a tear about Claire running the investigation about that Grambling boy's bones the night before. You showed your ass in front of a bunch of witnesses. Seems likely you just got mad and weren't thinking clearly. You decided to take revenge for my giving the investigation to Claire."

"No!"

Lester seemed startled by his own reaction. He lowered his voice to a more reasonable level. "I swear I wasn't doing that. Sure, I was mad. I was damned mad. You always look after her and leave me the shit list of things to do. But I wasn't wanting to kill you. I went home and started looking at want ads for other parishes. I figured to leave...not kill you."

"But yet you ran me off the road the very next morning."

Tears flowed down Lester's face. "But I don't remember doing it! I swear to you on a stack of Bibles. I don't remember."

The sheriff said nothing for a long moment in case Lester filled in the silence. The smaller man took the time to rub tears from his eyes and sniff. Finally, the sheriff changed the subject. "Tell me about the drugs, Lester."

Lester's hands began to shake. "I done told Sid everything. I figure he passed it on to you."

The sheriff leaned forward. "I want you to tell me. How did you become involved with them?"

When Lester didn't answer, Sheriff Willis's voice grew stern. "You say you aren't lying but you aren't coming forward voluntarily either, Lester. How did you become involved?"

Lester gulped and grabbed a tissue to blow his nose. "I was on night shift. I saw a truck coming out of the bayou without headlights. I pulled it over and they offered me a chance to work with them."

"What made them think that was a good idea?"

"I dunno. They offered about the time I was writing a ticket for no headlights. I was threatening to get a search warrant since they couldn't give me an excuse for driving without their lights." He shook his head at the memory. "I've thought about it over and over again. It almost seems like they were expecting me to stop 'em, and they already knew they would ask me to help them."

"How would they know something like that?"

"I've wondered the same thing." He lifted his palms in a helpless shrug.

The sheriff nodded toward Jess. "You're up to speed better than I am. You got any questions for him?"

"Yes." She pulled out a smaller copy of their map. "Here is an aerial view of Kalfou. Here is your place." She pointed to the rooftop Claire had identified as Lester's house. "This is your outbuilding here. You agree?"

He stared at the map curiously. "Yes."

Jess continued. "From what direction does the truck come to your house?"

Lester squinted as he stared at the map. "Most of the time I'm asleep and just hear a knock. But I've seen 'em come from the bayou or town. They switch it up sometimes. I've seen an older-looking van, an F150 and recently a black Chevy that looks like it just came off the lot." He tapped his finger at the appropriate areas on the map.

"Do you know where they go after leaving our parish?"

Lester thought a moment. "They never said it directly to me, but I heard one of them mention Baton Rouge once and Memphis another time. I don't know if they went to both on the same trips or if they switched up the drop-offs."

Jess pointed to the area they had found to be a path that was now leading from the bayou. "Is this on your property?" she asked.

Lester studied it a minute. "Yeah," he finally said. "Looks like it's in the back field."

"Back field?" Jess asked.

"That's what we always called it. I guess because it was the piece of land the farthest back from the house. He traced a finger just inside the section of trees at the bayou's edge. "It goes back about an acre or so in here. I rent the field to Arnold Beaumont. I ain't been in so long I don't even know what he's growing this year."

"Your land butts up to the water?"

He shook his head. "No. But it's not far from there. It's so thick with briars and shit it's pretty much useless. I used to go back there to hunt from my tree stand."

"Could these tracks have been made by you or friends?"

"Nope. Last time I remember being there was deer-hunting season three or four years ago. Even then, it wasn't traveled by anything but my four-wheeler. It wasn't enough times to make all them tracks."

"Why haven't you hunted there all this time?"

He shrugged. "A buddy of mine found us a better place."

Jess leaned forward. "We need to check that area, Lester. I can get a search warrant, but it would be easier on us all if you just agreed."

Lester looked at the sheriff. "I'll give my permission, but I want it noted that I'm working with you. I ain't fighting against you."

Sheriff Willis nodded. "Agreed."

With that settled, Jess pressed on. "Is it always the same number of people that come to your house? The same exact people or different guys at different times?"

He scratched his forehead before answering. "There are about five of 'em that switch out. I ain't seen any rhyme or reason for who travels with who. But it's most always two at a time."

"Describe them to me and anything that might identify them."

Lester described each of the men he had encountered. The information was rather vague, but just as he'd told Sid, he noted a few of the men had an accent.

The rest of the interview was unfruitful and ended with the sheriff warning Lester that it would be in his best interests to tell them anything he might remember later. Lester agreed that he would as Jess escorted him from the room.

Afterward, the three officers met in the sheriff's office once again. "So what did you take away from the interview?" Sheriff Willis asked.

Jess spoke first. "I thought your point about Lester not having a blackout since being incarcerated was valid. It shoots holes in his excuse of no memory during the wreck."

The sheriff pulled out his handkerchief and wiped beads of sweat from his brow. "I'll call his lawyer and see if he is willing to let Lester have a scan or something to make sure he isn't having a real problem. Don't know if he'll let Lester do it though."

Jess nodded. "He's got someone coming to do a psychiatric evaluation for him. As soon as it's complete we've got someone from your expert witness list to do the same thing. We'll need someone freed up to take him to Baton Rouge, though."

Sheriff Willis rubbed a hand along the back of his neck. "I'll call and see about them keeping Lester at Baton Rouge with the state police. We don't have the personnel to keep him any longer."

Claire nodded in agreement. "Something's been bothering me about all this. We're having all this criminal activity in our little parish. Big things like kidnapping, murder, drug-dealing. I wonder how they're all connected."

Jess made a note and circled it. "It's something to think about. We can't be certain about anything until we begin filling in some of the missing details. I'm interested in how they knew Lester might be a candidate to work with them on their drug runs. It tells me they have some knowledge of the officers here."

"Right." The sheriff leaned back in his chair. "Either somebody local is part of all this, or they took time to hang out and learn about all of us. In such a small population, it would be hard to just hang around without one of us knowing."

"That means we most likely have a local involved in addition to Lester," Claire stated.

Sheriff Willis grimaced. "You might be right. Get Maxine in here, please."

Maxine brought another cup of coffee that she sat in front of him. "What do you need? You ready to go home?"

He ignored her question. "Maxine. Me and you need to put together a list of people to come in for an interview. Jess and Claire can help us get started." As Maxine got out her notepad, he ticked off names. "Pastor Abel. Tell him he needs to come in today voluntarily or tomorrow we're coming for him. He is a big guy, owns the land near those graves, and hateful as hell. He hasn't lived in Kalfou for too many years."

"Who else?" Maxine pushed her thick glasses upward and they immediately slid down.

"Arnold Beaumont. I can't imagine Arnold doing something like drugs or killing anyone. But all it takes is getting behind in bills and you get mighty tempted to make extra cash. He's the one renting Lester's land where the tracks are going in and out of the bayou."

He continued his list. "Hopper Beaumont, Arnold's son that found that little boy's bones." He looked at Claire and Jess. "I plan to put the pastor, Hopper, and Arnold at the top of my list. Anybody else you can think of?"

Claire nodded. "There are just a few people in Kalfou who have airboats. Those can get places more easily so it makes more of the bayou accessible."

"All right. Maxine and I will find out who owns those boats and add them to the list. We'll set up appointments over the next few days leaving you two free to investigate that trail."

CHAPTER TWENTY-SIX

Lester's back field was easy to find as they simply followed a beaten path made from decades of farm equipment driving around its perimeter. They followed it to the tree line and found newer tracks diverting into the trees.

As Claire drove in, Jess wondered aloud, "With all these tracks why didn't Lester notice trucks coming in and out here. Was he lying to us?"

Claire kept her eyes on the trail. "No. I think he is telling the truth. He has no need to come out here since it's rented out. This looks like an old road bed used decades ago. Now somebody is using it again."

Jess checked her cell phone. "Darn. No service already. Do you know where we are in relation to the bodies and Dakota's skull? I'd like to check for the oaks if it's not too far. And if I'm walking near things that bite, I prefer to see them ahead of time. So now is better than later this evening."

Claire laughed. "I don't blame you." She stopped and checked the GPS. "Hmm. We're not too far from the larger burial site. We should be at a straight shot from here." Claire found a shady spot to park the SUV and they headed out on foot.

As soon as they entered the trees the swamp became eerie in its silence. Normally there were birds singing and insects buzzing. An intermittent breeze usually rustled the leaves while there was always the occasional splash. But today, there was no movement or sound except for their steps. The unnerving silence seemed to absorb the sound of leaves crackling beneath their feet. There was a feeling of eyes watching…waiting.

Perhaps the bayou was angry that the victims once interred within its black earth had been taken from her.

Claire stopped and signaled Jess to do the same. She allowed the quiet to wash over her, a moment of peace before going to the graves. Fear rose up as it had that first evening when diving around where Dakota Grambling's skull was found. She tried distracting herself by thinking of something else but couldn't.

A hand fell on her shoulder offering reassurance. "Are you okay, Claire?" Jess asked quietly.

Claire jerked her thoughts back to the present. She became aware of her labored breathing and clenched fists. She forced herself to relax her muscles and calm her breaths. "I'm good now. Thank you."

Jess said nothing, just rubbed her hand along Claire's back and shoulders.

The silence was broken by the flapping of wings. Claire looked up and saw a crow landing in the top of one of the trees. It was enormous. Three more crows, normal in size, joined it. The large one cawed at the others while ruffling its feathers. It seemed as if the sound signaled the three small ones to begin cawing. They lunged and snapped at each other, jumping from perch to perch, flapping around to a better spot only to be harassed again.

She recalled what Mr. Henri had said about crows. "A bad sign, Claire. A big crow means big trouble is coming."

Her thoughts were interrupted by the faint pounding of a drum. She blinked, trying to make sense of it. She listened intently before turning to Jess. "It's the rhythm of a ritual," she whispered. "Someone is calling Legba, one of the Voodoo loa."

Jess frowned. "Out here? How do you know that?"

Claire shrugged. "The drumbeats change depending on which god they are petitioning. Legba is always petitioned first because he is...sort of a doorway to the other loa. I've heard that particular drumbeat many times."

She didn't add that it had always been Mr. Henri who performed the rituals for the Voodoo followers in the parish. Her mother had taken her to Mr. Henri many times whether fighting a cold or asking for help with bullying at school. Mr. Henri had always done his best to help her.

She headed in the direction of the drumming, with Jess following closely behind. It became obvious the drums were close to one of the burial sites. Sure enough, the yellow police tape came into view, and there sat Joseph Trahan, tapping out the complex rhythm on a drum. Behind him was a small wooden coop with a rooster inside. The smell of incense alerted her to a makeshift altar placed near a fire. A vial of oil, a knife, candy, and a rolled up paper of some sort rested atop its surface. Claire looked for the symbol for a Voodoo loa drawn in flour on the ground. As expected, she saw the familiar pattern used to summon Legba.

Near the fire, Mr. Henri danced to the rhythm. He wore no shirt, only a tattered old coat from a suit that had seen better days, his legs bare beneath the ragged edge of his shorts. On his head was an old straw hat with a red rose in the hat's white band. His face and chest bore streaks of red paint that formed the same intricate pattern as the one drawn in flour. Mr. Henri grabbed a wooden cane and danced with it, alternating between whirling it as a baton and raising it above his head as he chanted to the beat.

He was calling for Papa Legba to take possession of his body.

Despite his advanced age, Mr. Henri's movements showed his strength and agility. With feverish intensity, he performed leaps and spins before the makeshift altar. Then with perfect control, he landed in a submissive posture, where he offered a silent prayer, his head inches from the altar's edge. After a short pause, he began it all again.

He danced feverishly as the music sped up until finally, his eyes rolled back in his head, and he collapsed onto his knees and began weaving in a trancelike state. His body slumped and immediately his demeanor changed. His features grew weary, older somehow as his movements slowed. He leaned heavily against the cane even though he no longer stood.

"What's going on?" Jess whispered in her ear.

"He is being possessed by Papa Legba."

Jess stilled as Mr. Henri began speaking. The language was French Creole, most often used in times past with some words still used among the locals. A glance at Jess showed she had some knowledge of it too.

"I am here," he said in a low voice that sounded nothing like the usual Mr. Henri. "What have you brought me this day?"

Joseph continued drumming but more quietly. "We bring you a sacrifice for your help, Papa Legba," he said.

With the help of his cane, Mr. Henri stood and hobbled over to inspect his offering. He picked up a cigar, moved to the fire and lit it, using a twig roasting among the coals. He took his time before leaning his head back and expelling smoke.

"Ahh. A good cigar."

He hobbled the few feet back to the offerings.

"Candy." He placed it in a coat pocket.

He shuffled through the papers. "Ahhh. You didn't forget." He lifted his arm with a small bottle of rum in his grip. He gripped the small cork with his teeth and pulled. Claire heard the pop of the cork and then Mr. Henri spat it out before draining half the small bottle at once.

"Ahh...very nice." He turned to Joseph. "What do you want of me?"

Joseph's drumbeat stopped and the silence was deafening. "We have much trouble here and need help of the loa."

Mr. Henri had begun swaying on his feet. One hand holding the cigar, and the other the cane. He closed his eyes, stuck out his tongue as a child might catch a snowflake.

"Yesss." The word sounded almost like the hiss of a snake. "I taste it in the earth here."

Joseph raised his hands in supplication. "Will you help us, Papa Legba?"

Mr. Henri nodded and spoke again in the low gravelly voice of Papa Legba that sent chills down Claire's spine. "Yes. I will help you. But you must call to Xango. I will speak to him so he will hear you." He stopped and sniffed the air, then placed his hand on the ground. "There is danger in this place, more than I knew."

With those words, Mr. Henri collapsed on the ground.

Claire rushed to his side and offered him some water. Disoriented, exhausted, he gratefully sipped from the bottle as he leaned against her.

"Papa Legba says to call Xango," he whispered between breaths. "I've never done that before. Xango doesn't think people deserve his help."

Claire patted his shoulder while still cradling his head. "Who is Xango? I haven't heard of him."

"Xango is strong. He is the lord of fire and lightning. He is a true warrior and helps us seek justice. If he answers he will help us rid the bayou of the evil that has found us."

He rested a few minutes and then handed Claire her water bottle. "Thank you, little one. I feel much better now. It's time to call Xango." A look of apprehension shadowed his face. "I hope he will accept my offering. I wasn't prepared to call such a one as him. I can only hope Papa Legba talks him into hearing my call."

Mr. Henri tossed his straw hat and cane to the side. Claire guided Jess toward Joseph and knelt on the ground. Claire began to sway to the music and clap her hands in rhythm with the drumbeat. After hesitating briefly, Jess did the same.

Mr. Henri also began to sway with the music and moved to the altar where he raised his hands in supplication to Loa Xango. He began to chant using words not unlike French Creole. Claire wondered whether it might be Haitian Creole.

Without warning, Mr. Henri sprang into the air. His motions and rhythm were nothing like before but strong as ever, as if he hadn't been exhausted just minutes ago. His movements reminded Claire of a bayou deer, agile and full of grace. He pranced, somehow making his legs lift him in the air effortlessly. He sometimes looked over his shoulder before leaping, spinning so he was facing where he had just been.

Then his movement changed completely, becoming rather ribald as he arched his back and thrust his hips forward. His eyes rolled back in his head and his bare feet pounded the ground before sliding to the side in a graceful gesture, clapping and gyrating to the beat. His eyes fluttered and his tongue flicked suggestively. He thrust his hips forward and he grabbed his crotch.

Claire sat, fascinated at the dramatic change in her friend. Mr. Henri was always so quiet and a little shy.

He changed his persona once again, hands remaining on his hips as he stomped around the clearing. His voice became deep and commanding as he continued to chant.

Claire was shocked at the transformation of sweet unassuming Mr. Henri. Not only had his personality and voice changed but his eyes had become almost white. His brown irises and darker pupil were barely visible behind the white haze, yet they appeared hard and judgmental.

Claire was terrified.

"Well," he announced. "Here am I. What do you want of me?"

Claire's mouth went dry and she had to fight the instinct to run from him. "I—uh…"

"Come now," he interrupted. "What do you want?"

His bass voice sent chills down her spine and made her mind go blank. Then, she felt Jess's warm hand on her arm. Claire calmed enough to reply.

"We need your help…Xango. Many have been buried here, all of them murdered."

Mr. Henri…or rather Xango…nodded. "Yes. Many have been buried here. The ground is stained with their suffering and death." His eyes rolled back in his head. He dropped to his knees again. His voice remained firm and imperious. "A wicked tree is in our bayou. It has three branches. One is vengeance, one is hate, and the other is madness. Roots of bitterness feed it and make it grow. You must kill the tree."

Claire frowned as she had no idea what Xango meant. "How do I kill it?" she asked. "Kill the roots?"

He shook his head. "No child. The roots grow too deep. First cut off the branches, and then chop it down."

"But—" He ignored her. "You must use my fire and strength to bring peace to the dead." He focused on Jess. "I will send Damballah to you. You must submit to him or perish at my hands."

Claire jerked in alarm at his words but had no chance to speak before Mr. Henri collapsed on the ground. The drumbeat stopped, and Joseph got to him almost as quickly as Claire.

"Henri is used up," Joseph muttered as he turned his brother over onto his back. He put a hand on Henri's chest to check his heart rate. "Xango has left him weak. I will keep watch over him."

Claire nodded. "Joseph, I've never heard of Xango. Who is he?" He answered her but his eyes never left his brother.

"Xango is a loa, rarely called upon. He doesn't particularly like humans, so he usually doesn't show up even if he is called. He pinned Claire with a stare. "But when he deigns to come to us, he comes because it is very important for both us and the gods."

Jess spoke up. "I don't understand."

Joseph looked at her. "Evil is here and is so terrible even Xango and Damballah are willing to help us. You and Claire are the ones to fight this evil."

"Who is Damballah?" Jess was confused by it all.

"Damballah is the loa that comes in the form of a snake," Claire murmured. "That's why you often see snakes in Voodoo ceremonies."

"I have no idea why Damballah would come to you." Joseph frowned. "He is the creator. He is not a warrior."

"But he will come to me as a snake?" Fear and dread filled her voice.

Joseph nodded. "Remember that when Damballah comes to you." He turned to Claire. "Go back now. I will look after Henri. You both have work to do this day." He gave them a nod and turned his back to them, an effective dismissal.

Claire wanted to stay and discuss what they had seen and heard but past experience told her Mr. Henri and Joseph couldn't add to anything the loa had said. They were instruments of the loa and nothing more. A glance at Jess told her she was beyond ready to leave, so with a quiet "Thank you" Claire escorted Jess back in the direction of their SUV.

Normally at ease in the bayou, Claire was jumpy this time, alert to any sound or movement. There were none which was eerie. The silence on the walk-in had been unnerving. Now it was frightening. And those damned crows seemed to be following them.

Jess kept touching her sidearm as if reassuring herself that it was still there. It was then that Claire realized she was doing the same thing. This is ridiculous, she thought to herself. I've got to get a grip…for Jess's sake as well as my own.

She stopped and took Jess's hand and gave it a squeeze before bringing it up to her lips for a kiss. "It will be okay," she said in what she hoped was reassurance. "This is good news for us. It means we don't have to do all this alone."

The crows stopped above them among the leaves, cawing at them.

Jess gave a wan smile. "Thanks. I'm kind of overwhelmed. I mean, Mr. Henri was darned convincing."

Claire couldn't let her believe it was all a lie. "Wait a minute," she said firmly. "That was real, Jess. It may not be easily explained but that doesn't make it fake."

Jess took a moment for her words to sink in. "Okay…" she said slowly. "I believe it because I believe you. It's just…a lot."

"Yes, but just remember that we have help when it's needed. That's all. We don't have to do this alone."

Jess took a deep breath. "Got it. But can we get out of here now?"

The fear lessened as their determination grew. As they continued on their way, the crows lost interest and headed back to the Trahan brothers. It seemed as if they took the fear with them. Or maybe it was because the SUV was in sight now. The closer they got to it the lighter Claire felt. "It's gonna be okay," she kept telling herself.

They drove back in record time where, groaning with pleasure, they entered the air-conditioned office. Before they could greet Maxine, the sheriff's door opened and slammed against the wall. Pastor Abel stormed out only to whirl around and shout while stabbing a finger at Sheriff Willis.

"I'll have your job for this, Willis. You can't go around accusing people of things."

The sheriff came into view. "I'm not accusing you of anything, Pastor, but I have to ask questions where the evidence leads me."

The pastor was as tall as the sheriff and much heavier, making Claire concerned for her boss, since he was so weak. She placed her hand on her firearm, her posture ready if necessary, but Jess shook her head.

Pastor Abel threw his hand into the air as if shoving the sheriff away. "Our small parish has been overrun by a murderer, and now drug dealers, while you and your female deputies are doing nothing to stop them." He turned to Claire. "What have you been doing when you should have been putting this killer behind bars?"

With his good hand, the sheriff grabbed the pastor by the shirt collar and managed to give the big man a rough shake. "Shut up. I'll throw you in jail if you open your mouth again."

Whatever the pastor saw in his eyes convinced him to be quiet. He took a deep breath and jerked out of the sheriff's grip. He adjusted his shirt and headed to the door. But he had to get in the last word. "Your election comes up next year. I'll make sure you never get elected again. We deserve better than you."

The sheriff stomped his foot at him and he scurried out the door like a child running from an irate parent.

CHAPTER TWENTY-SEVEN

A short time later, the phone rang and Maxine snapped her fingers at them to get their attention. "We have a three-vehicle wreck off highway ten. Patrol is on their way but request assistance. They need emergency response to highway 10 east lane between exits 54 and 55."

"Got it," Claire announced as she and Jess ran out the door. She flipped on the siren throughout the ten-minute drive.

Cars were backed up as they waited their turn to go around the wreck. A produce truck was wedged between a huge RAM pickup and an even bigger tractor-trailer, all three skewed across the road. The mammoth engine compartment of the eighteen-wheeler hovered at window level on the driver's side of the smaller truck, blocking it. A quick check showed the RAM was against the passenger's side of the truck effectively trapping two men inside the produce truck.

Jess announced their arrival over the radio and gave a description to be passed along to the Highway Patrol. The driver of the RAM was still inside, responsive but needing medical assistance. The ambulance had been called and its siren could be heard in the distance.

The driver of the tractor-trailer was already out of his rig. "I called you guys and an ambulance. The driver in the RAM seems to be the only one hurt. I'm fine and the two men in the produce truck just seem to be stuck."

Claire raised a brow. "Stuck?"

"Yeah. Their driver-side door is wedged shut and the passenger side can't open because the RAM is up against it so they can't crawl out a window either. Hell, they've even tried to kick out the windshield but haven't been successful. I don't know why they want out so bad."

While Jess went to the RAM driver, Claire checked on the guys trapped in the produce truck. The passenger side window was partially down. She noted it could have been completely down and the RAM would still prevent them from escaping.

She shouted so they could hear her. "Are you okay? Are you injured?"

The man closest to her ignored her completely, his cell phone to his ear but the driver nodded and gave a thumbs-up. Claire thought their response was a bit odd, but had more important things to worry about at the moment.

She radioed for a tow truck and the dispatcher advised one was on its way. Shortly after, the Highway Patrol arrived and the troopers took charge of the traffic movement. The EMTs now had the RAM driver in their care leaving Jess and Claire free.

While waiting on the fire truck to arrive with the equipment to release the men, she moved to the back of the truck and big rig to assess their damage. The tractor-trailer cargo had shifted but the giant spools of metal wire didn't appear damaged. The produce truck's cargo wasn't so lucky.

The load of vegetables and fruit was a sticky ruined mess in the back. And among all the smashed produce were plastic bags. A closer look showed the bags contained a white powder.

"Jess? Come here. You need to see this."

Jess came from the RAM. "What's going on? The men inside are going bonkers." Her mouth fell open at the sight. "What the fuck?"

Claire knelt and scooped a small amount of the powder. "I believe we've stumbled onto—"

A State Trooper came around the truck. "Deputies. The tow truck's here. We can move the RAM—." He stopped in his tracks. "Holy Christ. What the hell?"

Jess was the first to answer, laughter in her voice. "We've got a drug shipment. And two very unhappy dealers stuck inside the cab."

The trooper guffawed. "Can you imagine being stuck there, knowing what's going to happen, and you can't do a damned thing about it? They've got to be shitting bricks."

Word spread quickly and there was quite a bit of laughter at the drug dealers' expense. After the tow truck moved the RAM, the two men came out quietly where they were arrested and cuffed with no attempt at escape. Claire figured they were so humiliated they were happy to get away from the laughter.

Finally, something had gone right for the Kalfou Parish Sheriff's Department.

CHAPTER TWENTY-EIGHT

"You are being charged with drug trafficking," Jess announced as she sat at the table in the interrogation room. The larger of the two drug dealers sat across from her. Claire sat by her side while the sheriff sat at the end of the table. Gray from fatigue and pain, he was forced to assume a supporting role.

"Do you understand me?" she demanded when the man said nothing. "The amount in your truck is serious shit."

The man stared at her with hate-filled eyes, his slouching posture oozing defiance. He remained silent.

She tossed, onto the table, the drivers' licenses removed from the men's wallets. They were obviously fake. "What is your name? And don't bother referring to this piece of trash. The person who made these needs to change professions."

No response.

Jess's eyes were like flint. "You are in deep shit, right now. Co-operating is the only way you can help yourself."

A smirk was his only response.

"You're smiling when you're about to be locked up for decades? Drug trafficking is serious business, not to mention a driver was seriously hurt today. You're likely facing thirty years in federal prison."

His smile faded at her words.

Now it was her turn to smirk. "Uh-huh. You'll be a very, very old man if you don't co-operate. Now, what is your name?"

He hesitated a moment and then sighed. "Emilio."

"First and last name." Jess didn't try to hide her anger with his attitude.

He stared at her but eventually backed down as her own proved more intimidating. "Emilio Vergas."

"Where is your home?"

He shrugged. "I live wherever I am at the moment."

When he didn't offer further details, Jess slapped the desk. Claire jumped in spite of herself, but Vergas remained still. His demeanor signaled his experience at playing hardball.

"Houston, Texas," Claire said it quietly, as if of course, he was from Houston. He said nothing, but a narrowing of his eyes led her to suspect she might be close. Thank heaven for license-plate information, thought Claire.

"I want a lawyer. It is my right, and I am requesting one."

Jess snorted. "You're making it difficult to help you."

He didn't back down. "Lady, there is nothing you can say or do that is as bad as what would happen to me if I talked. Now I want a goddamned lawyer."

She glanced at the sheriff who gave a slight nod. She turned to Claire. "Let's bring in his partner. He looks like someone who's simply aching to talk to us."

Claire stood and escorted the man back to his cell. With such a small sheriff's department, they had two adjacent cells separated by a common wall of steel bars, normal for when the parish had built it. A newer solid wall design would be better but nowadays funding was tighter than ever. It would serve its purpose well enough with Lester in one cell and the new prisoners in the other. The arrangement would only be for the night as Lester would be transferred the next afternoon. At the moment, Lester was locked in another room speaking with his own lawyer.

Emilio entered the cell without a fuss but stared menacingly at his partner. "Shut up, Ernesto. You'd better shut up in there." He repeated it like a mantra, his voice rising each time as they cuffed and led the smaller man out of the holding area. Even after the door slammed shut he could be heard shouting.

Ernesto walked docilely alongside Claire to the interview room, his legs visibly shaking.

Jess decided to let him imagine the worst and ignored him as she fussed with her notepad. The paper rustling seemed overly loud in the small space. His arms began to quiver even with his hands held tightly in his lap and sweat beaded on his forehead.

Perfect.

"What's your name?" she began.

He gulped visibly. "Er—Ernesto Arnaz." His accent was much thicker than the other man.

"Interesting accent, Ernesto." Jess leaned back in her chair. "Where are you from?"

"Haiti," he answered quietly.

"Wow, you're a long way from home," she remarked. "Do you still live there?"

"I—um—consider it home though I have not seen it for a while."

"Where are you currently staying?"

He shifted uncomfortably. "I stay in Texas now." He kept his head lowered as he spoke.

"Ernesto, how did you come to have those drugs in your truck?"

He said nothing.

She tried again. "Where did you get the drugs? Houston?"

He jerked his head up as he hadn't mentioned the word Houston. "Why—why do you say that?" His voice trembled slightly.

She smiled cordially. "Your partner had a few things to say. As a matter of fact, he threw you under the bus." She looked at notes on her pad as if she were reading from them. "He said he was just a passenger and had no idea drugs were in the truck. He said to ask you where they came from as he was only helping you transport produce from Houston to Baton Rouge. He was riding with you as a favor."

His mouth dropped and his eyes showed how frightened he was. "No. Arturo. He would not say such a thing. We have worked together for two years now. I know he would not say this."

Claire jotted down the name Arturo. No surprise, the first man had falsely called himself Emilio Vergas.

"Oh, it was two years, all right. But your partner said you told him you've been friends about two years, but drugs have never been mentioned. He said he was riding with you to help with some produce but knew nothing of the drugs that you had in the back of the truck. That's right. He has agreed to testify against you, Ernesto. Do you understand what that means? It means we have a witness to all this."

She leaned forward and tried to appear sympathetic. "You're in deep trouble. You're looking at thirty years in a federal prison for your drug smuggling. Arturo says he is innocent, and you are the criminal."

"No."

Claire could hear his breathing from where she sat. He was on the verge of a panic attack. "If you aren't the leader, Ernesto, it would be in your best interests to work with me. Tell me what you know as a good-faith gesture."

"But I am just a mule for them," he whined.

"Who is them?"

"The bosses, yes? I am nothing of value. Arturo. He is also of little value. We are paid by an envelope of cash showing up in my mail. I am told nothing."

"Who is your contact here?"

"I do not know."

Her eyebrows rose skeptically. "You don't know his name? Of course, you do."

"No. I do not."

Jess turned to Claire and said, "Maybe we should take him back to his cell and let him stand trial. We have him dead to rights, and he isn't cooperating."

Claire looked at the man. "She isn't kidding, Ernesto. But we could make sure the prosecution is aware of your help."

He seemed on the verge of tears. "But I do not know the name of this man. We have given him the name, Dios Mio."

"My God?" Jess echoed.

He nodded emphatically. "Si. One time, Arturo was upset with him and shouted, Dios Mio. The man laughed and said something like, 'You got that right.' He has been Dios Mio to us ever since."

"What does he look like? Describe him to me."

"It is always dark. I cannot—"

"Tell me everything you can, Ernesto." Her voice held warning.

He heaved a ragged breath and wiped sweat from his forehead. "He is a big man."

"What do you mean by big? Is he tall? Is he fat?"

"He is big everywhere but mostly around here." He indicated his chest and stomach. "He is much bigger than me." He placed a hand over his head indicating height. This wasn't very helpful as Ernesto stood no more than five feet five inches. Most men would be taller than him.

Jess tried again. "Ernesto, is he white? Black? Latino?"

"He is white."

"Where do you meet him? When do you meet him?"

"We go to the swamp. To a special place few know."

Do you always meet him on land? There is a lot of water in the bayou."

"Mostly on land now."

"But you also arrive by boat at times, yes?" When he seemed surprised, Jess said, "I told you, your friend was talkative. All the more reason for you to help yourself and tell us everything."

"He says so much but tells me to say nothing." His voice was bitter.

"Maybe he isn't such a good friend after all," Claire said kindly. "Help us help you."

Ernesto bit his lip, weighing up his options. "We used to come by boat but now the water is drying up we are sending by truck."

Claire looked at Jess and tapped a finger against her notepad. "That matches with Arturo's story." Lying might not seem ethical but it was legal, and if it got the guilty behind bars, it was okay with her.

"You will help me not go to prison?"

Jess leaned forward staring him in the eyes. "You will go to prison, Ernesto. It's the amount of time you spend in prison that could change based on your cooperation."

He bit his lip as he thought a moment. "Okay. I will help."

He gave them details both about where they picked up the drugs and also where they dropped them off. It turned out most of the drugs were headed for Baton Rouge. Only a relatively small amount of cocaine was dropped off here. In Kalfou Bayou, their big money-maker was an expensive drug they called devil's breath.

"But Dios Mio calls it god's breath. I don't know why." With little prompting he explained the frequency and amount had grown over time until their source was having difficulty meeting the demand. "Very expensive, that one. But little is needed."

"What is it?"

He clamped his mouth shut.

"Ernesto, we will find out through the lab. Why not help yourself by helping us save time?"

"I'm not sure," he admitted after a moment. "I only know it must be handled with care as it takes very little and is very expensive."

Jess tapped her notepad with her pen. "Let me make sure I understand. The name of the drug is devil's breath. But the man you sell it to, calls it god's breath."

"Si. Another reason we call him Dios Mio."

"And you and your buddies make this drug in Houston?"

"Ahhh…nnoooo. It is made in Haiti and is sent as part of a shipment. The rest of the drugs go to a couple of places to be sold. But the devil's breath is only brought here. It is not well known."

Claire looked up from her notes. "What happens to the person when he takes the drug?"

"I have not seen it used. But sometimes, in Haiti, it is used in Voodoo ceremonies."

"Do you snort it like cocaine?"

"No." He shook his head vigorously. "It takes very, very little. Just blowing some in your face or drinking with a little in it makes it work. Dios Mio has said it makes you see things more clearly and act according to what God wants."

Jess frowned. "So, it takes small amounts and can be breathed in or ingested?"

"Ingested? Put in food or drink?" He was confused. "Then, yes?"

"Okay," she said while jotting down more notes. "The person gets the effects of the devil's breath by breathing it in or from eating or drinking it."

The man nodded. "Si."

Ernesto knew little more. It seemed to be a don't-ask mantra for him.

Jess's last question to him left them all hopeful. "Ernesto, if we took you with us, could you show us how to get to the place where you gave the drugs to Dios Mio?"

He nodded emphatically. "Si. Yes. Of course."

"Is there anything else you could tell us that would help our investigation or would help you?"

"No. I have told everything to you."

"We will want to talk with you again. Will you be willing to talk?"

"Si. Yes."

The sheriff, who had been quiet until now looked at both women. "Claire. Take Ernesto back and put him in Lester's cell. It will only be a few minutes while we wait on Lester and his lawyer to finish. Then we can head out."

As Claire took the prisoner from the room she caught the low conversation between Jess and Sheriff Willis. "… a few minutes for my medicine to kick in."

She heard Jess's calm voice. "Do you need me to call the doctor? We can do this without your having to—"

"I'm going," he broke in. "This happened on my watch."

She headed back to the cell with Ernesto in tow and before they reached the cells, Claire issued a warning meant for him alone. "I suggest you don't say anything to Arturo about what we've discussed. He will probably be upset that you got the better deal."

She put him in the empty cell with a stern warning to both inmates to behave themselves, then headed back to her desk. She opened her laptop and found out all she could about a drug called devil's breath or god's breath. She printed what she found with copies for herself, Jess, and the sheriff.

Devil's breath was a very potent hallucinogen. As Ernesto had described, it took very little to be effective. Ingested or inhaled, it immediately made the person docile and open to the will of others. The victim fell into a zombie-like state, and people had reported stealing items or doing things totally out of character because they were told to do so. They had little or no memory of the time while under its influence.

Claire was shocked. It seemed more like something from a movie. The article validated Ernesto's description. The drug was most often found in the Caribbean, whether by its point of origin or the region's familiarity with the substance.

She rifled through her notes from Lester's interrogation and found his report of a white substance blown into his face as a potential method for introducing the drug to a victim. If that was correct, she reasoned that Lester may have been under its influence and indeed have had no memory of running Sheriff Willis off the road. Lester may have been telling the truth. But who would be using him in this way? Who wanted the devil's breath and what was its ultimate use?

She put a copy of the website's information on Jess's desk and another in the sheriff's inbox. She was keen to discuss her findings with them. She pushed against the heavy door leading into the interrogation section of the tiny building when Lester's lawyer rang the bell to exit. She didn't bother looking at Jess as she announced, "I'm heading back to pick up Ernesto."

"I'll move Lester back to the cell," Jess answered.

Claire pushed against the door to the cell room. She was unprepared for what awaited her, and it took a moment before she began shouting for help.

Arturo had his arm through the bars of his cell and around the smaller man's neck. Ernesto was not struggling and was hanging limply, his feet dangling inches from the floor.

Claire fumbled for the key to Ernesto's cell and was just opening it when Jess rushed in. She headed for Arturo's cell while Claire entered Ernesto's. Claire yelled and braced herself against the bars to pry his arm away but the larger man's strength was too much. It was only when he felt the end of Jess's firearm against his neck that he stilled and let Claire take Ernesto to the floor.

Claire checked for breathing and a pulse. She could find neither so she began CPR while Jess called 911. Together they continued CPR until the ambulance arrived.

The EMTs took over. They hooked up the defibrillator. Ernesto's body jumped from the floor as the shock convulsed his muscles. They checked for a heartbeat.

"Again," the EMT announced and backed out of the way.

"Clear," shouted his partner and administered the shock a second time.

The first medic checked for a heartbeat yet again. He shook his head. "Nothing."

"Clear."

Ernesto did not recover. The EMTs moved him to a gurney and transported him to the hospital, still trying to resuscitate him. Dr. Siya Wason met them at the door of the ER.

Minutes later, Ernesto Arnaz was pronounced dead on arrival.

CHAPTER TWENTY-NINE

The wreck and drug bust were the talk of the town. A few locals owned police scanners and were eager to share the details. Pastor Abel and Chris Chevalier had both been caught up in the stopped traffic and saw the arrest. They were now inside the restaurant, describing it all to a captive audience.

Pastor Abel's voice rang out like he was in the pulpit on Sunday morning. "There had to be thousands of dollars' worth."

"Hundreds of thousands," Chris interrupted. "Street value—"

"Chris," Gil thundered. "Let Pastor Abel talk."

Chris shot a defiant glare in his dad's direction but quieted so the pastor could speak.

"Reckon what kinda drugs was it, Pastor?" one of the men asked.

"My guess would be cocaine. That's what you hear all over the television nowadays."

"That's right," another man agreed. "You cain't turn on the TV without seeing it."

"I never thought I would see the day when somethin' like that would come through our little parish," mused the lone woman in the group.

"Oh, it's everywhere," her husband assured her. He turned his attention back to Pastor Abel. "Reckon what will happen to them two men?"

He shrugged. "I would imagine they are in jail by now. They should be put away for a long time. This sort of thing would never have happened in the past. The sheriff is derelict in his duties. He hasn't even bothered to hire a full staff, and three out of four of them are women. You and I know a woman simply can't do the same job as a man."

Gil made an excuse to make more sweet, iced tea for the lunch crowd. But really, Gil was livid and needed time alone to gain his composure.

"Those fools," he thought furiously as he ran water into the large pot. "I need god's breath for the upcoming services. My plans call for everyone to partake in the Lord's Supper...My Supper. God's breath would guarantee everyone would be in the spirit on my Day of Wrath."

He sometimes called his day of transfiguration to Divinity the name Day of Wrath. After all, that was exactly what he was destined to bring. Nonbelievers and scoffers would be tried and found guilty.

He chose little Kalfou Parish to begin his reign because of the disrespect shown toward his mother when she was pregnant with him. It was only fitting that they be judged first among men. From here he would hit New Orleans as per his mother's wishes. Of course, Haiti would be the last to receive judgment giving them time to repent and accept their destiny.

The citizens of Haiti had gradually come to see his Divinity when New Orleans had turned its back to his mother so many years ago. Over time, Haiti had embraced Celeste Marie Dios and her abilities as she gained more knowledge in the cosmic plans for which she and her children had been born. Under his mother's tutelage, he had learned about Voodoo and Hoodoo, and the healing power of sacrifice and bloodletting.

Although his early years had been spent in Kalfou Bayou, he had had almost no interaction with anyone other than his mother and his father, Etienne Chevalier. It was in the bayou that Celeste had her first vision that told her what would happen to her baby boy, her firstborn, when he reached the Age of Perfection. Celeste had often rocked him to sleep as a child while telling him the stories of his past and the visions she had for his future. But it was in Haiti that he had grown spiritually. Haiti was where he realized his calling and the knowledge and wisdom that Celeste imparted.

When Gil and his mother had first arrived in Haiti, they had no money or place to stay. He had watched as his beloved mother had done whatever it took to have shelter and a little food in their bellies. When she had nothing to sell, she sold herself. Gil saw the bruises covering her face and heard her crying as she cursed those responsible for their predicament. He adored her for all the suffering and abuse she had taken to keep the two of them going.

As Gil became a man, she remained his sounding board when things seemed out of his grasp. It was Celeste who had discovered devil's breath could be used to help his followers overcome their basic inclinations and look toward the Divine. She always said, "In your hands it will be transformed from devil's breath to the very breath of God."

As always, she was right.

Gil cut the heat off as the pot of water began boiling. He moved the pot to a cool burner and put the tea bags in to steep for a few minutes. Having done this a multitude of times, he gave little thought to the process now. He heard one of the gossiping men mention Claire's name.

Gil wanted to curse both Claire Duvall's and Jess Morgan's names. He had been promised more devil's breath on this shipment and those two had prevented it. There could be no waiting for another shipment. He needed it in the next couple of days.

Fuck! Fuck! Fuck!

To give himself time to calm down, he began washing pots and pans. There were too many curious eyes in the dining area and their asinine conversation was intolerable. Better to stay here and figure out his next move. His blood boiled at the possibility that he would have to manage without the drug. His followers deserved to feel him in a way that only god's breath could induce but now…

"Gil? You fighting with them pots and pans?"

The man's voice jerked him from his thoughts and he realized he was slamming the metal cookware around in his agitation. He reached up and set the old-fashioned timer to four minutes and forced himself to appear relaxed. "Nah. I'm just hurrying so I can get back to hear what ya'll are saying."

Laughter sounded from the dining area at his words and the pastor replied, "We've already moved on to the next subject. We're talking about when the first thunderstorm is going to come our way."

"My bet is next weekend," he said as he came back and began wiping down the lunch counter. "Because I have some things to do outside."

The patrons laughed because they didn't see his earnest look as he turned away. He thought the timer would never go off and was relieved when its ringing called him back to the kitchen.

"You're always so busy. You gotta learn how to sit down and relax."

Gil forced a smile on his face. "I'm not a rich man like you, Vaughn. I have to keep working or the bills don't get paid."

The men laughed and tossed wisecracks in his direction as he headed back to the kitchen. Damn Claire Duvall and Jessica Morgan. Those she-devils had become thorns in his side. But the Devil himself would soon bow down to him and those bitches would too. His mind raced with thoughts of how he could overcome his Eternal Enemy and those standing between him and his perfect Transfiguration. It would indeed be a day of wrath.

The customers all left and Gil was alone when he finally decided his course of action. A smile spread across his face, his resolve renewed as he knew exactly how to deal with those two bitches. Death and sorrow would be theirs to reap as he and his followers rejoiced on his blessed Day of Transfiguration.

Glory to God in the highest...

CHAPTER THIRTY

The aftermath of Ernesto Arnaz's murder consumed the Sheriff's Department. In addition to the mandatory investigation for wrongdoing, there was the guilt and frustration that a man had died while in their care. This hit on both a professional level and a personal one as the traumatic experience took its toll on the already stressed group. A phone call ended with the prisoner being transferred to the prison in Baton Rouge at the same time as Lester. Although normal procedure when something of this nature happened, it was a glaring reminder of their failure to keep an inmate safe.

Sheriff Willis watched his people struggle with the trauma for a few days and finally decided to call a meeting. His tiny workforce was overwhelmed mentally and physically. They needed a morale boost, and he needed to give them a chance to blow off some steam.

"Okay ya'll," he said as he took in the group seated around the table. "Gil is bringing over supper for us in a few minutes. As I already explained, this is a time for everybody to say what's on your minds. I need to gauge how you're holding up and see what I can do to help you.

"Before we start, let me tell you I've hired two new deputies, and they will start next week. We'll need to give 'em some time to get trained but we can start giving out some of the more mundane responsibilities to the new help soon.

"Right now, I want to give you all a chance to talk. It's a terrible thing that happened. But we did nothing wrong." He looked each of them in the eye and repeated, "We did nothing wrong." An uneasy silence filled the room as no one wanted to speak. Sheriff Willis shook his head in reproach. "Dammit. Ya'll are making me go first?" Everyone chuckled but no one volunteered.

He had figured as much already so he had no problem starting. "So…I guess my biggest concern is I haven't been around while everything's been happening. Even now, I'm only doing part of what I should be doing. I'm sorry about that and appreciate all of you taking on the extra duties that have dropped in your laps."

Jess immediately responded. "Sheriff Willis, I admit we're overwhelmed but it's simply the circumstances in which we find ourselves. We know you're doing as much as you possibly can."

"Yes," Claire jumped in. "We're all worried that you're taking on too much too soon."

Maxine reached over and patted his hand. "Don't you worry about us, James. You need to take care of yourself."

The door opened and Gil Chevalier stalked into the room, his arms full of carryout plates. "Hey. I brought your food." His usual grin was missing. "Desserts are in one bag and barbeque in the other."

"Thank you, Gil," the sheriff said cordially. "I know it was short notice."

"Ahh, it was nothing." He sat the load on the table. "Looks like everybody is here. It must be an important meeting."

"Just letting them know what a good job they've been doing."

Gil nodded. "Well, that's good. I guess I'll leave you to it then."

He was almost to the door when he heard Sid say, "Don't you beat up on yourself, Sheriff. Me and Blanche are happy to have you with us. It helps me not to worry about her being home alone all the time."

Gil headed to his truck with Sid's words swirling through his mind. More devil's breath was arriving tomorrow night which prevented him from traveling to find a suitable sacrifice. With the extra heat from the drug bust and killings, he didn't dare take someone tonight and keep them forty-eight hours without devil's breath in their system. This meant he needed to get the sacrifice nearby.

CHAPTER THIRTY-ONE

The next evening, Gil closed the restaurant on time and headed into the tiny back room where he maintained a cot. He had things to do in the early morning hours and it seemed silly to head home when he would be driving in the opposite direction in a few short hours. He set his alarm and lay down, willing himself to sleep despite his racing mind. At 3 a.m., the alarm sounded and he woke eager to get started.

When Cammie arrived at the usual time of four thirty, Gil was in the kitchen sipping his morning coffee. She looked haggard, her hair unkempt, her eyes swollen from lack of sleep. Her voice was hoarse as it often was in the morning. "Where were you last night?" she asked dully without looking in his direction.

Gil's good mood immediately soured. "What does it matter?"

She shrugged. "I reckon it doesn't matter. Nothing's mattered in a long time."

She continued, unaware that Gil's face held an odd expression. "I guess you were getting ready for your big celebration, huh." This was a statement, not a question.

Gil paused before answering. When he did speak, his voice was weirdly neutral. "I slept here last night. I needed to go over the books and figured I would just sack out on the cot."

Cammie grunted her acknowledgment. "You mind getting me a cup of coffee while I start with my breakfast prep?" Gil stood and moved to the coffeemaker as if to do her bidding. He picked up something from the countertop and turned around with a smile that didn't reach his eyes. "I have a lot to get done today." He began walking toward her slowly... Purposefully.

She raised her head to see the butcher's knife in his hand.

Perhaps Cammie was too world-weary to care or maybe she had already resigned herself to the inevitable. Whatever it was held her in place as he walked toward her, the knife gripped so tightly his knuckles were white.

"No running from me?" he mocked as he stood looking down at her. "At least you never gave me drama, Cammie. You may have been a dimwit and nothing to look at, but you always kept the house clean and kept quiet about...things."

She stared first at the knife and then Gil. "I always figured I would end up on your altar someday." She stared up at him with dull eyes. "Just make it quick."

Gil's response was swift. He stepped forward and swept the knife's blade across her middle, exposing intestines that began sliding to the floor. Without pause, he snatched her hair, exposing her neck and slashed with the same speed. Blood splattered everywhere, its nauseating coppery scent permeating the room.

Ignoring the blood soaking his clothes as it gushed from her wounds, Gil drew her in a hug and whispered in her ear. "I was never going to use you as a sacrifice. You were never worthy."

With those last words to his wife of twenty-three years, he drove the blade into her chest. She slid to the floor where he heard her gasp for air and then a gurling sound as Cammie drowned in her own blood. The stench of a perforated bowel combined with that of the blood.

"God, you stink." He insulted her for the last time as life drained from her.

Cammie's final breath was faint, her eyes remaining open in accusation. He watched, oddly fascinated as blood became a narrow river that ran toward the drain in the floor's center. The blood loss was massive, a pretty bright red. His favorite color.

Gil stepped away from the growing puddle of blood to the sink to wash his hands.

The back door slammed, and Gil jerked as if shot. He grabbed another knife, and held it by his side, ready to strike. His son, Chris, entered the room, his sulky expression shifting to horror as he saw his mother lying on the floor.

"What the hell have you done?" he demanded, his face twisted in rage.

Gil shrugged. "It was time to take care of things. Cammie was never to rule with me."

Chris ran to his mother and knelt by her side. He made a high keening sound as he pulled the knife from her body. He felt for a pulse and found nothing. Weeping, he touched her face and brushed her hair from her lifeless eyes.

Chris turned to glare up at him, his features twisted in grief. "Why the fuck did you have to kill her...and like that?" He shook his head. "I always knew you were fucked up, but this..." He had no words for the tragedy before him.

"Watch how you speak to me, boy," Gil warned.

Chris's head jerked up, tears running down his face. "Why?" he sneered. "You gonna kill me with a bolt of lightning? A burning bush? Which god are you? Zeus? More like the devil."

Gil's own anger spiked. "Shut up," he demanded through clenched teeth. "Shut up." Chris had always been able to enrage him with his rebellious attitude and disrespect.

"Oh yeah?" Chris taunted, spittle flying from his mouth. "You gonna kill me too? Then who will do your drug running for you, huh?" He stood, hands by his sides, still having to look up several inches to stare his father in the eye.

In a flash, Gil drew his son into a deadly hug. He stabbed the knife into the soft flesh of his belly and watched the anger in his son's eyes turn to disbelief. Still holding him close he whispered in his ear. "You have always been a disappointment to me…and now, I don't need you anymore."

He gave the blade a vicious twist.

Chris opened his mouth to say something, but nothing came out. Gil pushed him, making Chris slip in the pool of his mother's blood, the knife still sticking out of his abdomen. He fell next to her and placed a hand on her arm. "Mom," he muttered as his own life's blood mingled with hers.

His eyes closed.

"How precious," Gil mocked. He turned away and began gathering up his things. He inspected the area for signs that might point to his being the culprit. All he needed was time to perform tonight's ceremony, and no one would be able to harm him.

He checked his watch. It was time to go.

As he took a last look at his worldly family, he shook his head. "We all have our cross to bear. I just got rid of mine."

He left the room, whistling to himself.

With coffee in hand, he headed out to his truck and drove to Sid and Blanche's house. He shut off his lights and parked across the road from the small field that adjoined their yard. He could see anyone coming or going without being seen himself. He had a little time before the sun rose close enough to the horizon to be seen. Sid Rochon was doing his usual night shift and the sheriff hadn't left yet so there was nothing to do but wait. The light in the house showed the sheriff was on schedule to leave about five thirty or so as usual.

It wouldn't be long now.

With dawn on the horizon, the tall figure of the sheriff left the brick home and headed to his pickup. The sheriff was barely out of sight when Gil left his truck and hurried over to the car parked underneath the carport.

No one ever locked their car doors in their small town and Blanche was no exception. He slipped inside and lay down on the back seat. This was the most dangerous part. If she glanced in the back seat before sliding into the car, she might escape and place his entire Transfiguration ceremony in jeopardy. He refused to allow that to happen.

He thought about the perfect timing of his Transfiguration. His Day would be on his forty-ninth birthday. The number seven was a perfect, holy, and complete number, as opposed to six being the mark of man. Just as God took six days to work, he rested on the seventh day as he was finished with his work of creating the world. The Hebrews had followed God's command to use the forty-ninth year as a year of Jubilee. Debts were forgiven, slaves were freed, and lands returned to the original owners. What better year could be determined for his reign on earth to begin?

He thought back to his seventh birthday, when his mother had prophesied his Transfiguration. It was another important announcement on another important day in his life. Even that long ago, she knew his destiny. From that day forward, she had taught him the knowledge and skills he would need to ensure he was ready when his day to reign came. With her guidance he sifted through the beliefs and rituals of many faiths, and discovered what was truth and what was of false prophets.

The crunch of gravel caught his attention before there was a slight pause and then the car's interior light came on as the door opened. There was enough daylight to see him if she happened to look. He positioned a hand-rolled cigarette in his hand while Blanche slipped beneath the steering wheel and squirmed to get comfortable. His heart raced as he waited to spring into action. What would end with exhilaration always began with tension.

"Blanche?"

As he had expected, his voice startled her. He sat up, and placed the paper cylinder between his lips. She screamed in surprise, her eyes wide with fear as he blew a small amount of powder into her face.

"What do you want?" she asked breathlessly. "Why are you here?"

He grinned as he saw her body beginning to collapse. "I'm here for you, Blanche. I need you for my Kingdom."

She didn't hear the final words as she slumped unconsciously in her seat. He pulled her small limp body from the car and tossed her over his shoulder. He hurried as he carried her to his pickup. The Rochons' neighbor lived too close for comfort. He needed to get away from there quickly.

He heaved a sigh of relief when he had her in his truck and pulled away without a light showing through a window at the neighbor's home. He headed toward the bayou where she would stay for the next twenty-four hours. He had always liked Blanche and was glad she would play a part in his ascension to power. He would make sure she understood the honor he was bestowing on her. He checked his rearview mirror. Blanche was awake and docile, just as he knew she would be. God's breath was a useful tool to be sure.

His fishing shack and the outbuildings nearby were made of the typical weathered wood boards, many of which needed to be replaced. His cabin stood on stilts with the living space on the upper level. Below had room for parking his truck between the posts. He had enclosed the area where a second vehicle could have been parked. Many hunters and fishermen used their enclosed area for storage. All in all, it looked similar to hundreds of others in southern Louisiana.

He commanded Blanche to get out of the truck. She did as he said and waited for more instructions. "Come with me." He kept his hand on her back as he escorted her upstairs. The layout was similar to an apartment, with a bed in one room and a full bath.

After telling Blanche to go to sleep, he watched as she lay on the bed and closed her eyes. He had used this room many times as a holding pen for his upcoming sacrifices. The windows nailed shut and deadbolts on the door made it escape proof.

He whistled a happy tune as he strode toward his truck. His day drew nigh.

Praise God from whom all blessings flow

Praise him all creatures here below...

CHAPTER THIRTY-TWO

"Good morning." The sheriff began the meeting as he always did. "I told Sid to head on home this morning. I don't have anything new for him and he was tired after—"

Maxine hurried into the room. "Sid is on the line, Sheriff. He's pretty upset. I told him I would put him on speakerphone for everyone." She didn't wait for an answer but placed it in the middle of the table and hit a button. "Sid?"

His voice came back immediately. "Sheriff? She's gone and she left without her cell phone. Something's happened to her."

"Calm down a minute, Sid. You're talking about Blanche? Did you call the hospital? Maybe she—"

"Her car is still in the carport. She didn't go to work, and she didn't take her cell or pocketbook. They were left in the car." Sid's voice was rising as he spoke. It was evident he was panicking.

"All right. We're heading to you right now. But give the hospital a call anyway. Better to cover your bases, okay?"

"I will, Sheriff, I got to find her." His voice was cracking.

"We will. Just hang in there while we come over."

The call disconnected.

Claire caught sight of Maxine's wan face and took the time to give her a hug before leaving. "I'll let you know what happens as soon as I can."

"Thank you, honey," Maxine wore the stricken look they all shared. "Poor Sid."

As they exited the building, Sheriff Willis was speeding down the road, lights flashing. Moments later, Claire and Jess were doing the same.

"What do you think happened? Has this happened before?" asked Jess.

"No," Claire answered as she took a turn, tires squealing. She backed off the gas a bit. "Sid and Blanche have always been joined at the hip. It's serious for Sid to not know where she is. And leaving her phone and purse?"

In ten minutes, they were pulling into the driveway, the squad car already parked. Claire and Jess jogged into the house to find Sid sitting on his couch, his head in his hands. The sheriff was sitting next to him.

"Thank you all for coming so fast," Sid said automatically without looking at them.

Sheriff Willis remained calm. "Tell us what you found when you got home, Sid. Bring us up to speed."

Sid took a shaky breath. "I came home and saw her car in the carport. I was surprised because she should have already left for work. I worried that she might be sick. I went in and couldn't find her. After checking all the rooms, I went out to the car and found her pocketbook. Her phone and keys were in it. I know her cell's password and there was no call today."

Claire was at a loss for words. This was so out of character for Blanche that it was difficult to not think the worst. "Did you call the hospital?"

"Yeah. They were wondering where she was too." He sounded defeated.

The sheriff put a hand on Sid's. "Is there anyone Blanche has mentioned having a rough time? Maybe someone she might want to visit or might call her for help?"

Sid cleared his throat. "I thought about that, Sheriff, but why would she leave her purse? Or go with somebody without letting us know she'll be late?"

"Before we panic, let's check her phone over the last several days and call everyone to make sure she isn't helping with a broken arm or something. If it's too long a list, then we can help you."

Claire pulled out her phone. "I'll call the hospital and see if they know of anyone she has mentioned lately."

Jess already had hers in her hand. "I'll do the same thing with the EMTs. Just to cover the possibilities."

The sheriff said, "Blanche was in the kitchen making coffee when I left this morning. She planned to leave around six."

Sid looked up from Blanche's phone. "That would be about right. She always gets there early and takes her time doing the changeover for each patient. I got here a little after seven so that narrows it to about a one-hour window."

The two women went outside to use their phones leaving the sheriff with Sid. The two men had a close bond. If anyone could keep Sid calm, it would be Sheriff Willis.

Jess finished up with the EMT station while Claire was still on the phone. She went inside and emerged again as Claire was disconnecting her call. "Anything?" Jess asked.

"No. What about you?"

Jess headed toward the car. "Nothing. I'm going to start looking for anything that might point us in the right direction."

"I'll help. But let me report back to Sid and the sheriff."

Claire went inside and gave them the bad news. A few minutes later, she joined Jess inspecting the car's interior.

Jess was frowning as she stared at the front seat. "It seems odd for Blanche to leave her stuff in her car. I can see going with a friend in their car, but she would have taken her purse or at least put it back in the house. The car's interior is spotless. It puts mine to shame. Except for the floor in the back seat. Check it out."

Claire opened the door to the back and saw a couple of muddy black streaks that stood out in stark contrast to the lighter color of the floormat. "I see what you mean. It's not much but it stands out."

Claire took the keys and moved to the car's trunk. She opened it and announced, "Even the trunk is spotless."

Jess pulled back from the car. "Let's talk to Sid. It may make sense to him." They went inside and the two men looked up, their conversation put on hold for the moment.

"Got anything?" the sheriff asked.

"Not sure," Jess turned to Sid. "How long has Blanche had this car? It's cleaner than some new ones I've seen."

Sid smiled weakly. "Blanche loves her car. She has it cleaned every week and won't even let me in it unless I'm wearing my civilian shoes. Most of the time she makes me bring a towel and lay it on the floor."

Jess took the opportunity to ask, "Can you take a look at the back seat floormat for us, Sid?" They walked outside to the car. "It's the one on the driver's side." Jess leaned into the front seat so she could see over Sid's shoulder. He opened the door and immediately frowned.

Jess explained, "It's not bad at all, but it made us question it since the rest of the car is absolutely spotless."

He pursed his lips in thought. "She just had it cleaned yesterday. Vaughn's boy does it every Thursday."

"Would the boy have left it like this?" Jess moved in farther and placed a knee on the driver's seat as she leaned over the seat's back to point to the mat.

Sid shook his head. "That's easy to clean up and he does a good job. Besides, I don't think Blanche would have let it happen in the first place."

The sheriff frowned. "Well, half the parish has black dirt. Any ideas on how to narrow down where the mud came from?"

Silence was his answer.

"Well, we have something to think about. Have you found anything else?"

"Nothing," Jess answered as she got out of the car.

Claire immediately noticed white powder on the front of Jess's navy uniform shirt. "What did you get on your shirt, Jess?"

"Huh?" She looked down and frowned. She started to brush it off but stopped.

"Claire? Did I have this on me before I leaned against the seat?"

"No," Claire answered and turned to Sid. "Any idea what it could be?"

Sid's frown deepened. "I don't have any idea."

Claire turned toward her SUV. "Let me get a bag from my kit." She grabbed the evidence kit and a spare T-shirt she kept in the back. She hurried back and placed the floor mat and Jess's shirt in bags. The men focused on tagging them.

They decided to give the home and property a thorough search. Claire and Jess would begin outside while the men checked the house. Afterward, they would switch to ensure no one had overlooked anything.

Jess began her search in the backyard while Claire started near the car. She checked for black mud but found nothing in the driveway or yard. Frustrated, she headed back to the vehicle to rethink her strategy. Then a thought occurred to her. She stuck her head in the home's front door. "Sid? Do you have a sprinkler system for your yard?"

He came into the room. "Yeah. I've cut off the one in the back but still using the one in the front."

"Did you run the sprinklers last night?"

"Yeah. They're automatic at one in the morning."

"Can you show me where they're located?"

"Sure." He came outside and walked to the side of the house. "Here is where it's connected."

She checked for any disturbance underneath the faucet where a small patch of earth was exposed but the soil wasn't black and there was certainly no footprint. They moved a few yards and Sid found the first sprinkler. He started to move to the next one, but Claire stopped him. "Let's look around as far as the sprinkler can reach and see if we find any exposed earth."

He looked puzzled momentarily, and then, "Dang, Claire. You're a smart woman."

"I don't know about that," she denied. "But it's worth a try."

The two of them traversed back and forth but found only grass. They moved to the next one which was closer to the yard's edge. "This is the closest one to the road," Sid mentioned. "It comes out to about here. From here it's the neighbor's land."

Claire stared at the ground. "Sid? Look at the tree." She pointed down to the ground near the lone tree on that side of the house.

He came over and saw the large patch of exposed earth beneath the tree. Part of it was black. "It's remnants of an old flowerbed Blanche tried to grow. I moved everything out a while back but some of the black potting soil is still there."

"Let's see if there is a footprint."

His response was almost immediate as they drew close. "Right here. It's a lot bigger than my footprint, too."

She looked where he pointed and there was a perfect print of a boot. "Could a neighbor or someone walk around here recently?"

"No. Things have been so busy, we haven't had time for visits. Our closest neighbor is about Lester's size. I don't think it could be him." He wrapped her in a bearhug. "Thank you, Claire. Looks like he walked right by here and his boots picked up enough in the deep tread to keep it all the way to the car."

"Yeah," she agreed. "He wouldn't have seen it if it was still dark when he got here. We need to get a cast of that print."

Sid fetched the others while Claire kept looking for more prints. She found nothing but knew the footprints under the tree and in the car placed someone there. That's what really mattered.

When the group was assembled again, Claire and Sid explained their findings. At first, Sid became excited at having something to go on in their pursuit of evidence, but then, reality set in. There was a very real possibility that his wife of forty-two years had been taken from him.

Without warning, Sid fell apart and sobbed. Tears welled up in Claire's eyes as she watched Sheriff Willis wrap an arm around Sid's shoulders and let him cry. These two men had always been pillars of strength and it was heartbreaking to see them so upset.

Finally, Sid tried to gain control of himself. "I don't know what I would do without Blanche," he whispered, his voice thick with tears. "I always said I wanted to die first."

Claire had no idea what to say. Her heart broke for the sweet man and she worried about Blanche too. Claire counted them among her circle of friends and Sid's pain was hard to bear.

Sheriff Willis helped him back inside where he could sit down. Needing to keep busy, Claire made some coffee for Sid.

"I just don't understand what somebody wants with Blanche," he was saying as she came into the room with a cup of coffee. "She hasn't got an enemy in the world. She would give you the shirt off her back."

Jess's face was unusually solemn as Claire sat next to her on the sofa. "Did you talk to Arturo about anything, Sid? I'm wondering if the powder is related to the drug shipment in some way."

"I talked to him a little before he was transferred, but not much. He didn't do much besides sit there and smirk."

"What about Lester? Maybe he talked to him?"

Sid lifted a mug in trembling hands. "Lester was scared of the guy. He wanted nothing to do with him."

"Do you believe his story about blacking out?"

"I know it sounds outlandish," he admitted. "But I think Lester believes it's true. I guess that's all that counts."

Claire looked toward the sheriff. "So, what's the plan?"

"I think it's time to start thinking about the drugs and Blanche's disappearance being linked. And now we've found some powder that might be something important, too. That's a lot of coincidences for me."

Sid looked helplessly in his direction. "So, what do we do?"

The sheriff ran a hand across his jaw. "Me and you are going to make phone calls and put word out that Blanche is missing. If she can, she will let you know where she is. If we don't hear from her, we will get the evidence bags shipped to the lab. I wanna see if the powder on Jess's shirt matches either of the drugs from the produce truck. Ernesto talked about a powder you can inhale or ingest. Seems like it could be connected."

"I guess you don't have the results of that yet?" Sid looked up, eyes hopeful.

"No. And one of us personally going there might put a burr under them to get a move on." He leaned forward and put a hand on Sid's knee, I'm going to do everything I know to get Blanche back. I swear it."

He turned to Jess. "I want you two to swing by and ask Mr. Henri to head over here with his dogs. They aren't professionals but they have helped us a lot in the past. Sid and I will be with him while you two check the swamp."

When Jess raised her brows at his direction, he explained. "You haven't had a chance to check on the trail yet. We need to know where that trail goes. Maybe that's where Blanche is."

Jess borrowed a pen and pad from Claire. She wrote down something and handed it to the sheriff. "Here is the name of the guy we use over in Lincoln Parish when hounds are needed. If you need more dogs, he is a good man to use. You could cover twice as much ground. Give him a call."

He stuffed the paper in his pocket. "Thanks. Will do."

Jess turned to Claire. "You ready?"

"Yeah."

Jess and Claire headed toward the door. The sheriff stopped them with a stern order. "I want ya'll to be extra careful. I don't know what is going on, but we're spread awfully thin and it sounds like Sid and I will be in the field."

Claire frowned. "You're supposed to be taking things extra easy. You're going to be okay?"

He sighed heavily. "I know, Claire. I'll let the dogs' handlers communicate with me using their phones while I'm in the squad car. Kind of central command where I can drive wherever I'm needed."

At Claire's dubious expression, he shooed her off. "Don't worry about me. Take care of yourselves."

Knowing that was as good a compromise as the sheriff would allow, they headed out.

CHAPTER THIRTY-THREE

With a renewed sense of purpose, the two women headed toward the bayou. Blanche was missing and there was the possibility that this trail could lead to her. Claire kept her eyes on the narrowing path while driving faster than Jess would have liked. However, she said nothing. If Blanche was in the bayou, they needed to find her. If she wasn't they needed to get back quickly to look somewhere else.

Jess pulled out her firearm and double-checked the chamber. "Be careful out here, Claire. If someone tries to hurt you, use your weapon. I want you safe and sound next to me when all this is over."

Claire drove with one hand for a moment as she reached over to pat Jess's leg. "You have no idea how good it feels to hear that from you."

Jess lifted a finger to her lips and reached over to Claire's to repeat it. "That's as close as I can get to a kiss. We've got to concentrate." Jess broached a painful subject. "So…do you think Blanche's disappearance is related to the drugs?"

Claire thought before she answered. "To me, there are three options. One: she had a change of plans that Sid didn't know about and she didn't mention to Sheriff Willis this morning."

"That's highly unlikely."

"Right. Option two is Blanche is somehow abducted because of the sheriff and Sid being a part of the department that messed with their drug shipment."

Jess nodded but remained silent for Claire to finish her thoughts.

"Last option is the person responsible for all those buried victims has begun the same thing in our parish now." She looked at Jess solemnly.

"Try not to think about it, too much." Jess patted her hand. "We all want her back."

The path narrowed even further leaving only just enough room for the SUV. Black water sat on one side with soggy swamp mud on the other. The smell of sulfur and decay was strong even with the windows up.

Claire said, "This area must normally be below water level. The path has been built up a little. Someone has gone to the trouble of hauling dirt and heavy equipment to make it."

"Wow, I—" Jess began. Then she shouted, "Claire, look out!"

At that moment, a deer jumped in their path. Reflexively, Claire wrenched the steering wheel to avoid it. The SUV careened off the path and into the black water, stopped from submerging fully by the numerous cypress knees rising from the water.

Shaken, Jess slowly opened her eyes and looked around. Both the driver and passenger-side airbags had deployed. Hers had hit her full in the face, leaving scratches and patches she was sure would bruise. She looked over at Claire. "You okay?"

There was no answer. "Claire?" She touched her shoulder and shook her gently.

Still nothing.

Black water was almost to the level of the windshield allowing water to stream inside the SUV. "Claire? Wake up!"

When Claire didn't respond, Jess grabbed the mic to the police radio. "Station One? We have a cop down. We need emergency response." The radio remained silent except for the hum of static.

"Dammit, we're out of range here." She checked her cell phone. There were no bars either. "Fuck," she muttered in disgust. "Now what?"

More water was seeping inside. It was almost to their knees.

She attempted once again to radio the station. "Station One…Maxine or Sheriff Willis. If you can hear me, I need you to head to the location we spoke of this morning. We need help and EMT personnel with you."

There was no response, but she crossed her fingers that someone had heard it.

"Ugh." Claire began to stir.

"Claire? Wake up. We need to get you out of here."

Claire opened her eyes. "Jess, are you all right?"

"I'm not the one that got knocked out." She put a hand on Claire's shoulder. "Let's get you out of here. Can you make it up the bank?"

"Yeah." She tried the electric window and watched the glass move downward. "Glad they're still working. The battery is still good at the moment."

Jess did the same and they exited through the windows and into the water. It took a few minutes of slipping and sliding before they scaled the bank. Once at the top, they surveyed the scene.

The vehicle was at an approximate thirty-degree angle with the back half still resting on the bank while the front was in the water pressed against cypress knees.

Jess saw Claire gingerly touching the lump on her forehead. "Is that from the steering wheel?" She came over and inspected it for herself.

Claire stood still. "I'm sorry about this, Jess. I didn't see—"

"Don't apologize. It was an accident. That's all." Jess looked around.

"So what now?" Claire was still a little dazed.

"I tried to call on the radio but don't think it went through. My phone got wet while I was climbing up the bank. I need to go back and get help."

Normally Claire would have argued but she knew Jess was right. She wasn't sure she could walk in the hot sun all the way back without fainting. The lump on her head was throbbing and she still felt a little dizzy. Ever practical, she advised, "Your gun is wet too. At least get some dry ammo out of the box. It probably won't hurt anything but better safe than sorry."

"Where is it?"

"In the emergency kit," they said simultaneously.

Claire grinned weakly as Jess muttered something about a hoarder.

Jess found the ammo box and took a few minutes to dry the weapon as much as possible. "You know. I'm beginning to believe your emergency kit is a bottomless pit. Clothes and towels, water, extra ammo. What else do you have in there?"

"Everything in that kit is something I've wished I had at some point or other. I guess I was a girl scout in a former life." She sat up and groaned.

"Just stay still and it won't hurt. I promise to be back as soon as I can."

Claire grimaced. "I need to get up. Blanche may be out here somewhere needing our help."

"Let's get you changed into something dry before I leave. I saw clothes in your kit."

Claire shrugged. "You need them more than I do. Walking in those wet things will chafe like crazy. You'll get blisters long before you can find a signal. Take whatever I have there."

Jess tried to argue but knew Claire was right. She found socks and a pair of hiking pants that unzip at the knee to become shorts. The pants were on the short side and her slimmer frame had them drooping slightly, but they were dry. And the socks were a welcome barrier against the wet shoe leather.

"Okay, then," Jess said. "I'll start off. I'll be back as soon as possible." She bent down and gave her a fierce kiss. "Stay safe, please," she ordered.

Claire snorted. "You're the one that's got to do all the walking. You be careful, huh?" She got another kiss before Jess reluctantly turned to go.

CHAPTER THIRTY-FOUR

Yowl! Yowl!

Noses to the ground, a bluetick hound and a beagle were running madly in circles around Sid and Blanche's front yard. Mr. Henri had worked with the sheriff's office a few times before, once for a missing child and again when an Alzheimer sufferer had wandered from home. Sheriff Willis had seen the dogs find the victim both times but still waited anxiously for the professionally trained dogs Jess had organized.

He planned to search the swamp in case Blanche had been taken there. The adjoining parish sheriffs were sending officers to assist in the search and volunteer responders and firemen would arrive soon.

Sheriff Willis knew he was doing all he could, but the stress was making his chest tight. On top of that, his damned rib was hurting like a son of a bitch making it difficult to catch a deep breath. And dammit, he needed to get some deep breaths. He wasn't sure if the pain was his injured lung or if postponing the angiogram had been a mistake.

To make things worse, he felt helpless...and he hated it. His department now consisted of a "borrowed" undersheriff, a young deputy working her ass off, a terrified husband, and him...barely keeping himself upright after such a short time watching the hounds.

"Damn it! Where are those extra deputies from the neighboring parishes? And where are the other dogs I requested?" he sang out to his empty vehicle. He reached in his shirt pocket and took one of the pain pills the doc had given him.

All thoughts of his health fled when his cell phone rang. He snatched it from the seat next to him and barked, "Sheriff Willis."

The voice on the line was the same one he had spoken with earlier when asking for more scent-trained dogs. "Sheriff? Clyde Johnson again. I'm over here at a place called Gil's. I ain't sure which way I'm supposed to go."

Sheriff Willis broke in. "Stay right where you are. I'll come to you."

"All right," the man's slow southern drawl replied. "Uh... while I got you. My best hound is having a fit at the back door of this place. He's kinda my boy, ya know, and I keep him in the truck with me instead of the dog box on the back with the others. When I got out, he did too, and got all squirrelly when he nosed around the back of the place."

Sheriff Willis's brows shot to his hairline. "Stay right where you are," he repeated. "I'll come to you. We'll check it out when I get there. I won't be long."

"Sounds good to—"

Clyde didn't finish before the sheriff cut off the conversation and was stalking across the Rochons' yard. "Sid...Mr. Henri," he called above the noise of the baying hounds. "I'm going to Gil's to meet Clyde Johnson and his dogs. I'll bring them here." He looked at Sid. "You got your phone?"

Lines of worry were etched across Sid's face. "Yeah."

The sheriff nodded and headed back toward his squad car. His body was begging him to rest but he had more important things to do right now.

Gravel flew beneath the tires of the squad car as Sheriff Willis turned into the parking lot at Gil's. Clyde Johnson met him at the car and offered his hand in greeting. "Sheriff. Good to meet you."

The sheriff shook his hand vigorously. "I'm sure glad to see you. We've got a missing woman." He turned toward the nonstop howling coming from behind Gil's restaurant. "It's not like Gil to close. Even when he has to be gone, his wife and son keep it open."

They strode toward the rear of the building, the pain med having kicked in. They found Clyde's bluetick hound excitedly pacing back and forth at the back door, repeatedly standing on his hind legs as if trying to tree something.

"Something in there is setting him off," Clyde announced. "But I didn't want to break down the door."

The sheriff nodded. "Now that I'm here with you, I'm sure Gil won't mind. He's a good guy. If it's nothing, I'll pay for the door out of parish funds. But something is sure getting your dog excited." He stepped to the door and pounded on it. "Anybody here? Sheriff Willis here. Open up."

When there was no response, he raised his foot and kicked the flimsy lock on the door. The crash of the door opening didn't muffle the groan that escaped between his clenched teeth.

"You all right, Sheriff?"

"Getting over some surgery, that's all. Just a little sore."

They entered the open door and closed it to the dismay of the overwrought dog. His frustrated howls followed them into a large supply room. It smelled of disinfectant, the floor still tacky from the concentration of cleaner when it was last mopped. Sheriff Willis smelled something else but couldn't quite place it. The disinfectant was too strong. As they passed through another small room housing miscellaneous pots and pans, the smell grew stronger and he finally recognized it...

He entered the kitchen and was horrified. Cammie and Chris Chevalier lay in the middle of the kitchen, the center of a red lake of blood. The smell was overwhelming in the small space.

"My God," he heard Clyde Johnson mutter. "What the hell happened here?"

Sheriff Willis immediately thought of Gil and how in the world was he going to deliver the bad news to the poor man. He pulled his cell phone from his pocket. "Here," he said as he tossed the phone to Clyde. "Call 911 to come to Gil's restaurant. They will know where it is."

He moved carefully toward Cammie and Chris. He knelt by the young man who was lying on his side, his arm resting on his mother's shoulder. "Could this be a murder suicide?" he pondered, "but why would Chris do such a thing?"

He felt for a pulse on Chris's neck and felt a small thump under his finger. Chris was alive? He felt the carotid again. Sure enough, there was a weak, slow beat that stirred beneath his fingers.

"Chris?" he shouted. "Chris, can you hear me? You stay with me, do you hear? You stay with me, son." He ensured his airway was open but had little idea of how else to help him. He moved to Cammie and checked but her heart was silent. This was no surprise as he saw the damage done to her body.

Clyde Johnson stuck his head inside. "Jesus! I'll wait outside for the EMTs."

Sheriff Willis didn't blame him. It was a grisly scene.

"Thanks. I believe this young man is still hanging on."

Clyde gave a thumbs-up and left while the sheriff pulled out his cell phone and began taking some photos. This was a crime scene that was going to be trampled upon soon. He would need to gather as much information as possible between now and then.

CHAPTER THIRTY-FIVE

Jess jogged along the path. Sweat poured down her back as she tried to hurry in the heat and humidity. The T-shirt Claire had given her earlier exposed her arms for the most part. Although cooler, the mosquitoes were out in full force today, buzzing around her, alighting wherever bare skin offered a convenient place to have a meal. She wished she had taken the time to apply the spray Claire kept in the vehicle as part of her emergency kit.

Inevitably, the heat and humidity took its toll and she had to stop for a minute. She hunched over, hands on her knees as she sucked in deep breaths. Sweat dripped onto the ground from the tip of her nose and she took the tail of her shirt to wipe her forehead. The damp cloth smelled like swamp water.

She started off again at a steady albeit slow jog. Head down, she was focused on controlling her breaths when she almost stepped on a copperhead viper sunning in the middle of the path. It wrapped itself into an angry coil, its bronze scales blending with the surrounding dead leaves. Copperheads didn't grow long and lean like most other snakes. Instead, they maxed out much sooner in length while their body kept thickening. She had seen the thick girth of the snake and wanted nothing to do with this poisonous pit viper.

"Whatcha got there?"

Already jumpy, Jess whirled around while trying to keep an eye on the snake. A few yards away, a large well-built man clothed in camouflage pants and T-shirt stepped through the brush running along the roadbed.

"Who are you? What are you doing here?" she asked, her voice sharp as a cold feeling of danger swept over her.

The man smirked, and she had to resist the urge to touch her sidearm. He brushed by her and quick as lightning grabbed the snake. With ease, he guided it into a bag he held in his other hand. Hissing inside the sack indicated there were more snakes in there.

"People call me Peter, ya know? Like the disciple?" His smile had a decided edge to it. "And what I'm doing is snake hunting." He lifted the bag higher. "You want to see?"

Jess tried to hide her revulsion. She forced herself to stay in place even though the bag was close. "No thanks. Why would you be doing that, Peter?"

He shrugged. "Why not? It's good money for the skin. People pay top dollar for snake-skin boots, and women's bags. If you can make it with gator leather, then they will make it with snakeskin."

Jess chose to ignore that for now. Every inch of her was taut and ready for attack. The man had done nothing out of the ordinary, but something was off about him. She didn't know what, but something was definitely wrong. She managed to keep her tone neutral. "Are you hunting alone? It seems rather dangerous." She could probably handle one person but two could be a problem.

He stepped into her space and leaned over her. His eyes looked almost wild and she realized his pupils were pinpoints. This man was high on something, making him dangerous. He wouldn't be thinking clearly. But neither that nor the snakes accounted for her fight or flight response as her heart rate soared and her mouth grew dry.

Jess didn't back up as she recognized it for what it was—intimidation. She knew to stand her ground. This time she had no problem putting her hand on her gun.

He backed up and sneered, "You going to shoot me?"

She raised a brow in warning. "Am I going to need to shoot you?"

He laughed and raised his hands in surrender, the bag still in one hand. "Now why would you do something like that?"

Trying to defuse the situation, she said, "Good point. Just don't give me a reason, right?"

He shrugged, his hands still high. "We're just out here hunting snakes, officer," he repeated.

She stiffened. "We? Who is here with you?"

"Me," a familiar voice said right behind her.

Jess whirled around and saw Gil Chevalier standing a foot behind her. "Gil?"

His answer was to blow a fine powder in her face. Immediately, everything turned black. She felt herself falling but her arms and legs wouldn't move. Her last thought was picturing Claire as she had left her, alone and needing her.

Late that evening, Jess began to stir. She was regaining consciousness but couldn't get her eyes to open. Her mouth had a bitter taste and her tongue stuck to the roof of her mouth. She needed some water.

A soft hiss came from nearby.

Her eyelashes began to flutter a bit. She was making a little progress toward waking up. She detected a scratching sound several feet away, and another hiss, this time louder, or maybe she was becoming more aware of her surroundings. She noticed an earthy smell mingled with oil and gas.

Where am I?

It took several attempts to open her eyes and bring the world into focus. Slowly, she looked up to a metal ceiling above exposed rafters. Its mostly gray coloring held random patches of rust from the humid climate. She sat up and immediately regretted the movement. Her head throbbed. She placed her head in her hands and felt something sticky. Blood. It was partially coagulated but the bold color indicated it could easily begin flowing again. She touched her head gingerly and hissed in pain. Besides the cut, she felt an egg-sized lump.

What happened? The last thing I remember was Chris Chevalier. No—that's wrong. It was Gil Chevalier and some man I've never met before.

She gave herself a mental shake to try and clear the cobwebs from her mind. Yes, it had been Gil's voice. But when she turned to him, he had blown something in her face…white powder.

Did I start to wake up after blacking out and they hit me with something? Oh God. Were Gil and the man involved in all those murders? Had they taken Blanche too?

Another scratching sound came from a few feet away. This time it was a dry oak leaf scuttling across the floor from a slight breeze.

She was in a shed or barn of some kind, the earthy scent due to the dirt floor. She turned her head gingerly and saw a few windows covered in heavy dust. However, outside light still penetrated with a vibrance that told her it was early evening and soon only moonlight would illuminate the building.

Hiss…

She looked toward the sound and squealed in protest as she curled her legs into a ball. Just a few feet away was a rattlesnake, coiled and ready to strike. Luckily, it wasn't upset with Jess, but with another snake a foot or so away from it.

Oh Fuck! Two snakes!

Her gaze swept over the area in a quick inventory of the situation. She stood to go toward the door on the wall opposite her when she heard another hiss. She jerked to the sound, catching a glimpse of yet another viper, this one a copperhead.

Her movement agitated the snakes lying so dreadfully close, but more hissing throughout the area pulled her eyes away from them. She took time to focus in the dim light. Her blood ran cold. There were snakes everywhere. It was straight out of the nightmares that had terrified her as a child.

She had always accepted her fear of snakes was irrational and bordered on a phobia but she was rarely in a situation that put her anywhere near the slithering reptiles. Panic set in and she choked back the bile that rose in her throat. She crept to the door and shook its knob in desperation. She did some breathing exercises that told her body to calm itself. Too bad her mind didn't calm at the same time.

She looked around for another door but found nothing. She went to the tiny window and tried to push it upward, but it had been nailed shut. She groaned in fear and frustration. Her movements were making the snakes agitated.

She was more awake now, and as her thoughts gained clarity, her memory gathered more details from the odd encounter with Gil Chevalier and that stranger. There was now no doubt in her mind Gil was either an accessory to the murders or the killer himself.

A hiss accompanied rattles shaking just inches from her foot. She instinctively jumped as the snake struck. A guttural scream erupted from her throat.

As evidenced by the incessant rattling, the snake wasn't amused.

CHAPTER THIRTY-SIX

"Sheriff?" Dr. Avi stood in the doorway of the waiting room. Sheriff Willis stood up. "What's going on, Doc?"

"We have Mr. Chevalier stabilized and will be sending him to LaFayette Regional for surgery. The ambulance is on its way."

"Is he going to make it?"

The doctor hesitated as if to choose his words carefully. "He's lost a lot of blood, but nothing that can't be sorted. A major issue is that intestines have been cut open, so he has peritonitis. Sepsis is a very real danger."

"When can I see him? It's vital that I talk to him."

The doctor shook his head. "I'm sorry Sheriff, but—"

The sheriff took a step forward. "You don't understand, Doc. We don't know who did this or if it was self-inflicted. But it's possible the same person that may have done this to Chris Chevalier and murdered his mama has kidnapped Blanche Rochon. I am going to talk to him and find out what he knows."

The doctor paled. "Blanche Rochon...that works here? Deputy Rochon's wife?"

"Yeah. Now I need to see him ASAP."

"Okay…But he is on heavy duty pain meds so he may be incoherent."

The sheriff was already heading toward the door. "Show me the way."

Chris Chevalier's eyes fluttered as the sheriff sat down in the chair next to him. "Sheriff." His voice was hoarse. "I guess you saved my life."

Sheriff Willis wasted no time with pleasantries. "I need to know, Chris. Did you kill your mama and try to kill yourself?"

Chris's eyes rounded in horror. "What? No…I would never do such a thing." He rattled the arm handcuffed to the bed rail. "Is that why I'm cuffed to this fucking bed? I didn't do it. I swear."

The sheriff ignored his question. "Then I need you to tell me everything you know. Who did this to you? I believe this person may also have Blanche Rochon as well. Tell me what happened."

Chris turned his head and with haunted eyes stared at Sheriff Willis. "The bastard that sired me. Gil Chevalier. He killed mama…and almost killed me."

Sheriff Willis was stunned. "Gil Chevalier! Why on earth would he do such a thing?"

Resentment toward his father darkened Chris's features, "Because he is a sick son of a bitch," he spat out and winced in pain. "The bastard thinks he's God Almighty and can fucking do whatever the hell he wants."

"I'm sure most kids your age—"

Chris snarled, "I'm twenty fucking years old, asshole. My dad has been crazy my entire life. It's you fuckers that have been fooled all this time…not me!"

"Let's talk about where he's keeping Blanche."

Chris put a tired hand against his forehead. "He'll have her at his fishing shack. But it's not fishing that's going on out there."

He began tossing and turning. "Nurse," he croaked. "I'm hurting like shit. Please…"

The sheriff had no time to question him further before the doctor came in. "The ICU transport to Lafayette Regional is here, Mr. Chevalier. We're going to send you on your way now."

As he spoke the nurse injected something into his IV line. Within seconds Chris calmed.

His eyes closed but he managed to murmur, "You get him, Sheriff. And you'd better get there by the time the sun sets tonight if you want Blanche Rochon alive."

CHAPTER THIRTY-SEVEN

Claire nursed her bottle of water as she watched Jess move out of sight. Her head was pounding but the discomfort of soaking in fetid swamp-smelling clothes overrode her headache.

With nothing else to do but wait, she examined her firearm. She wasn't happy about her beloved Sig Sauer P226 handgun having been submerged in the black swamp water. She emptied the magazine and picked up the wet bullets Jess had removed from her gun as well. The high heat in the car wasn't the best place to store them so she stuck them in her pocket. She wiped the gun down thoroughly and loaded a fresh magazine, her actions as much to keep her occupied as it was to ready the gun.

Her shirt had dried in the sun's heat. Her pants were still damp but feeling better against her skin. Her watch showed Jess had been gone quite a while.

The thrum of a truck's motor drew near causing a moment of panic until she saw Gil Chevalier behind the wheel.

Thank God.

"Hello Gil. How are you?"

"Hey there." He wore a serious expression instead of his normal affable grin. "Looks like you're in a mess here." He eyed the SUV.

"Yeah," she answered sheepishly. "A deer ran out in front of me."

"Come on and get in. I can take you wherever you need to go."

"Thanks, Gil. I appreciate it. I need to catch up with Jess. She's headed toward town." She frowned as a thought occurred to her. "You didn't pass her on your way?"

"I didn't see her."

Claire hoped that meant she had run into someone and hitched a ride. Maybe Arnold Beaumont had been in the field and she flagged him down. "Let me write her a note and I'll leave it here."

"Take your time."

He waited in the pickup while Claire got out her emergency kit. She kept a notepad stashed there along with a couple of pens. She was searching for the pen when she was grabbed from behind. A cloth covered her mouth and she fought to breathe. She reached for the arm wrapped around her neck and tried to pry free, but it was too late. Whether it was the tight grip withholding air or whatever saturated the cloth, she lost consciousness once again. Her hands had no strength and they slowly slid downward until they hung suspended along with her body. Within seconds, her world grew black.

Claire woke, her head throbbing as mercilessly as before. She opened her eyes and found herself looking into the face of Blanche Rochon. She sat up straight, her heart pounding. "Blanche!" She hugged her tight. "We've been so worried about you."

Ever the nurse, Blanche zeroed in on her wound. "Be careful," she advised. "You've got a nasty crack on the head."

Claire reached up and gingerly touched her forehead. "I had a car accident and hit my head somehow." Claire threw her legs over the side of the small bed and sat hunched over, her hands supporting her head. "Have you seen Jess?"

"No. Was she with you?"

"How did you get here, Blanche?"

"Gil Chevalier." Blanche's frustration and anger was evident.

Slowly she remembered Gil's attack. "Me too," Claire replied as she tried to understand what was happening.

Claire had no idea where Jess might be. Hopefully, she had made it back and was on her way with the sheriff and Sid to the rescue. She refused to consider the possibility of Jess running into Gil or her lifeless body lying in the bayou somewhere. She chose to believe she was okay and getting help.

She glanced around the room. It was obviously a bedroom, small and rather spartan. She tried the three doors in the room, one to a bathroom, one was a closet, and the locked entry door. A glance out the window showed them to be on the second level of the building, a two-story cabin like so many in the bayou.

She turned to Blanche. "Do you know what he plans to do with us?"

Blanche clasped her hands together. "No one has said, but it sounds like there is a big celebration that starts tonight and will go until sometime tomorrow morning." She leaned closer to Claire and said, "They keep mentioning a transfiguration. They seem to think a massive change is occurring tomorrow morning that will change everything for everybody."

The door swung open and Gil walked in. He smiled in amusement as Claire reflexively pulled Blanche behind her for protection but said nothing. He carried bottled water and handed one to each of them before sitting in the barrel chair across from them.

"I see you're awake," he stated without bothering with pleasantries. "Good. I want you both awake to understand what is happening."

"What do you mean?" Claire asked cautiously.

Gil's voice resounded as if giving a sermon. "Tonight, we give thanks to God and what he is about to do. My people will show their loving devotion with sacrifices worthy of the God most high. Afterward, there will be joy and feasting of the brethren. Then, at dawn, we shall turn to the east. As the sun rises so shall I rise with a magnificent Transfiguration."

Both women stared at him in confusion. "What is a transfiguration?"

He gave a self-satisfied smile. "My Transition. I'm fulfilling my destiny." He laughed at their blank faces. "You don't know what I'm talking about, do you? You see, tomorrow is my birthday. I will be forty-nine years old. The age of perfection."

Claire still had no idea what he meant and a glance at Blanche showed she was confused as well.

"You know nothing of God, do you?" He slowed his speech and spoke more slowly to ensure they understood. "Turning forty-nine is important as seven is the number of perfection. Forty-nine is seven times seven, perfection times perfection. You see?"

Claire was pretty sure the transformation had nothing to do with the Bible. "So what is your transformation?"

"Why, transformed to God, of course." He seemed a little peeved that she had to be told.

"You're transforming into God?"

"Yes."

"But how can that be, Gil?" Blanche spoke up for the first time.

Gil turned his gaze to her. "I am God."

"What?" Blanche cried. "What kind of craziness is this?"

He leaned forward to rest his elbows on his knees. "This isn't crazy. It's destiny."

Claire forced herself to appear reasonable. "So what happens to cause you to transform? And if you're God, why can't you just snap your fingers and change?"

A supercilious smirk crossed his face. "As with all things, there is a perfect time. I have known my destiny since my seventh birthday but just as Jesus learned from the priests in the temple as a child, I learned at my mother's knee."

Claire knew now she was talking to a delusional madman but understood from her training that it was best to keep him going, to humor him. Maybe he could provide a clue as to how to get out of this mess. "Celeste taught you that you are God?"

That smirk finally slid from his face. "Cammie told me you noticed the picture and asked about it. I guess it was meant to be that you and I would come to this conclusion."

It was all falling into place for Claire. Gil's ever-present smile and kind heart was simply a mask. He had fooled everyone. He had killed and dispassionately listened to the embellished tales spouted by the old men that hung out at his diner. He had asked the occasional question or commented when all the time, he knew more than anyone else what had happened. "Cammie has been by your side helping with all the sacrifices?"

He shook his head in annoyance. "You still have no idea what is going on, do you? I never intended for Cammie to rule by my side. She wasn't fit to be elevated as the Most High Mother. I've never thought otherwise." His eyes glittered as he continued. "I had once thought to make you my wife, Claire. I knew you were damaged but just as Mary Magdalene was delivered of evil you could also become my follower. But Jess Morgan has confirmed your unholy nature."

Claire easily brushed off his delusional comment and pushed to learn more. "Help us understand, Gil. Blanche and I deserve the chance to repent and follow you." She ignored the slight intake of breath along with Blanche's tightened grip on her arm.

He thought a moment and began magnanimously. "All right. I will give you a chance. My mother's parents were missionaries in Haiti. They sent her away from her home at a young age... like the first mother Mary."

"She was pregnant?"

Gil's face flushed red. "My mother's hypocritical parents chose to maintain their standing in society over their own daughter's needs. They didn't believe that my birth would be a new miracle as Jesus's had been. My mother was sent to live with her grandmother, a heartless woman who did unspeakable things to force her to abort. But Etienne, the man who would become my stepfather, wrote to Mother asking her to marry him. They had been dear friends and he longed for her. That's how I ended up in Kalfou Parish as a child. Mother raised me with little contact with people around here because of their inability to appreciate my divinity."

He paused and Claire encouraged him to continue. "So you left Kalfou Parish and moved to Haiti at some point?"

"Yes. After Etienne died when I was nine years old, my mother found she couldn't stand the foolish locals any longer. We went to New Orleans where it was better for a while. But then things changed. She was forced to leave and return to Haiti. Even there the non-believers belittled her…at least at first."

His gaze lost focus as he thought about the past. Claire glanced at the door wondering if she should try to make a run for it. But how could she get past Gil? He was an enormous man. If unsuccessful, it would put him on guard. She rationalized it was better to wait, at least for the present.

Gil continued in a voice that bore little resemblance to the man she had known for years. "But my mother did what she must to survive. She sold herself for a while when we had nothing to eat or a place to stay. Even I, the new Lord Almighty, had to be sold once. After all, sacrifice is demanded of us all."

Blanche opened her mouth to say something.

Gil glared at them. "No more interruptions. Where was I?"

He paused a moment before continuing. "Where she had been unwelcome and pushed into a vile life of brutality, she clawed her way up to be respected and revered in Haiti. My mother's people learned of her gifts and finally gave her the respect she deserved."

At their expressions, he thundered, "Don't you dare pity me! Wasn't Jesus beaten and ill-used? I am as worthy as he is! It was then that I came to believe Mother when she explained my future. Pain and ill-treatment are how we are molded into who we become."

He stared at Claire. "All your life people like Pastor Abel have hurt you. I've seen them cast proverbial stones, forming you into a vessel worthy of me. You were so close to the time of my Transfiguration. But you turned your back on it all for that woman."

Claire refused to be cowed by his words. "So you were in Haiti when you decided you were Jesus but then traveled back here."

He rolled his eyes. "I am not Jesus. He was a victim...a martyr. I am the *new* Christ. I, the Messiah, am to come again when I transfigure to my Godly form, as Mother prophesied from the beginning. My mother learned she was the Holy Mother long ago before I was even born."

Blanche spoke up hesitantly. "How did your mother know?"

"She took the truth that Voodoo offered. The night I was born she had her first vision after conversing with Legba. Over the years she has had many more that only confirm it. You see, Mother's destiny is to be the Holy Mother but only I can give you life everlasting."

A visible shiver ran over Blanche at his lunacy. "What do you want with us?" she asked in a subdued voice.

"The Bible teaches that sacrifice is necessary to show your willingness to give up what is dear to you to gain what you desire. It also shows God your respect. Just as Abraham's sacrifice demanded a son, my Transfiguration demands a sacrifice just as great. Only a person can fulfill that requirement when much is desired. You, dear Blanche, are a sheep without blemish. You are that sign of respect I mentioned. Claire exemplifies that I am willing to push my old life behind me." He turned to Claire, his eyes angry and hateful. "Sinner, I can lift you to paradise if you will follow me."

Claire glared at him in defiance. "I think you've twisted the Catholic faith into a pretzel, Gil. It seems to me that you pervert the Bible into what you want it to say. And why do you think sacrifices are necessary now? I thought Jesus became the ultimate sacrifice so that no other was needed."

Gil lifted her by her upper arms with little effort and glared into her eyes. She glared right back. After a long pause with neither of them backing down, Gil placed her feet back on the ground and said, "Your courage is notable, Claire, but it only makes you stubborn now. As for sacrifice, I see you don't understand. I found long ago that no religion or denomination holds all truth. Catholics, Protestants, Jews all have a piece of truth that put together is the one great truth. In Haiti, my mother discovered the divinity of Voodoo, which has its own piece of the greater truth. The poorest people on the island of Haiti still understand a price must be paid for help to be granted. Much of the rest of the world has forgotten that."

Claire challenged him. "You're crazy."

He ground his teeth in anger. "Before sunrise tomorrow morning, you and your lover will both know the meaning of pain and suffering. Then you will learn about sacrifice."

He was becoming angrier with every word and Claire decided she had pushed him enough. He would only retaliate if she continued. She needed time now to think about the conversation and try to figure out what he meant about Jess. Was she here or looking for her somewhere?

Believing he had switched Claire's defiance to respect, Gil smiled at both women. "I believe I have made my point. I suggest you both get some sleep. Repent and follow me so that you may leave this world of pain and suffering behind to be with me forever. Worshipping me would be your greatest honor."

He turned and left the room, and they were locked in once more.

"What do we do?" Blanche asked, her voice trembling.

"I'll have to think about it but obviously we need to get out of here as soon as possible. It sounds like more crazies will be arriving to begin the festivities."

A woman's scream caught their attention. Claire and Blanche ran to the window and stared out. They saw a flurry of movement near a small window of a barn across the yard and then Jess's face pressed to it, her arms pushing with all her might to raise the window.

"Oh my," Blanche breathed. "It's—"

"Jess." Claire finished for her. "What the hell made her scream?"

CHAPTER THIRTY-EIGHT

As the day drew to a close, Claire and Blanche sat staring through the cabin window toward the building where they had seen Jess's face.

"She's so close but I can't get to her."

"Any ideas?" Blanche asked as she twisted the top on her bottled water.

"No," Claire admitted.

Blanche took a long swallow of her water. "At least he brought water. I haven't had anything for most of my time here."

Her words barely registered to Claire as she focused on a plan for escape. The beat of drums began, interrupting her thoughts. She went to the window and saw people dressed in white beginning to mill around, some dancing to the rhythm of the drums, most with some kind of drink. Gil's celebration was beginning. They were crowding around the giant campfire and what appeared to be a wooden altar of sorts, large enough for a tall man to be strapped down on it as a sacrifice. Her mouth fell open when she noticed the large, rounded stone sitting on it.

She glanced at Blanche and saw the older woman lying on the floor.

"Blanche!" Claire raced to her and patted her cheek, but the woman didn't respond. "Blanche! Come on. What's wrong?"

Blanche's eyes opened but were unfocused. Claire saw the water bottle next to her. He must have spiked it. She heard voices nearby and knew she had to decide quickly. She grabbed their bottles and poured both into the bathroom sink. She forced herself to remain calm as the voices grew louder.

She hurriedly replaced the caps and sat on the floor waiting, the empty bottle lying next to her. Their only chance of escape demanded that they believe Claire was drugged. She would try to emulate whatever Blanche did to make them believe she was no threat. It wasn't a great plan, but it was all she had.

After several minutes of silence beyond the door, Claire got up to watch the proceedings from the window. More and more people danced as the music became nothing but the beat of drums, its rhythm calling to Legba. Everyone removed their shoes and tapped out the cadence in the sandy soil while children tried to copy their movements.

She saw a few men dressed in white robes with gold stoles similar to the Catholic albs. They wandered through the crowd, stopping to speak with many people, smiles on their faces but were quick to change if they didn't like anyone's behavior. Those men must be Gil's enforcers.

Gil was dressed in gold with a red alb. He also wandered about, smiling and acknowledging the congratulations and comments. He didn't have the look of a killer, but he also seemed very different from the Gil Chevalier she had known the last couple of years.

She turned back to Blanche who still hadn't moved but at least her eyes were open. "Blanche? How are you feeling?"

Blanche looked at her as if it took time to focus on Claire. "I am fine. And you?"

Claire frowned at her odd greeting. It was as if she were meeting a stranger on the street. "Blanche, do you need to rest?"

Immediately, Blanche answered, "Okay." Then she lay down on the floor saying nothing.

Footsteps sounded outside the door and Claire hastily lay down beside her, imitating Blanche's expression. The door opened and a man she didn't recognize strode in. He came to stand over them and picked up the two empty bottles.

"Works every time," he muttered. "Both of you, stand up."

Blanche rose, so Claire did the same. She watched Blanche closely to copy whatever she did.

The man spoke again. "Come with me." He led them downstairs with only a cursory glance to ensure they followed.

They entered a room that Claire assumed was for people preparing to participate in Gil's ceremonies. It was large enough for no more than four to easily move around with a door leading to a small closet, or maybe bathroom in one corner.

"Sit." The man pointed to a couple of chairs set up against a wall.

He began rifling through a rack of white cotton robes. While he did so, Claire took in the rest of the room. Another wall appeared dedicated to herbs and liquids in small bottles. Knives featuring handles carved with Voodoo symbols were interspersed among them. She shuddered at the memory of the unearthed cadavers and how these knives had probably been used.

Bunches of sage hung above while shelves held containers of dried herbs, powders, and even a quartz skull. A shelf held several goblets that reminded her of medieval chalices portrayed in movies.

Next to them, on the same shelf sat a picture Claire recognized as Gil's mother standing with three young boys. One of them was obviously Gil and Claire wondered if the others were his brothers.

She froze, her eyes fixed on the picture as Mr. Henri's voice whispered in her ear.

"A wicked tree is in our bayou. It has three branches. One is vengeance, one is hate, and the other is madness. Roots of bitterness feed it and make it grow. You must kill the tree."

Claire shook her head to clear it. Had she heard Mr. Henri or was she simply remembering what Xango had said? Did Xango mean this family constituted the evil tree and branches?

The man's voice cut through her thoughts.

"Take off your clothes and put this on." The man held a white robe in front of Blanche.

While Blanche did so, he turned his back and chose three chalices from the shelf. Two were simple unadorned metal with a smooth surface. However, one was much more ornate. It had lots of scrollwork along the base with red faux rubies around the rim.

The empty spot on the shelf revealed a bag of the familiar white powder.

Devil's breath.

The man retrieved a couple of bottles of wine and poured some into all three goblets. He lifted the ornate one, sipped and heaved a sigh before filling the chalice again. Afterward, he opened the bag of devil's breath and shook a small amount into each vessel. He stirred them with his finger before putting the bag back in place.

He turned to Blanche who had donned the robe, her feet peeping out from beneath its hem. He looked at Claire. "Now it's your turn." He moved to the robes again and pulled out another one. "Try this one."

Without warning, the door slammed open and another man wearing a similar white robe with a gold stole rushed in. "There you are. I've been looking everywhere for you. I need help carrying the casks of rum. Gil wants at least five of them and I can't pick them up."

"You and your bad back. It only bothers you when work is involved."

"Just shut up and help me," the other man shot back. "These two won't do anything. Just lock them inside."

They left, still sniping at each other. For a brief moment Claire had hope of a possible chance at escape. That is, until she heard the telltale click of the door's lock.

Her heart raced as she tried to come up with a plan. She could always simply lunge for the nearest dagger and take the man by surprise. It was a poor plan at best as she had no way of getting Blanche away from the others. Even if she overpowered this guy, there would be others to replace him. Unfortunately, that was the only idea that sprang to mind.

Knowing she could be caught at any second, Claire went to the wall and grabbed a dagger, but as she held it in her hand, a strong negative feeling washed over her. A deep, powerful voice inside her head bellowed.

"No!"

Without understanding what was happening she found herself putting the dagger back and picking up another. Identical to the first, it nevertheless felt comfortable in her hand, and she had a rush of confidence while holding it. She inspected it more closely and recognized the scrollwork as the one Mr. Henri had used that day in the bayou.

The symbol for Xango!

She shivered at the sudden chill that swept over her.

First, Mr. Henri and now Xango. Am I going crazy?

Mr. Henri's kind voice whispered again. "Use the devil's breath."

She looked at the chalices and understood what she needed to do. Whether her imagination or something paranormal, it didn't matter. She had no better plan and no time to waste.

She reached for the chalices and poured white powder into all three. Without knowing the appropriate amount, she put at least as much as the man had done. She had no idea what and when they would be used but it surely couldn't make things worse.

"I need you all to conduct yourselves in a way worthy of me. No! I don't want excuses. I want you to follow my commandments." Gil's voice sounded close.

She returned to her chair. Thankfully, the robe was a little too long for her. No one would know she had her clothes on beneath if they didn't check. She lifted up a prayer that no one noticed her boots.

Just as the door's bolt slid from the lock, she sat down and tried to look unfocused in a similar fashion to Blanche. With her heart thumping madly, this was no easy task.

Gil opened the door, a smirk smeared across his face. He strode to Claire and cupped her jaw lovingly. "Your girlfriend is making a little noise in the barn. I heard her panicked squeals as she found my friends out there. I keep my ceremonial snakes in that part of the barn. I wonder which one will kill her. Maybe one of the rattlers or copperheads? Or my personal favorite, the coral snake. It's such a beautiful killer. Silent, deadly, and it doesn't let go immediately after a strike. So many lovely ways to die." He pulled her toward him and kissed her.

It took all of her self-control, but Claire managed to stand still as he captured her lips in a sloppy, wet kiss, his hand behind her head smashing her face against his own. The smell of rum made it worse. Although repulsed and outraged, Claire forced herself to allow it. Jess and Blanche needed her. Their lives depended on her.

His assault lasted an eternity and only stopped when he needed breath. He pulled back and offered the smirk she was beginning to recognize. Try as she might, Claire couldn't keep the hate from her eyes. Gil saw it and eyed her suspiciously. "Oh, I can see the hate in you, Claire," he slurred a bit. "You want to do something, but the breath of God prevents you."

"Blanche is next, dear Claire. You will get to watch as she dies under my knife. But you will wait until the sun begins to rise to meet your death. You will watch all the festivities and then my Transfiguration while knowing each second draws you closer to death."

"Your choices have put you here, Claire. You could have chosen life, but you chose death and destruction instead. And your penalty is watching your friends die."

He turned his back to her. She moved to retrieve the knife but had only touched the handle before he turned around, the bag of powder in his hands. He poured just a little into each chalice before putting it back on the shelf.

"After giving him extra time to get god's breath, that bastard cheated me on the amount this time. Mother will fix him. She will fix him good." His hands shook a little as he mixed in the powder. "I'll take that up with him after my Transfiguration. His hubris is going to be his downfall."

He stared at Claire, anger stirring in his eyes. "This cost me dearly, Claire. Market value for this is always high but you put it through the roof when you found the truck. But I must keep this on hand. I want to show my love and desire to make my people happy."

Then as if giving a military command, he ordered, "Stand up and follow me. Bring the chalices."

Blanche, expressionless, rose from her seat and stood behind him. Claire did the same. Then with a grunt of satisfaction, Gil grabbed the ornate chalice and headed through the door while Blanche and Claire carried the other two.

They marched outside to sounds of shouts and clapping, enthusiastic adulation greeting them. Gil took the goblets and placed them on the altar. He held up his hands and the people instantly fell silent.

"Tonight, we are on the crest of Eternity. An eternity where we yield power. Powerful joy and pleasure for the devoted. Powerful destruction and vengeance to the unbelievers and deviants."

He turned to the two women. "Here we have both. The one is pure and unblemished like a perfect lamb. Her sacrifice shows our purity of thought and absence of sin. The other," he pointed to Claire, "is a fallen angel. Once lifted up as a dove but now sin and desecration have brought her to desolation."

He turned his back to the two of them again. "We shall sacrifice a perfect lamb to Heaven above that I might show respect for the promise that awaits me. Then we shall eradicate this fallen one. Afterward, when the sun rises in the east, the day of Transfiguration is at hand. We shall rise up as the Christ and my chosen." He motioned to the crowd. "You are my chosen."

The crowd cheered and clapped at his words.

Throughout his speech, Claire seemingly hung her head in shame. But in reality, she was hiding the anger that was ready to burst forth at any moment. She must wait for her chance.

CHAPTER THIRTY-NINE

A wave of helplessness washed over Claire as Gil lifted Blanche onto the altar and buckled the strap around her wrists. Gil leaned down and shouted to be heard above all the noise from his followers. "Rejoice, Blanche, for you have been chosen to be my special sacrifice. Your blood will help me transform while your flesh will gift me with wisdom and power. But I must have you pure and holy."

He patted her foot after strapping her to the table without a whimper from his captive. "Understand. The god's breath will soon wear off. There wasn't much in the water as I must have you uncorrupted as your blood runs free.

As she saw how Blanche was waiting to be slaughtered, Claire's eyes misted at the very real possibility that Blanche and Jess might lose their lives this evening. It terrified her to know their life or death was based on her actions.

Gil stepped back from the altar and glanced dismissively in Claire's direction before lifting the silver chalice. "All my people, come to me," he announced in a loud voice.

"'Come to me all who are weary and heavy laden. I will give you rest.'" He began offering sips from the silver cup. "'Taste and see that the Lord is good: blessed is the one who takes refuge in me.'"

As they partook of the wine, people fell backward while others caught them and helped them gently to the ground. Several times after sipping from the cup, the person's eyes rolled back, and they began to jerk as if having a seizure. Claire wasn't sure if their reaction was due to their spiritual emotions or the devil's breath.

Many were still waiting in line to partake of the drink when a hush fell over the congregation. Claire turned to see what brought the silence and saw a woman dressed in a black cape and heavy black veil covering her features as if in mourning.

She slowly made her way toward the altar and Gil. She was so close that Claire had to take a step back to get out of her way. She remained near enough to hear the conversation.

"Mother." Gil's tone was reverent. "I'm so humbled that you came."

The woman reached out and touched his cheek with a black glove. "I wouldn't miss this day, Gilford. Your destiny is near."

Gil took the woman's arm and escorted her to the chalices. "I would be honored if you would offer the cup to my men and me."

"Of course."

She picked up the cup and absolute silence fell over the crowd. "Come to me, my son and his disciples." She didn't shout but it seemed her voice rang throughout the crowd.

Gil knelt before her. The men with the gold stoles knelt behind him. Gil's mother took a gloved hand and pulled away her veil to reveal her face. Her wrinkled skin was tanned but the black penned symbols covering her cheeks were still clearly visible. Claire didn't know the meanings of the symbols but recognized them as those connected with Voodoo rituals. The woman's hair was white, her eyes black. When she looked toward Claire, they seemed to burn into her soul.

Mr. Henri's voice began chanting inside Claire's head once again. Instead of frightening her as it had once, it somehow gave comfort.

The older woman removed her gloves and revealed the black symbols weaving around each hand. She lifted a tattooed hand to her throat, pulled at a string and her cape fell to the ground. One of the disciples picked it up and held it to his cheek in adoration.

The woman wore a simple white cotton dress devoid of color except for a scarf and matching waistband colored in gold and white. There was something odd about the scarf that Claire couldn't put her finger on, and she stared as she tried to figure it out.

Oblivious to all except her son, Celeste picked up the chalice and raised it above her head. "This is my Son in whom I am well pleased." She brought the cup down and offered it to Gil who drank a large amount. He immediately sagged to the ground, his mother miraculously grabbing the cup before he fell. The crowd clapped and shouted at this good sign.

Celeste remained unfazed at her eldest son lying on the ground. Then one by one she offered the cup to each of what Gil must regard as the twelve disciples, with the same results. To anyone who didn't know about the drug, it must have looked as if they were entranced by a spirit.

Finally, after the last one drank, she raised the chalice high and said something in a language Claire didn't understand. Then she brought it back down and drank the last of the wine.

The drums began again, pounding out a simple rhythm that seemed to permeate Claire's brain. Every beat reverberated inside her. Celeste wavered and two of the disciples caught her. As they helped her to the ground, she glared at them, wide awake. She said something and they immediately helped her back to her feet, looks of terror on their faces. Upon seeing the strength of the woman, the crowd grew wild.

Mr. Henri's voice began to explain it all in her mind while sounding as if he were whispering in her ear. "She is the Voodoo Witch that has brought chaos to us. She has strength that her son does not."

Xango's deep voice took over without warning. "She is the tree and her sons are the branches."

It had the opposite effect to Mr. Henri's whispers. Claire's throat closed, making her fight for breath. The day in the swamp and his words came rushing back to her. "The roots grow too deep. First cut off the branches, and then chop down the tree."

The drums began once again, beating rhythms she knew from her childhood. She could almost feel her mother beside her, joining in the celebration while smiling down at Claire's childish attempts to copy her movements. Her breath became calmer, her heartbeats slowing to the rhythm of the drums.

Celeste then picked up a chalice and began motioning those who had not done so before she arrived to come forward. Long lines began forming again in front of them. One by one, people sipped the cup, stepped away and slid to the ground, unconscious. Each time the crowd would reverberate with shouts and trills, as the drums continued their beats.

This was Claire's opportunity.

She stepped to the altar to stand at Blanche's side. Still under the influence of the devil's breath, Blanche lay quietly as Gil had ordered. Claire glanced around to see if anyone noticed her movement but everyone seemed focused on receiving the wine. Those that had awakened from fainting were under the power of the drug. Her hands fumbling in her haste, she began unbuckling the closest strap binding Blanche.

Blanche grew restless, making Claire wonder if the drug-induced daze was ending. "Continue to lie still," she ordered Blanche who obediently kept her hand in place, her eyes glazed.

Claire laid the strip of leather over Blanche's wrist so it would be less noticeable that her hand was free, then moved to her feet. She tried to look as if she were getting out of the way, which wasn't difficult with people stretched out on the ground nearby. Thankfully, all eyes remained on their Savior and his family.

Gil began to stir. Slowly, his movements unsteady, he knelt once again before his mother. She looked down at Gil to say something and he nodded.

Celeste raised her hands and shouted in victory, "The Day of Transfiguration, the Day of Wrath is at hand." Then she lifted her hands to the scarf at her throat and began unwinding it. At that moment, Claire realized it wasn't a scarf. It was a snake, a constrictor with yellow-gold and white markings. Celeste had miraculously worn it as a scarf and belt without the snake cutting off her air. Did this woman have power of some kind?

"Yes," Xango's deep voice answered in her head. "She is a powerful Voodoo witch."

The words made Claire's blood run cold. Voodoo witchcraft was a vile twist of the otherwise healing religion. Where most Voodoo practitioners used only potions and spells to help people, Voodoo witches perverted their abilities and knowledge to harm others.

The boa remained calm as Celeste lifted it above her head and danced. She twirled in circles while the crowd encouraged her with chants. The woman never faltered with the heavy snake. She simply spun and chanted, the drums growing louder and faster.

With no forewarning, she stopped abruptly, her chest heaving from exertion. The crowd silenced immediately. "Bon Dieu," she said breathlessly. "Most High God. Give the spirit god to my son that he may ascend to your most high place." She kissed the boa's head and placed it around Gil's neck.

He rose to his feet and patted and stroked it while the crowd began clapping in rhythm to the drums chanting, "Bon Dieu, envoyer loa."

Claire knew it meant "Good God, send your spirit god." A spirit god was a lesser spirit, more a spirit guide. The way Gil had twisted things, she was unsure if they were chanting for a permanent spirit god or one to show him what to do as he rose to immortality and became God Himself.

With everyone's attention on Gil, she was able to work on the leather strap more easily. She leaned over to let as much of the robe hide her movements as possible. The buckle co-operated and she quickly had Blanche's feet freed.

She moved to the other side of the altar and pretended to be enthralled by the Voodoo ritual Gil was performing. All eyes were fixed on him as he began to dance with the serpent.

She glanced around the crowd to ensure no one was watching her before attempting to unbuckle the last strap. The buckle appeared to be broken and Gil had tied the strap instead. Cursing to herself, Claire struggled to untie the knot. She thought about pulling the dagger she was hiding beneath her robe but worried someone would notice. Instead, she steadied herself and worked at the knot holding Blanche's arm in place.

Gil began swaying with the snake, lifting it above his head and twirling as he stomped his feet in rhythm to the drums. He brought the snake back down and kissed its head, anointing it as holy, before lifting it high once again. He returned it to his mother and accepted another snake.

Claire noticed the bins lined up behind Gil and realized they must house snakes. She thought of Jess and her phobia. She fervently hoped Jess was safe and sound and was already escaping. Although tears threatened, she forced herself to concentrate on the task at hand. The chances of escape were slim but lack of focus would diminish them further.

Gil repeated the dance with this new snake while his mother performed the same movements with the brightly colored boa. They danced in perfect unison within a large circle that opened up amid the crowd.

When the dance steps concluded and Gil had kissed the serpent, he handed it to someone in the crowd who now joined them in the circle. Gil received another snake and together the three of them danced.

Gil continued until his body was sheened with sweat. His chest heaved as he took deep breaths each time he handed another snake to someone. He anointed at least two dozen snakes of various sizes and species before falling to the ground, exhausted. He lay there while his mother ministered to him and the others continued dancing with their snakes. The music and chants rose higher. The dancing became more vigorous, the movements jerky as if the dancers were possessed.

Claire untied the last of Blanche's straps.

"Claire?" Blanche's voice could barely reach Claire amidst all the noise.

Claire moved to her side. "Don't move, Blanche," she ordered. "Don't do anything until I tell you, okay? You must make everyone believe you're still unconscious."

"Unconscious? But what's going on?"

"I can't explain right now, but don't move. We're in danger and it's very important that you stay still."

A quick glance around showed no one paying attention to the altar. The attention was on Gil and his mother in the midst of the crowd. Even the bonfire was devoid of people as it blazed between the crowd and the altar. Claire forced herself to walk rather than run to the large bonfire. She didn't want to do anything that called attention to her movements. She pulled out all the bullets from her pocket and tossed them into the fire. Then she walked back to the altar to stand guard over Blanche. She said a prayer and crossed her fingers that the bullets would activate even though she had no idea what to do next. It was simply her only idea.

Gil slowly began to stir as if a spell had been lifted. His mother stroked his arm with one hand and the snake with the other, speaking loudly in an unknown language. All eyes were on the elderly woman, who paused momentarily, and then screamed. She turned to stare directly at Claire with a venom that sent chills down her spine.

Claire involuntarily took a step back as if from a physical blow to the gut. She watched with both dread and fascination as Celeste began talking animatedly to Gil. He stood, his height towering above everyone. His face was emotionless. He stalked toward Claire and she prepared for an assault by gripping the dagger tightly in her hand. There came a large whooshing sound and then an explosion that caught everyone by surprise.

"Fire! Fire!"

"The shed is on fire!"

CHAPTER FORTY

After her initial panic, Jess forced herself to calm down. Taking great care, she moved to the double doors that provided the only access to the outside. The doors didn't budge and a closer inspection of the tiny gap between them showed a heavy piece of lumber resting across them. There would be no way to break it or lift it from inside.

Feeling helpless, she turned to lean against the doors. To her horror, she heard the distinctive sound of an irritated rattlesnake. She slowly turned, trying not to antagonize it, only a foot away, coiled and ready to strike. It lay among the items on the table next to the door and her movements had aroused its attention. Reflexively, she jumped to the side a split-second before the snake struck. It missed and turned toward her new position, rattling furiously as it sized up her position.

She instinctively jumped backward and bumped against an old wooden ladder. She grabbed it and climbed up a few feet. This wasn't ideal but at least it got her above harm's way momentarily.

The snake rattled furiously at her but was unable to give chase where she stood above. At least, she hoped so. Jess shivered in terror, her breathing ragged until she feared she might pass out and fall to the ground. Images of lying unconscious as snakes slithered across her body made her legs tremble so violently that the ladder shook in response.

She drew on her officer training in dealing with dangerous situations and managed to calm herself to the point of thinking more clearly. She wanted the hell out of there and being composed and rational would be her only chance.

Unwilling to climb down, she ticked off her options. There was the large door that wouldn't budge and two small windows that a six-year-old couldn't wriggle through.

A small tractor sat in the center of the building. Could she use it to ram through the door? She climbed down the ladder and slowly climbed onto the tractor seat. She could have cheered when she saw the key in the ignition. She turned the key but nothing happened. She put her feet on the pedals and tried again. Nothing. She moved every lever and the gear shifts and tried every combination she could think of, and it still made no sound at all. Tears came to her eyes as a feeling of hopelessness overcame her resolve.

The light was fading fast.

The smell of a nearby fire caught her attention. Its flickering light cast shadows along the back wall almost as if demons danced at her predicament. She felt as if the situation was increasingly hopeless. She saw a huge BBQ grill against the wall. Sitting beside it was a container of gas and one of lighter fluid.

She climbed the ladder again and could see the people all staring at something hidden from her line of sight. They seemed to be enraptured. She watched for a few minutes as she debated whether catching their attention would make things worse or better. The man she had confronted earlier along the trail was adding wood onto a bonfire. The fire blazed upward making several people jump back in alarm.

That's when inspiration struck. Perhaps she could douse a small section of one of the walls, start a fire, create a distraction and somehow escape. But how to set the fire? She had found no matches or a starter. From her perch, she looked around the shed and a plan slowly emerged. She would use the old manual bench grinder as a firestarter and the oak leaves on the floor would be perfect kindling.

Enthused, she tried to ignite the leaves. Sparks flew as she touched a mower blade to the stone but even though some sparks fell on the chips it wasn't enough to start a fire.

Frustrated, she looked around for a better way to start a fire when she got an idea. She removed her T-shirt and saturated it with the lighter fluid. For good measure, she used the rest of the fluid on the rotten wood and the wall of the building. After giving the liquid a few minutes to soak into the wood, she returned to the stone grinder and once again used the mower blades to produce sparks. After several attempts, the shirt caught fire.

She quickly tossed the shirt against the leaves and wood chips and was rewarded with the flames growing as the wood fueled it.

The fire was irritating the snakes but climbing back onto the ladder would most probably have her suffocate from the smoke. Smoke inhalation, burning to death, snake bite, or a crazy killer. So many ways to die. All she could do was wait and see if the flames did their job.

CHAPTER FORTY-ONE

As the flames engulfed the shed, the bullets in the bonfire began exploding, sounding almost like a machine gun. The effect was chaos as people had no idea whether to run or put out the fire.

Claire decided to help them make up their mind. "Run! Save yourselves. Run! They have us surrounded. Run!"

At her shout, Blanche rolled off the altar and crouched next to Claire. "Go," Claire shouted in her ear. "Run into the trees and hide. Don't let them find you."

Blanche's eyes were dazed and Claire worried that she was too unsteady to leave. "Blanche," she said urgently. "You've got to go. Save yourself."

Thankfully, Blanche shook herself and her expression grew more lucid. "Come with me, Claire."

Claire shook her head. "Not yet. I've got to find Jess. Then we'll head to you. Go ahead," she urged. "I'll meet you as soon as I can."

Blanche grabbed her arm. "Hurry, you hear?" Then with unsteady steps, she headed into the safety of the bayou shadows.

Claire turned toward the building now engulfed in flames. She had to find Jess. But she had barely taken a step when she was brought up short. Gil and his mother stalked toward her with murder in their eyes.

"You bitch!" Gil thundered as he tossed people out of his path. "Do you know what you've done? I'll kill you!"

Claire crouched, ready for the attack, every muscle tensed.

Gil came straight at her, his bulk towering over her. His eyes never wavered from her own, so he didn't see the dagger's blade beneath the long billowing sleeve of her robe.

Celeste either saw the dagger or had a vision as she screamed just before Gil got to Claire, "Gilford! Watch out!"

But it was too late. Gil moved within Claire's reach. She thrust the dagger upward, aiming to slide under his ribs. Unfortunately, the extra girth of his abdomen coupled with the short length of the dagger, made her attempt unsuccessful. However, the pain was stunning, causing Gil to stumble back against the altar while Claire and his mother looked on.

"Son!" Celeste cried out, her voice a mixture of rage and pain. She turned toward Claire and spat at her. Then she pointed a finger, shaking with the intensity of her fury at Claire. "Ou modi."

The expletive, damn you, wasn't something which usually bothered Claire. She heard it almost daily. But the vehemence with which Celeste said it, coupled with the hand gesture, sent shivers down her spine. Madam Celeste, the powerful seer, had placed a curse over her.

With outstretched arms, the woman grabbed for her, her hands clawing as a wild animal might. Claire crouched once again, preparing to use the dagger, now coated with Gil's blood. Celeste Chevalier's maniacal screeches were terrifying.

Claire readied herself for the attack, her body automatically preparing for it as her police training had taught. Without warning, she was struck from behind by a frantic cult member as he scrambled away from the chaos. Claire was knocked to the ground, unable to regain her footing before Celeste careened into her.

The larger woman dwarfed Claire's small frame. They rolled several feet, stopping when Claire's back became wedged against a tree stump. The sudden jolt of pain took her breath away and Celeste was able to settle on top of Claire's chest. The older woman's weight made the pain of the stump beneath her pressing against her spine almost unbearable.

Claire was in a position in which a law enforcement officer never wanted to be—on one's back with an arm out of commission. The knife was useless, held in the hand pinned to her side.

Like a woman possessed, Celeste slapped Claire's face hard and fast in such a frenzy, Claire couldn't recover from one until the next landed on the other cheek. Her blood splattered as Celeste's sharp nails tore across Claire's face. She brought up her free arm in protection while raising her hips trying to buck Celeste off. After almost flipping over Claire's head, the older woman changed tactics. She stopped slapping Claire and gouged at the younger woman's eyes, the long fingernails like rapiers.

Claire brought her free arm down to the ground, searching for anything that might help. All she felt was the sandy bayou soil. She threw it in Celeste's face, aiming for her eyes. The older woman's cry of dismay coupled with her hands leaving Claire's eyes and clutching her own gave her the opening she needed.

Claire bucked her hips again, rotating as she lifted her arm and pushed Celeste to the side. She freed her arm holding the knife and stabbed it into Celeste's thigh with all her strength.

The deep voice of Xango thundered in her head. "You must chop off the branches and then kill the tree."

In other words, kill Gil and whoever the other branches were before she could kill Celeste. The woman screamed in pain and rolled away, the knife slicing as she did so, soaking her white robe.

Celeste looked at her with hate-filled eyes, the pupils so large as to appear totally black. It seemed a perfect match for the black tears rolling down her dirt-streaked face. "You hurt my son. You will pay for that."

She pointed a finger at Claire and said with authority, "I invoke Kalfou, god of sorcery and black magic. Kalfou, king of chaos and mischief, place a hex on this woman. Make those she loves die a horrible death. Make her life empty, without laughter or happiness as she travels her life's journey alone. Kalfou, I ask that you speak to your brother, Legba. Upon her death this woman must not be allowed to ascend at death but to wander the wasteland, forever alone."

Claire's blood ran cold. She had seen firsthand during ceremonies the power of the loa as they possessed Voodoo followers. Mr. Henri's possession at the burial sites had been awe-inspiring, his power unmistakable. But never had she seen the dark side of Voodoo. Mr. Henri only helped people when invoking the loa. Celeste was invoking a hex spell, the most powerful and dangerous of black magic Voodoo and now she focused that power against Claire. Had Kalfou responded to Celeste's invocation?

A siren pierced the night and headlights shone brightly from several vehicles that blocked escape via the road. Sheriff Willis's voice boomed from a bullhorn. "This is the sheriff of Kalfou Parish. Cease and desist immediately."

Seconds later, several explosions erupted as flashbang grenades sailed through the air from different directions into the crowd. A heavy mist and the smell of pepper were the telltale signs that pepper bombs had been deployed.

The detonations were literally stunning as Claire and many others reflexively dropped to the ground. Shock registered on Celeste's face and Claire wondered what kept the woman on her feet.

As the peppered mist wafted into the area, most of the crowd began coughing, tears streaming. The skirmish between Claire and Celeste had taken them away from the crowd so they were momentarily unaffected by the spray. Claire threw off the long robe and held it to cover her mouth and nose. When she looked toward Celeste, the older woman was gone.

Reluctantly, she decided to trust the law to apprehend Celeste. She had to find Jess.

CHAPTER FORTY-TWO

Flames crackled as they licked the walls and rafters of the outbuilding. Smoke burnt Jess's eyes. But that was the least of her problems as the agitated snakes were becoming much more aggressive. The fire was burning quickly but the smoke from the wood and hay was filling the shed. She still had no way out. She crouched lower to the ground to avoid as much of the deadly smoke as possible.

Through the haze, a snake came sliding almost regally across the ground. It was enormous, its skin the bright green of a young corn stalk. All the other snakes moved out of its path.

Jess was mesmerized, her legs rooted to the ground as it slithered to her. She watched, trembling, as it lifted itself high enough to look into her eyes. It stared at her for a long moment, weaving slightly in the air before lowering to the ground.

A man's voice sounded in her ear as if he stood next to her. "Damballah is with you."

She swung around to confront the man but no one was there.

As if demanding her attention, it tapped her leg with its head, mouth closed. Jess screamed and backed away.

A great cracking sound erupted from above. There came a large crash as a beam dropped to the dirt floor just feet away from where she stood. Snakes scattered everywhere as hiding places were exposed and heat seared their flesh.

My God! It fell right where I had been standing.

Jess couldn't hold back her terrified scream any more than she could stop her arms and legs from quivering. She had known it was risky, but now, faced with the fire and no exit, she wondered if she had created her own death.

"Stay strong!" The same deep voice sounded inside her head. "Damballah is here to help but you must allow him to do so. Do not reject him or you will die this day."

She looked down and saw her green companion hiss and strike at a rattlesnake sending it in a different direction when it drew too close. The snake rose up as it had done before and stared at her.

Mr. Henri's voice sounded in her ear. "You must trust Damballah. He was sent to help you. Remember?"

Oh God! She was on the verge of panic but forced herself to stand still. Her body trembled as the snake came closer.

Once again, the huge bright green snake rose until they were eye to eye, its tongue flickering in and out. Slowly it moved forward to bump its head against her forehead. Then moved back and stared at her once again.

Tears streamed down her face, her body jerking uncontrollably, but she stayed in place. As she watched, the snake drew its head down in a pose reminiscent of a swan. Then it moved back down to the floor hissing at any snake that dared get too close.

Meanwhile, the fire roared around her.

CHAPTER FORTY-THREE

Claire looked where Gil had fallen and was surprised to see he was no longer there. Fuck! The lucky bastard couldn't be hurt very badly. As much as she wanted to deal with him, she felt an overwhelming need to make sure Jess was safe. Eyes watering, she hurried toward the building and the fire.

Flames licked through the roof of the shed and thick gray smoke billowed from every crack and crevice. Red and orange peeped through the smoke in several places where fire was breaching the walls.

"Jess!"

As she removed the board from its cradle fastening the door, she became aware of a low chanting. For a second she froze as she recognized Mr. Henri's voice. This time it was definitely not in her head. The sounds of chaos and the fire should have drowned him out, but the sound was there just beneath it all.

She turned and there he was, standing at the edge of the trees, his arms raised, standing firm as he invoked Xango. That distinctive rhythm was calling the Voodoo god of fire and strength.

For a moment she lost herself in his chant, all things around them becoming background noise. He stared at her and she saw flames burning in his eyes. She felt a rush of warmth sweep down her spine, as if hot water had been poured down her back. A sense of calm enveloped her, and she knew it came from him.

He gave Claire a simple nod and then set his gaze to the night sky, arms still raised above his head. The sounds of the surrounding chaos returned, the smoke choking her. She stepped to the side, threw open the barn door, and went inside.

At some point she had lost the robe covering her mouth and clutched her shirt instead. She bent forward to stay as low as possible. Her hope was to stay conscious long enough to locate Jess and get them both to safety. If not—well then, so be it.

"Jess?" Her hoarse shout received no reply.

A king snake slithered by her as it searched for safety, barely stopping to pause as it slid over a much larger one. There was no danger from the big constrictor. It was dead. Its tail was alight, just like one of the rafters that rested beside it.

The smoke robbed her of her voice and her cries weakened as she called for Jess, desperately hoping for an answer. Was she mistaken? Had the scream come from somewhere other than the shed?

At that moment, a large brilliant-green snake emerged through the smoke. It moved in an elegant, almost regal fashion, its unblinking eyes focused on her.

"Follow Damballah," she heard Mr. Henri say clearly. "He knows the one you seek."

The snake stopped and stared into Claire's eyes. Drumbeats began beneath the roar of the fire. Claire was sure it was inside her head, just as Mr. Henri's voice, but when the serpent swayed to the rhythm, she began to second guess herself.

Without warning, the snake dropped to the ground and slithered away.

"Follow," Mr. Henri's voice whispered urgently. "Hurry."

Claire took a cautious step in that direction, unsure of what she was hearing.

"Hurry."

Her lungs felt as if they would explode, her skin burned in several places now, but she somehow knew she was safe. She coughed violently, and almost fell when she stumbled over something.

"Jess!" She shook her violently. The figure moved.

"Claire?" The raspy voice was unrecognizable.

"Oh God Jess. Let's get you out of here." She knelt down and with a herculean effort pulled the taller woman into a standing position. Claire offered up a small prayer that God would carry them to safety before heading in the only direction possible.

"You cunt!" a deep voice yelled, raw and thick. Gil had followed her inside.

"Let it go, Gil," her hoarse shout barely audible above the fire's roar. The door was only feet away but so very far to go. "The cops are here. You're through. You're going to jail for the rest of your life."

Gil's eyes glittered with hate and he took a step toward them. "You still don't understand. I. Am. God." He lifted his arms in triumph. "My time has come, and you will pay."

Claire didn't understand how he could stand there amid the raging inferno and not be falling down. It was as if her knife wound had done nothing and he had no concern of the furnace surrounding him.

"Prepare to die, Claire." He stood between them and the door and Jess needed help badly. She felt a tap against her leg and looked down to see the green snake.

"Follow Damballah," Mr. Henri's voice told her.

Knowing she needed to find a safe place for Jess, Claire followed the snake a few feet to a corner of the shed where the flames had not reached. As soon as Jess slid to the ground, the snake curled on top of her.

A yell pierced the roar of the fire and Claire barely had time to draw her dagger before Gil was upon her. She managed to duck in time to avoid his meaty fist. It slammed into the wall just inches from Jess.

The green snake hissed and raised its head to stare at Gil.

"Damballah! You have Damballah helping you?" He gave the snake a wide berth and then charged Claire. She had been trained to deal with individuals much larger than her. She waited until the last second to dodge while swiping with her knife. Blood on the blade let her know she at least nicked him and his roar of outrage corroborated it.

The smoke cleared momentarily, and she saw blood coming from a second wound to his abdomen. He stood still a moment as he appeared to devise a new game plan. He found a board that was only a few feet long still burning on one end. He grabbed it and walked to her.

Claire was cornered. Both of them knew he had the advantage this time. He stabbed the board toward her. Claire had little defense.

"Ahhhh," she screamed as the board's hot ember branded her belly.

"Die, you bitch," he growled as he stalked toward her. "You've ruined everything. My entire life came down to this moment, and you fucked up everything!" His voice rose in vicious passion.

"Wait for him," the deep voice in her head commanded.

Gil stood over her, a diabolical grin smeared across his face. "You're about to burn, Claire. And this is just a taste of the flames you'll soon be feeling. Yes. I judge you, Claire Duvall, and find you lacking. You will feel the flames of hell after I kill you."

She stared up defiantly.

He laughed and leaned down until face-to-face with her. His eyes were black with no hint of pupil. "Once you're dead, your partner will be next. She'll scream for mercy while I carve her sentence into her flesh. Just a reminder to carry throughout eternity."

Claire listened to his words and something primal burst forth as he threatened Jess. She screamed and swung the dagger as hard as she could into his side.

"Fuck you, Gil! You're evil and twisted. Go to hell where you belong."

Gil grabbed at the knife in his side as she tried to tug it free. He roared in pain as the blade slid out, slicing his hand as they fought.

An overhead beam creaked ominously seconds before it gave way. With a hoarse screech, Claire let go of the knife and dived out of the way of the falling timber. When the smoke cleared Gil was standing with the bloody knife in hand, his face twisted diabolically.

Surrounded by fire, flames scorched his robe, turning its edges to black char. He lifted his arms, the knife gripped tightly as blood ran down his arm.

"This world no longer has power over me." She somehow heard him clearly above the roar of the fire. The flames licked upward now from the hem of his garment, but Gil remained oblivious, consumed in his madness.

"Look," he said in wonder. "I see the face of God. He has come to consume me as we become one." He raised his arms as if to embrace something invisible to Claire. "You are mine and I am yours. The fire will not harm me. Just as the children walked in the fiery furnace, I shall be kept safe."

Gil disappeared amid the smoke and Claire heard what she thought were his screams but then second guessed herself. Could it be the roar of the fire?

She decided it didn't matter. She had to get Jess to safety. She moved to the place she had left Jess and found Damballah still protecting her. Without embarrassment, she thanked Damballah for helping Jess. The snake stared for a long moment before moving into the smoke as Claire dragged Jess the last few feet toward safety.

Holding Jess as best she could, they clung to each other coughing and retching as they exited the building. Claire checked over her shoulder more than once to ensure Gil wasn't coming after them. But they were alone.

She listened for his voice but, there was just…nothing.

Strong arms grabbed her but she couldn't open her eyes enough to see who it was. "I've got you, Claire," she heard Sheriff Willis's gruff voice. "Let me get you and Jess to an ambulance."

His voice had never sounded so good. She tried to talk but nothing came out, so she contented herself with holding on to Jess tightly and allowing the sheriff to guide them.

Jess was taken off in the ambulance while the sheriff set Claire on a gurney and stepped back. An EMT placed an oxygen mask over her mouth and she took deep blissful breaths. Her throat was raw and it was simultaneously painful and divine.

"Don't try to open your eyes." The sheriff's voice had never sounded so kind. "Let's wash them first."

The cool clean liquid felt wonderful, and she lay quietly, allowing him to do it. She caught the smell of the sheriff's aftershave and realized it was him ministering to her rather than the EMT.

"Blanche is with Sid." He spoke quietly as he ran a wet cloth over her face. "She told us that you saved her life, even though she was sketchy about just how you did it." Water sprinkled in her hair and on her throat. Then he used the cloth gently once again. "We have a lot of talking to do, honey…a lot of talking."

Claire found it difficult to focus on his words. All she could think about was the sheer misery of her irritated eyes and the pain of burns and wounds she had sustained. Blackness swirled behind her eyelids making her dizzy. She knew she was losing consciousness but couldn't change it.

The last thing she heard was, "I need you over here. My daughter needs help."

CHAPTER FORTY-FOUR

The next few days were a mix of blurred images and pain. At some point, she woke up to the sound of Maxine's hushed voice as she spoke with someone. Claire tried to say something but her throat was too sore and she was sedated.

"They haven't found him yet?"

"No. That's what has everyone stumped. We caught his two henchmen, the ones he called Peter and John. Neither of them took the deal to help us locate Gil. I don't know if they are too involved in the cult or if they don't know where he is. I just can't believe he survived being stabbed and burned. I think he probably died in the swamp and a gator had a mighty big meal. That's why they can't find him. I mean, here Claire and Jess are burned and battered and Gil was still inside while they got to safety. He couldn't have got away."

"I heard they have checked at hospitals all over the state and maybe further but no one matching his description has shown up."

Claire was having difficulty catching all of Maxine's words. "…men have been searching…that man from Lincoln Parish… his dogs….no sign…Gil."

Claire woke up later as a nurse was changing out her IV. She started to give a sign that she was awake but stopped when she heard Lester's name.

"The sheriff has made up his mind about Lester. He has dropped the charges and talked to the DA about it." She recognized Sid's voice.

The next voice belonged to Blanche. "Why?"

"He said that devil's breath made Lester do stuff without knowing it. Besides, he's been in jail while all this stuff has been going on. The sheriff says just firing him will be enough."

"Well, he has proven he can't be trusted by helping the drug dealers and all that mess."

"Exactly. The sheriff figures that will be punishment enough since Lester loves the job so much."

Claire fell asleep again.

At some point they reduced the pain medication. Claire was able to stay awake more often and think clearly between bouts of sleeping. Her abdominal burns from the burning poker were the most painful. Although she was curious about the doctor's treatment plan, her first words were to inquire about Jess.

Blanche and Sid came in together, both dressed in face masks and scrubs. Sid first noticed she was awake. "Hey there. Glad to have you back with us."

"How is Jess?"

Blanche explained what was happening. "Jess is still in the Burn Unit's intensive care, honey."

"Burn unit? Where are we?"

"You're in Baton Rouge's Burn Unit. You've been here four days now."

At Claire's confused look, she continued, "You were both in intensive care for a couple of days. All that smoke hurt your lungs and your burns needed to be handled carefully. Jess is still needing that extra care."

Claire tried to throw back the covers but only succeeded in groaning at the pain in her abdomen and arm where the worst burns were. "Blanche, I gotta go see her."

Blanche put a firm hand on her shoulder. "You can't go anywhere yet, honey. Jess isn't awake anyway, so she won't know you're there."

"She's unconscious?" Claire exclaimed, panicking. "Is she going to be okay? Can you at least let me see a picture of her?"

Sid and Blanche looked at each other for a moment.

"I'd kick the door down to see you, Blanche. She should at least get to see a picture of Jess."

"Okay then. I'll try to get a couple of photos a little later."

Sid nodded. "I'll go get us some supper while you're doing that. But first, help me understand what happened in that shed. The sheriff is still with the SBI combing the bayou for any trace of Gil."

"The State Bureau of Investigation is involved now?" She was surprised. "Why now?"

"Well, we're down to only two of us experienced officers. One of the new hires never showed up for his first day, and this is literally the first job for the other newbie. Not to mention that we may still have a serial killer out there. From what I hear, they were about to send a couple of people anyway. Gil just made his move before they did."

He looked at Blanche. "I think we need to catch Claire up on everything that's happened." Sid told them about Gil's attack on Cammie and Chris. Claire found herself shaking. She knew it could have easily been Blanche, Jess, or herself.

Blanche blurted out, "What in the world was he using? Chloroform?"

Sid shook his head. "Dr. Avi got the tox reports back on that white powder. It is a hallucinogenic drug mainly coming out of Colombia now, but there is growing use in Haiti. They call it devil's breath. It doesn't take a lot. First you pass out and then you wake up to be susceptible to the influence of others. You'll do crazy things for someone and have no memory when it gets out of your system."

Claire interrupted. "It's like a date rape drug on steroids?"

Sid shrugged. "Probably as good a description as any."

"Are there any lasting effects?"

This time Blanche answered. "Dr. Avi said it's temporary. It takes just a small amount since it is processed in the body quickly, leaving little trace. As a matter of fact, the amount is important. If the victim gets too much of the drug then they can hallucinate."

"I wonder if Gil was doing that in the shed," Claire mused. "He probably had a very high dose. They took us to a little room to put on our robes. While I was left alone there I saw the bag and put some in their wine. Then one of his goons put more in so they got a heavier dose than usual. When Gil came in he added even more. He drank a bunch more wine from the chalice than the others. I think it may have influenced him to think he wasn't going to burn in the shed."

Sid frowned. "Why did Gil think he was supposed to turn into God anyway?"

Claire spoke up again. "I think it came from his mother. According to what I read, she fell from fame in New Orleans and became ridiculed to the point that she left and moved to Haiti. Gil was a little boy at the time. She rose to prominence again, this time with a dark Voodoo influence." She shivered. "I saw it in the ceremony."

"Any trace of Celeste?" Claire added.

Sid shook his head. "Nothing."

"Why have so many people been killed?" Blanche asked as she read over Claire's clinical notes.

Sid shrugged. "Apparently, Gil has been sacrificing people on special occasions for years. I wouldn't be surprised if he had begun killing back in Haiti. But we can only speculate as to the number of victims."

"Damn, what a mess." Claire sipped some water.

"Yeah. Hard to imagine all this happening in our little part of the world."

"By the way. I saw a lot of people at the ceremony. Who were they? I recognized some but maybe only half?"

Sid shook his head. "He had danged people coming from all over. We caught some that night that were visiting from Haiti. Most everyone else was within driving distance but not everybody. Some were squatters at the old beach houses, and some were doing the same at fishing shacks in the bayou. I guess if you don't go to your cabin very often, you never know somebody's living there."

"How did we miss all this?"

"Well. We've been short-handed for quite a while. Nobody wants the low pay, on call so much of the time, and—"

"The danger." Blanche butted in, her tone letting them know how she felt.

Sid's voice remained as calm and unhurried as ever. "Plus we never got a call from anybody saying they had seen a stranger in a neighbor's cabin. Everybody that could, probably just drove back home after their ceremony."

Together they left as Claire's supper was delivered. Claire's first reaction to the food was to long for something from Gil's Grill. Then it hit her that this man who had lived in their small parish and been well thought of had been a serial killer. How had she not seen it? Had she missed something that could have saved lives?

Her thoughts were interrupted by a timid knock on the door. The large metal handle turned and in walked Sheriff Willis. Or maybe her father. Had she imagined that?

"Hey there." He removed his hat and stood fidgeting with it. "Sid told me you were awake and alert. Uh…how are you feeling?"

Claire didn't know what to say. Had she really heard him say she was his daughter? It would be beyond embarrassing if she had imagined it. "Did—did I hear you say something kinda important before I passed out?" She stared at her hands clenching the sheets tightly.

He cleared his throat and shoved his hands into his pockets. "Yeah. I did. I called you my daughter." He took a step toward her. "I came here to see if you feel up to talking." He backed up a step when she turned a belligerent gaze toward him.

"We haven't talked about anything in my entire life. Why start now?"

He grimaced. "I deserve that and a whole lot more. But I'm hoping you will hear me out."

Claire stared out the window and waved her hand toward him. "Go ahead."

He pulled a chair close to the bed. "Thank you for letting me explain." There was an awkward pause as he gathered his thoughts and she refused to look at him.

"I was seventeen and your mother wasn't quite sixteen when we got to know each other. It was the end of my senior year. She was a freshman. We thought we were in love but didn't know what to do about it. Back in the eighties and nineties, it was harder to date outside your race than it is now. You might remember that girl that was beaten almost to death and then left for dead behind the football field?"

Claire had heard the story many times and didn't answer. She simply continued to stare out the window, listening despite herself. He continued, his voice insecure, a stark contrast from normal.

"We kept it secret because Nessa's father would have hit the roof. It was just easier to keep it quiet."

Claire noticed her mother's shortened name that only a select few were allowed to use. Almost everyone called her Vanessa.

"After graduation, I enlisted in the Army during Desert Storm and deployed just as it was ending. When I came back Nessa had a toddler…you."

"Why didn't you acknowledge me?" Claire's voice rose with each word. "I needed a dad. Mama needed help. She was raising me and working all the time to make ends meet. And then there were hateful things people said to her…said to us," she amended, tears flowing.

"I know." His voice grew soft. "I stayed here instead of moving to another parish so I could be near you both. I got a job as a deputy and sent money to Nessa. It was for both of you. I paid for your schooling and such. I tried to do good by you without anyone knowing about your mom and me."

Without anyone knowing…The words stabbed like a knife. "But why didn't you want us? Were you ashamed of me?"

"Claire." He reached out before stuffing his hands in his pockets. "Claire, you were being raised as a white child. If I had said anything, you would have suddenly become a biracial little girl. Things just aren't the same for black folks, not anywhere, but particularly not in the south. Your mom and I felt it was best to keep it quiet. We had both moved on with our lives and never planned to get married. The truth would have just opened the three of us up to all the racist garbage. Ya'll already had enough on your plate."

When she said nothing, he swallowed a lump in his throat. "I've watched you grow up, Claire. I've seen you become a beautiful, strong woman. I was never so proud as when you graduated from the academy and joined me."

"Is that why you hired me? So you could stop putting out money?"

For the first time, his eyes flashed in anger but his voice remained calm. "You deserved a job with us. Your grades were topnotch. It seemed like a win for you, a win for the department and a win for me. I could get to know you better and be a part of your life."

When there was no cutting remark from Claire, he continued. "I want you to know how proud you've made me, Claire. You're a good deputy but mainly you're a wonderful person. Your mother did a great job and I'm grateful for the years we've had to get to know each other. I can understand you're angry, you're hurt. And I'm sorry for all the years your mama and I kept the secret. I just pray that I've done the right thing by saying you're my daughter now."

He rubbed the back of his neck. "That wreck got me thinking. I could've died and you would've never known the truth. I couldn't stand the idea that you never knew me as your dad. It sorta popped out without me thinking it through. I don't want you hurt any more than you've already been."

His words stabbed her in the heart. Her mother had known and thought it best to keep it secret as well. And dammit, he was still not happy about publicly accepting her as his daughter.

"This is a lot to take in. I'll think about what you've said. But I will hand in my resignation. I can't have everyone whispering about nepotism on top of everything else they gossip about."

He started to argue but thought better of it. "Please think it over and don't do anything rash. We can work our way through it."

Claire closed her eyes, effectively dismissing him. When Sid and Blanche came in quietly, she pretended to sleep. She supposed the sheriff had spoken to them on his way out. Blanche placed a couple of photos they had sent through to a printer and left the room as quietly as they had arrived.

Claire picked them up as soon as she was alone and immediately burst into tears. Jess was unconscious, wrapped in bandages mostly on her left side and hooked up to monitors. She had known her still being in intensive care meant she was in worse shape than she was, but seeing it for herself was heart-wrenching. Jess was so close, just a few floors above. But they were so far apart.

Sleep was a long time coming that evening.

CHAPTER FORTY-FIVE

A couple of days later, Claire was released to go home. Her throat was almost back to normal and her burns could be tended at home with Blanche volunteering to come each day. She was dressed and waiting on her bed when Sid came in pushing a wheelchair.

"Are you ready to ride, young lady?" His grin was almost as wide as her own. "I'm driving you home, but first, Blanche has a little surprise for you."

Claire's curiosity was piqued. "She doesn't need to do anything, Sid. The both of you are already doing more than you should."

He stood up and crossed his arms over his chest. "If you don't want to go visit Jess…"

"What?" She squealed like a child at Christmas.

"Come on…let's go." She hopped into the chair without argument and barely contained her impatience to get there.

As Sid rolled her into the room, her excitement was quickly subdued. Her beautiful Jess was lying on her right side with her left covered in bandages. Her beautiful long hair had been cut short as it had not escaped the fire unscathed. Seeing her misery firsthand was difficult.

Blanche saw her expression. "Jess is going to be fine, Claire. It's just going to take longer for her than it has for you."

Jess opened her eyes. "My hero," she whispered hoarsely.

She lifted a shaky hand and Claire took it gently. "Your hair looks cute like that."

Tears welled up in Jess's beautiful amber eyes. "You think so?"

Claire squeezed her hand before placing a kiss on it. "Yes, I do. You're absolutely gorgeous."

A tear rolled down one cheek. "It's going to be a while with the burns, Claire. I'm going to have some scars."

Claire kissed her hand again, as if it were the most precious thing in the world. "I love you, Jess. The scars are nothing to me except as a reminder of your bravery." Jess looked unconvinced but listened as Claire continued. "Do you realize you overcame your phobia and dealt with all those snakes? Not to mention coming up with an escape plan. The courage you showed in facing your fear is amazing. You're my hero."

"Do—do you want to..." Jess's voice trembled as she couldn't finish.

"To love you?" Claire kissed her hand. "Yes. To live with you and make a go of it?" She kissed Jess's hand again. "Yes. I'm going to take a leave of absence while we both recover. That will give me time to put in applications at other parishes."

"You're leaving?"

Claire kissed her hand yet again. "There's nothing left for me here. I have a few friends I will miss but I can always come visit. I'm tired of the hateful gossip and narrow minds that believe it's okay to treat me like I'm a lesser human because of who I love. Of course, if you want to stay, I'll stay. Wherever you are is the right place for me."

Jess smiled. "I love you, Claire. I love your heart and your soul."

Claire bent down for a kiss on the lips this time. It began soft and gently as she didn't want to hurt her. Jess returned the kiss just as gently. There would be time for passion later.

"We will get through this, and come out the other side, Jess. I promise." She kissed her again. It was reassurance for what had happened and a promise of better things to come.

EPILOGUE

Six Weeks Later

Claire pulled her truck to the side of the road outside Mr. Henri's home. A large table made of plywood lying across two sawhorses was already set up in the garden. A blue checked tablecloth covered the plywood while various styles of chairs sat ready for the upcoming meal. She hurried around to the passenger side and held out her arms for Jess to hand over the enormous bowl of Cajun slaw, leaving Jess to carry the sweet potato pie.

"Hey there, you two," Blanche called out as she came out the door with a platter of dipping sauces. "I wondered when ya'll would get here. Maxine and the sheriff have been catching Sid up on things at work since he retired, and I haven't had anyone to talk to."

"You know you've been holding up your end of the conversation," Sid said as his long strides caught up to his wife. "Let me help with that."

"Lord, is Claire and Jess here? I've been waiting and waiting to see them. Come here, girls, and give me a hug. I've missed you so much." Maxine began mothering them before she even got within eyesight.

The Trahan brothers were focused on two giant steam pots. When Joseph pulled the lid off one to check on the food, the aroma of a flavorful shrimp boil wafted out.

Claire called out to them, "Mr. Henri. Joseph. That sure does smell good."

Mr. Henri laughed. "It should be. I caught the shrimp this morning. That's about as fresh as it gets."

Joseph pointed to a large cooler. "Get a drink. They're ice cold."

Jess handed over the sweet potato pie while Claire placed the slaw on the table.

As they went to get their drinks, Sheriff Willis and his newest deputy, Mia Sanchez, walked out with him. Actually, with Sid's retirement and Claire's resignation, Mia was the only deputy at the moment.

"Hi, Mia. Good to see you again." Jess's voice was back to normal, thankfully. An inhaler was about the only remaining treatment for the smoke inhalation. Her left thigh had undergone a skin graft and was healing nicely. It would scar but the doctor had promised it would be minimal.

"Hello, Jess…Claire." Mia's slight Spanish accent suited her perfectly.

"Let's eat," Mr. Henri called out as he and Joseph brought the first steam pot to the table. They tilted the pot to spill its contents on the disposable tablecloth that covered the length of the table. Everyone would have their food directly in front of them. Two containers were strategically placed for easy disposal of shrimp shells.

Mia sat next to the sheriff. "I've never seen a meal like this."

Sheriff Willis grinned at her. "This is our version of a barbeque, I guess. Just eat all you want."

Sheriff Willis looked over at Claire. "How have you two been doing? Have you started looking for a job yet?"

Claire wiped her hands before answering. "I've begun putting in résumés. But I haven't heard anything."

"You're always welcome here, Claire." When she began to reply, he held up his hand. "I know you don't want to and I respect that. I'm just letting you know, you have a job here if you want one. As a matter of fact, if you want to work even part-time that's fine."

Claire was ready to protest but the idea of part-time or maybe temporary was tempting. After all, it took money to live. "I'll think about it."

Word of Claire being the sheriff's daughter had spread like wildfire throughout the parish. The emergency technician that heard the sheriff's request to help his daughter had seen to that.

For the most part, Claire and the sheriff tried to ignore the gossip. He promised not to push her too hard while she had promised to think things through rather than cut off the relationship altogether.

"Good enough."

Sid looked at the sheriff. "I saw a sign saying Vote for Pastor Abel. Sounds like you have a competitor for sheriff this election."

"Yep. He's already saying he will be the best thing that ever happened to Kalfou Parish."

Everyone began voicing their opinions of the pastor until Sheriff Willis held up his hand. "Let's not ruin our time by talking about him. I want to hear about how Sid's retirement's going. Is Blanche keeping you busy?"

"I'm a man of leisure, now. Doing what I want. Sleeping as long as I want."

Blanche broke in. "Do you know how hard it is to get up in the morning while he's snoring in bed, going to work, and then coming home to see him on the couch taking a nap?"

Several offered free advice.

"Give him a honey-do list."

"Kick him off the couch and ask where your supper is."

Blanche looked over at Sid and he gave a small nod. "Actually, I am doing something about it. I'm retiring in a few months too, at least before the end of the year. We're going to do things we always wanted to do. With everything that's happened, we realized the future isn't guaranteed."

As all the congratulations calmed down, she raised her beer bottle. "A toast to our Kalfou heroes…Claire and Jess. Thank you for giving me a chance to make it to retirement."

Everyone shouted encouragement as both women blushed at their praise. When it died down, Claire raised her bottle for a toast.

"Thank you, Mr. Henri and Joseph. Your guidance and prayers made all the difference."

Everyone shouted their agreement, when Maxine's voice cut through the noise.

"Claire. What's that on your hand? Is that a ring I see?"

Claire laughed and wriggled her fingers to make the light dance across the stones. "That's right, Maxine. Jess and I are getting married."

Shouts of congratulations and teasing erupted from everyone, with Claire and Jess grinning from ear to ear. Claire leaned over and gave Jess a sweet kiss. "I love you, Jess. I think I fell in love the morning you arrived all starched and formal."

Jess chuckled and kissed her again. "I fell in love with you at the same time. But even more so while watching you those first couple of days. You have such a beautiful spirit. You're amazing, both inside and out, hon."

The rambunctious group teased and applauded as Jess wrapped Claire in her arms and kissed her. As they drew apart, Claire realized she had everything she had ever wanted—a wonderful woman who adored her and friends who supported and loved her. She knew now what she wanted and it all was right in front of her.

She looked at all the smiling faces surrounding her. Then she stared at the hand entwined with her own.

I'm the luckiest woman in the world.

Bella Books, Inc.
Happy Endings Live Here
P.O. Box 10543
Tallahassee, FL 32302
Phone: (850) 576-2370
www.BellaBooks.com

More Titles from Bella Books

Hunter's Revenge – Gerri Hill
978-1-64247-447-3 | 276 pgs | paperback: $18.95 | eBook: $9.99
Tori Hunter is back! Don't miss this final chapter in the acclaimed
Tori Hunter series.

Integrity – E. J. Noyes
978-1-64247-465-7 | 228 pgs | paperback: $19.95 | eBook: $9.99
It was supposed to be an ordinary workday...

The Order – TJ O'Shea
978-1-64247-378-0 | 396 pgs | paperback: $19.95 | eBook: $9.99
For two women the battle between new love and old loyalty may prove
more dangerous than the war they're trying to survive.

Under the Stars with You – Jaime Clevenger
978-1-64247-439-8 | 302 pgs | paperback: $19.95 | eBook: $9.99
Sometimes believing in love is the first step. And sometimes it's all
about trusting the stars.

The Missing Piece – Kat Jackson
978-1-64247-445-9 | 250 pgs | paperback: $18.95 | eBook: $9.99
Renee's world collides with possibility and the past, setting off a tidal
wave of changes she could have never predicted.

An Acquired Taste – Cheri Ritz
978-1-64247-462-6 | 206 pgs | paperback: $17.95 | eBook: $9.99
Can Elle and Ashley stand the heat in the *Celebrity Cook Off* kitchen?